REGULATION 19

P.T. HYLTON

1

UNDER THE LAW

I.

Frank Hinkle was staring at the murder weapon in his hand when Correctional Officer Rodgers called his name.

"Hinkle!"

Frank squeezed his eyes shut and muttered a near silent curse.

He had been standing in the prison yard, drifting. Not even thinking. Just drifting. It had been happening more lately, the sense that his mind had become un-anchored from reality. He would find himself standing in the middle of the yard with no idea how long he'd been there. The old timers said the longer you were inside, the more it happened. You would find yourself losing bits of everything —time, your personality, even the reality of the prison walls around you. Still, common or not, it was damn unsettling.

If he had seen the Newg striding toward him, he would have turned and walked the other way. But he had been drifting hard, and he didn't see the Newg until the other man was up in his face.

The day Jerry Robinson arrived at NTCC, one of the

men in the yard called him 'the New Guy'. As a reward for this burst of wit, Robinson punched the inmate in the throat. In spite of the throat-punch, the nickname had stuck. Over the years, it had morphed from 'the New Guy' to 'the Newg.' and somewhere along the way the Newg had come to embrace his new name. He even had it memorialized on his right bicep in prison ink.

While the Newg wasn't opposed to a good old-fashioned throat punch when the need arose, he now preferred to repay perceived slights with a shank. He'd doled out one such repayment only two days ago, and the COs were in an unusual hurry to find out who had stabbed the kid in the shower.

The Newg gave his shoulder a gentle squeeze as he spoke. "Man, I need your help. I know I ain't paid you back for what you did before, so I feel real bad asking. But I ain't got no choice."

Frank blinked hard. His mind snapped back to reality, but he still felt like he was playing catch up, jumping into the middle of a conversation he didn't fully understand.

The Newg must have taken Frank's silence as permission to continue. "Need you to hold on to this for me."

Something slipped into Frank's hand. He didn't have to look to see what the Newg had handed him. Frank's mind, and his pulse, sped to life.

"Whoa, Newg," he said. "I respect you, and you know I'd love to help. But you also gotta know I'm not putting a murder weapon in my bunk."

The Newg's face scrunched up in desperation. The man wasn't handsome to begin with and the look did nothing to improve the situation. "You were at the laundry, right? They got you signed in at the time of death, and at least three guards laid eyes on you while you were working."

"It doesn't matter where I was. They're going to keep tossing bunks until they find something. How did they not find this already?"

The Newg glanced around and lowered his voice. "I got a hiding spot in the yard. But it's not the kind of spot that's gonna withstand a full sweep."

That was the moment the voice came, shouting his name like it was a cuss word. "Hinkle!"

The Newg looked up and the color drained from his face. He backed up. "Looks like Rodgers wants a word."

"Newg!" Frank whispered as loudly as he dared. He still hadn't turned to acknowledge the CO's call. "Get back here and take this thing!"

The Newg wiggled his head back and forth, his eyes never leaving the figure behind Frank. "I appreciate this. I owe you double." He turned and hustled away.

Frank remained frozen. There was nothing to do but wait for the inevitable. He snuck the shank into the waistband of his pants and pushed it down as far as he dared. If he shoved it down too far, it would fall down his pant leg and onto the ground. Guards tended to notice stuff falling out of the leg of an inmate's pants. It was an all too common, last resort option for getting rid of contraband in the loose-fitting, pocketless prisoner's clothing.

"Hinkle! You got shit in your ears? I've been calling your name for two minutes."

Frank felt a hand on his shoulder, this one from behind him, and he grimaced. He turned and saw Correctional Officer Rodgers standing there, the light hint of a smile on his face. When CO Rodgers smiled, it was never a good sign.

Frank had most of the guards figured out, but Rodgers...Rodgers was different than the others. Rodgers was smart. He was good looking. He was an athlete. Fifteen years ago, Frank had been in the stands the day Rodgers had led the Bristol, Tennessee High School football team to a stunning victory over Virginia High. The kid had been a natural athlete.

Rodgers went on to play for UT his freshman year of college before being cut from the team as a sophomore. He finished school and got his degree in criminology. And then, for some reason, he had come to work with a bunch of dunces and thugs who'd barely made it through high school.

"Sorry about that," Frank said. "I was spacing out. Didn't hear you."

Rodgers grunted. He nodded his head toward the Newg who was now halfway across the yard. "Having a little conversation with Robinson?"

Frank nodded, not quite meeting the other man's eyes. "Yes, sir."

"Every time I give you a little bit of credit and start thinking maybe you're an actual human being with a functioning brain, you gotta turn around and prove me wrong. Why is that? Did you have to train hard to act so stupid or does it come naturally?"

The shank in Frank's waistband felt huge. Rodgers had to see it. Any moment he would blow his little whistle and ten guards would sprint across the yard and tackle Frank to the ground.

Frank said, "I guess it comes naturally, boss."

The smile faded from Rodgers's face. "That was a rhetorical question, Hinkle. See what I'm saying? You just proved my damn point." He grabbed Frank's right arm and marched toward the administration building. "Come on. Warden wants to have a chat."

"What?" Frank asked. He struggled to keep up without

dislodging the shank from its precarious position. "What's the warden—?"

Rodgers stopped and spun to face Hinkle. He leaned in close to the prisoner's face. "Do me a favor. Keep your feet on that side of the yellow line and don't speak unless you are asked a direct question."

Frank may not have understood the inner workings of CO Rodgers's mind, but he did know enough basic guard psychology to understand that Rodgers had no idea why the warden wanted to see him.

They stopped outside the door to the administration building. "Hands in front."

Frank held out his wrists, and Rodgers clicked the handcuffs into place. "Okay, let's move," Rodgers said.

They entered the administration building and walked down a long, institutional gray hallway. It didn't look much different from the other buildings in the NTCC except for the doors. They were standard office building doors with nameplates instead of the heavy metal monstrosities found in the rest of the prison.

Northern Tennessee Correctional Complex wasn't a terrible place, at least as far as maximum security prisons went. The bizarre rule changes during Frank's nine years inside had made things worse, but the location was still hard to beat. The prison was located in Rook Mountain, Tennessee, and the prison yard views of the Smoky Mountains could be outright breathtaking. Still, even after nine years, the sight of the administration building unnerved him.

He had been in this building once before. He had been scared that time, but at least he had known why the warden wanted to see him. He could reveal or withhold the facts as he wished. That little bit of power had been something to hold on to, something to savor. Even though they had him in handcuffs, he chose whether to talk. This time, he had no power.

Also, last time he hadn't had a murder weapon in his elastic waistband.

Rodgers led Frank into a room with no windows. The warden sat in a chair behind a large metal table. The fluorescent overhead lighting gave his already weathered face a sickly hue. He looked uncomfortable, like maybe he was suffering from a bout of gas. He nodded to Rodgers, and the guard moved Frank to the lone chair on the near side of the table. Frank sat down, and Rodgers locked the handcuffs in the latch built into the table for this purpose. Then Rodgers took a few steps back until he was out of Frank's field of vision.

The warden leaned forward and folded his hands on the table. "We've only got a few moments, so listen to what I am about to tell you."

Frank shifted in his seat.

"An hour ago I got a call from Rook Mountain City Hall. They told me Becky Raymond needs to meet with you. I know you haven't had the chance to keep up with politics lately, but Ms. Raymond is the city manager of Rook Mountain."

The warden stared at Frank for a long moment.

Frank had the feeling that he was supposed to say something. He couldn't quite keep the smile off his face. "This the same Becky Raymond who used to work at the Road Runner gas station out on Dennis Cove Rd?"

The warden leaned even closer. Frank saw beads of sweat forming on the big man's forehead. "Ms. Raymond is going to be here any minute, so don't be cute. I need answers. What the hell does the city manager want with you?"

Frank shrugged. "I have no idea."

"Come on. Think!"

"I...I guess it could be something to do with my brother. He works for the city. Maybe he's up for a promotion, and they want to interview me for some background check or something."

Rodgers snickered behind him. "I'm pretty sure your brother isn't up for a promotion."

The warden smacked the table. "You expect me to believe the Rook Mountain city manager would come down here and walk into this prison about a background check?"

Frank paused, unsure of how to continue. "All due respect, but it seems like you may be thinking about this a little too hard. We're going to find out what she wants in a few minutes, right?"

The warden shook his head. "You don't understand. Things have changed in Rook Mountain. The city manager represents the board of selectmen, and the Board..." The warden paused. He glanced at Rodgers as if looking for an assist, but the CO remained silent. The warden continued. "The Board has done amazing things since you've been inside. Wonderful things. But there are rules –"

If Frank hadn't been looking at the door behind the warden, he wouldn't have seen it. But he was, and he saw a flash of blue light through the crack below the door.

The door opened and a tall, sharply dressed woman in her early fifties marched into the room. She moved toward the table and held out her hand to the warden. "Warden Cade?"

The warden leapt to his feet and shook her hand. "Yes ma'am. It's an honor. Thanks for coming down. I think you'll

find what we are doing here is in keeping with the Regulations."

"Fine." She slid into the nearest chair and looked at
Frank. Her face was all sharp angles. Her deep brown eyes
perfectly matched her hair color. "Mr. Hinkle," she said,
"how would you like to get out of prison?"

2.

Will Osmond drew a deep breath and concentrated on
putting one foot in front of the other. They were hiking
through a dense stand of pine trees, but it wouldn't be long
now. In a few moments, they would step out of the trees and
onto the round bald top of the mountain. The view would
be worth it. It always was.

Henry Strauss said, "You holding up okay?"

Will stopped and glanced back at the other man. Henry
was red with heat and slick with sweat. Both men were in
their late thirties, but, when Will compared his own stamina
with that of the six twelve-year-old boys hiking with them,
he felt much older.

The two men held up the rear of the procession. Osten-
sibly, this was so that they could keep watch on the boys in
front of them. In truth, it was so they could go at a non-
lethal pace without the kids stepping on their heels.

Will grunted in reply.

"Yeah, me too," Henry said. "It sure was easier when we
could drive up."

Will ignored that last comment. Sometimes it was better
to let things slide.

He said, "We made it. That's the important thing. Almost
made it, anyway."

Two years ago, the board of selectmen had decided vehicles were not allowed past the old ranger station on Rook Mountain. Before that, you could drive all the way up to the parking lot at Carter's Gap. A stroke of a pen turned a fifteen-minute hike into an excursion that took a whole afternoon. Will had no idea why the board had passed the change or what danger a vehicle near the summit of Rook Mountain might pose, but he had long ago stopped asking those types of questions out loud.

When it came to the board of selectmen, trust was a must.

Will stopped for a moment and waited for Henry to catch up to him. Then he fell in step with the other man. When he spoke, it was quiet enough that only Henry could hear him. "Did you see what I saw half a mile back?"

Henry nodded. "Under that boulder by the overlook?"

Will smiled. "Good eye. We have to deal with it on the way back."

Henry arched his eyebrow. "What about the boys?"

"The boys are the reason we have to deal with it," Will said. "What if one of them saw the backpack wedged under that boulder? The hiker wasn't even trying to hide what he's doing."

Henry nodded. "So the kids might have seen it. That's not the end of the world. We'll report it when we get back to town and let the boys sign the testimony. It'll be good for them."

Will snorted. "We're supposed to be teaching these kids to be men, right? How's it look if we just go back and report it? Sure, we're fulfilling the letter of the Regulations, but we aren't doing our duty. Is that what you want to teach Carl? 'Cause it's sure as hell not what I want to teach Trevor. By the time we go to town, file our report, and the law gets back up here, the hiker could be long gone."

Henry squinted at him. "What are you suggesting we do?"

"You know what I'm suggesting. I'm suggesting we teach our boys to uphold the Regulations."

Neither man spoke again for a few long moments. Only the call of distant birds and the excited chatter of the boys on the trail ahead cut the silence.

Finally Henry said, "You're right. We don't have a choice. We need to take care of it on the way back down."

Will nodded. "Good man."

Henry was the leader of their Rook Mountain Scout troop. Henry's son Carl was Trevor's best friend, so Henry and Will saw a lot of each other. The two men weren't close. It was mostly a quick hello when dropping off the kids at some activity or a little chat around the dessert table at a school function.

It had come as a surprise when Henry invited Will to help out with this camping trip. Will knew Henry wouldn't have called if he wasn't desperate. The Scout troop's usual co-leader had come down with a case of something or other, and Henry had nowhere else to turn. People got a little nervous around Will because of his job. Combined with his wife Christine's job and...well, they didn't get invited to a lot of cookouts. Sometimes he thought it wasn't fair the way they were cut off socially just because they served the community. Other times he felt like it was a necessary evil.

Truth be told, he had been a little thrilled at the invitation. Things between Trevor and Will had been strained recently. It was natural. The kid was growing up and finding himself. He was feeling the need to rebel and he was just starting to discover what form his rebellion might take. So far it was a lot of moping around and disdainful glares when he thought Will wasn't looking. Will could deal with that, and he thought he would be able to deal with whatever rebellion came in the next few years. Still, he couldn't help hope that the weekend would be a time to reconnect, a time to teach the kid a thing or two about nature, about being a man. It hadn't worked out that way so far. The kids had kept to themselves, and Trevor had interacted with Will only when required.

And now the thing with the hiker. He hoped it wouldn't embarrass Trevor too much. Either way, it couldn't be helped. The Regulations were the Regulations. Trust was a must. Will was a leader of the community, and he was expected to uphold the Regulations. Appearance was everything in Rook Mountain.

The kids had disappeared around a corner, but Will could still hear them talking and laughing. They were out of the dense part of the forest and surrounded by bushes. A few months earlier, this spot had been covered with the blazing purples and reds of rhododendrons. Now, the season of the flowers had passed and the bushes were bare, spindly as a tangle of fishing line left unattended.

The pitch and volume of the boys' conversation went up a couple excitement levels.

"Sounds like they made it to the clearing," Henry said.

Will rounded the corner and there it was—the summit.

Rook Mountain and the surrounding peaks were grassy balds—blunt rounded mountain tops covered with dense vegetation. The balds of the Southern Appalachian Mountains were unique because they were well below the tree line. The peaks' lack of trees was a scientific mystery. Some researchers cited long centuries of grazing by a wide variety of large animals, many of which had gone extinct. Other scientists said it was the composition of the soil. There was no conclusive verdict.

Just another damn Rook Mountain mystery, Will thought. Add it to the list.

The thought snuck into his mind before he could suppress it. He was usually good at blocking those kinds of thoughts before they took shape.

Whatever the origin of the grassy balds, the end result was a clear three-hundred-sixty-degree view of the surrounding landscape. From up there the land looked untouched, an endless sea of deep green forest. Will had lived in the town of Rook Mountain for sixteen years. It had been the center point of his whole adult life. At the summit, it seemed tiny, just a series of small gaps in the thick trees that blanketed the landscape below.

When Will first moved there, the town of Rook Mountain had been a small village to the north of the mountain. The town limits had been expanded eight years ago, and the mountain itself was part of town now, all the way to where it bumped up against the North Carolina border. The prison was in the town limits too. But regardless of what the maps said, the mountain top had always been the real Rook Mountain for Will. It was his favorite place on Earth. The view, the crushingly beautiful, endlessly green view below him, was a large part of the reason he had settled there while most of his college friends had migrated to cities like Chicago, Denver and Phoenix. Up there, more than anywhere else, Will felt like he was home.

But there was a job to do.

The boys were gathered on top of a large boulder near the summit. Just a couple of years ago they would have been playing King of the Mountain, the boy at the top of the boulder fighting to keep his position as the other boys struggled to take it. Now they were too cool or too proud. Or maybe they were just growing up.

Will and Henry stopped a few feet from the boulder.

"You wanna tell them?" Henry asked.

Will nodded.

"Guys," he said in a voice full of hard-won authority from sixteen years standing in front of a classroom. "Listen up."

Their roar of conversation diminished to a soft murmur.

"I have something important to tell you. On the way up here Mr. Strauss and I spotted something."

The boys turned to look at him. They went silent.

"Before we came up, we checked with City Hall. There shouldn't be anyone on this mountain but us. Unfortunately, we saw someone. They appeared to be camping. Maybe even living up here."

"Regulation ii," muttered the boy at the top of the bolder.

Will nodded. "That's right, Russ. This individual is in violation of Regulation ii."

There was a long silence. Finally Carl Strauss said, "What are you going to do?"

"Not me. We. We are going to do what we have to. We are going to find this Regulation breaker, and we are going to carry out his sentence."

3.

Frank looked at the city manager for a long time before speaking. "I'd like to get out of prison very much, but I guess you already knew that."

Becky Raymond smiled. "I guess I did. Let me restate that. I have it within my power to release you from prison today."

Frank sat up a little straighter in his chair. The shank in

his waistband dug into his side as he moved, reminding Frank of its presence. Was that what this was about? Did they want Frank to give up the Newg?

His palms were sweaty. They always got sweaty when he was nervous. He wished he could wipe them on his pants the way he always did back in the day before reaching for a girl's hand, but his wrists were handcuffed to the table.

He waited to see if Ms. Raymond would continue. She didn't, so Frank said, "What do we need to do to make it happen?"

Her lips curled into a smile. "When was the last time you saw your brother?"

Frank recoiled under the pressure of her cold brown eyes and the unexpected question.

The warden spoke before Frank could. "Ma'am, as you know, our prisoners have not been allowed any contact with the outside since Regulation Day."

Regulation Day. That was a term Frank hadn't heard before. He could infer its meaning from the context: the day eight years ago when everything had changed at NTCC.

The first year of Frank's stay at NTCC had been difficult, but there had been contact with the outside world. The prisoners were allowed regular visitors and TV time. There were phone calls and magazines and letters. It had been a lot like the versions of prison Frank had seen in movies, only noisier and smellier.

Then, eight years ago, everything had changed. With no explanation, televisions were removed, mail was cut off, and the phones were taken out. The prisoners were told there would be no more visitors. They had reacted with predictable fury. They'd threatened lawsuits, but since they weren't allowed contact with lawyers that hadn't gotten them far. There had been a series of riots, but the guards had violently put those down.

Eventually, the prisoners had come to accept their new circumstances, taking out their anger on each other more than on the prison leadership. New prisoners were kept in a separate cell block, cut off from the prisoners who had been inside before the day everything changed. Except for the occasional new guard, Becky Raymond was the first new person Frank had laid eyes on in eight years.

Ms. Raymond ignored the warden's comment about Regulation Day and kept her eyes fixed on Frank.

"My brother came to see me once," Frank said. "Right after the trial."

"Only once?"

"Ma'am, I'd be happy to pull the visitation records if you'd like to verify Hinkle's story," the warden said. "We could get the exact date for you. Wouldn't take but a moment."

Ms. Raymond shook her head. "Why didn't he visit you more?"

Frank shifted in his seat again and the shank wedged deeper into his side. If they were serious about letting him out, what would happen if they found the shank?

"I killed a friend of his," Frank said. "Jake didn't take it very well. He didn't have much to say to me after that."

"You look like him."

Frank couldn't help but smile. "I've been hearing that my whole life. It's been a while, though."

"A lot has happened while you've been incarcerated. With the town. If you get out of here today, you won't believe the changes we've made. The things we've been able to do."

"The warden mentioned something about that. I think he called it wonderful."

The warden practically glowed at the comment, but Ms. Raymond didn't seem to notice.

"That's an accurate statement," Ms. Raymond said. "And I don't say that out of pride. It's the simple truth. I think it's fair to say you won't find a town like Rook Mountain anywhere else on Earth. It is truly a marvel."

"What's this have to do with me getting out?"

Ms. Raymond reached forward and touched Frank's hand, a casual gesture that made him flinch in surprise. It had been a long time since a woman had touched him.

"I'm sorry to tell you this," Ms. Raymond said, "but your brother killed three people."

Frank drew a deep breath. "That's not possible."

"I'm afraid it is."

Frank let this idea, this horrible idea, roll around in his mind. Sure, Jake had hit a rough patch and got in some trouble as a teenager, same as Frank. Unlike Frank, Jake had met a nice girl and made a solid life for himself. Jake was a husband and a father. He was the only person Frank knew who could accurately be described as content. The idea that Jake could have taken three lives was absurd.

Something wasn't right about this. Something seemed off in a big, bad way. The sudden meeting where even the warden was caught off guard. The way Ms. Raymond had walked through the door as if she owned the place. All this talk about the board of selectmen like they were the President's Cabinet or something. And now this lady was saying Jake was a killer? Had she come to prison just to deliver this horrible news?

Why was Becky Raymond really there?

Frank's hands were dripping a fair amount of sweat onto the table. He really wanted to wipe them on his pants.

"Okay. So my brother's a killer. You still haven't told me what I need to do to get out of here."

"After the killings, your brother realized that we were on to him, and he ran."

A chill went through Frank. He pictured Jake on the run, living out of hotel rooms and dying his hair unnatural colors. "When was this?"

Ms. Raymond smiled her hollow smile. "Seven years ago."

"What about his family?"

"He left them behind."

Frank's stomach felt like lead. Christine and Trevor had been going it alone for seven years? "I don't understand. Why didn't anyone tell me?"

The warden cleared his throat. "We discussed it. But the selectmen decided, and I agreed, of course, that telling you wouldn't serve any purpose. Time in prison is hard enough without that on your shoulders. Besides, Jake had only been here the one time. We assumed you two must not be close."

The smoldering lead ball of emotion in Frank's belly was growing hotter by the moment. He wanted to lash out at them, to scream. Not close? A thousand childhood memories flashed through his mind in an instant. A hundred inside jokes. A dozen secrets. Not close? Frank had been closer to Jake than to anyone else in the world. Jake and his wife and son were the only real family Frank had. Maybe things hadn't been friendly since the trial, but this went deeper than that. This was family.

Frank took a deep breath and reminded himself of what the city manager had said. He could get out of here today. He couldn't help Christine from behind the walls of this prison. Whatever emotions he was feeling, he had to remain calm and figure out what the city manager wanted to hear. Whatever he needed to say, he would say it.

"You still haven't told me how I get out of prison," Frank said.

Ms. Raymond leaned forward and took a deep breath before speaking. "We have reason to believe your brother is still in town. We believe he's been in Rook Mountain all this time, deep in hiding. We have used everything we can think of to ferret him out. We've failed. We are not one step closer to finding Jake than we were seven years ago. We've turned over every stone in this town. There is nowhere we haven't looked. We've investigated every angle. And we have nothing."

Frank spoke cautiously. "And you think I can help?"

The city manager nodded. "We're hoping you can."

"You must be pretty desperate."

"Watch your mouth!" the warden said.

"It's okay," Ms. Raymond said. "We are desperate, but we also have our first clue in seven years."

Frank cocked his head and waited for her to continue.

"Do you remember Sally Badwater?"

Frank nodded. Sally had lived a few doors down from the Hinkles when Frank and Jake were growing up. She was two years younger than Frank, but the boys spent a fair amount of time with her because of the trampoline in her backyard.

"Sally claims that your brother came to see her three days ago."

"Why would he go see Sally Badwater?" Frank asked.

Ms. Raymond reached into her briefcase, pulled out a stack of paper, and slid it to Frank. Frank repositioned the pages as best he could with his restrained hands.

"Top of page four," Ms. Raymond said. "Jake approached

Sally in the Food City parking lot. She was putting her groceries in the trunk. She turned around and there he was."

Frank flipped over the first three pieces of paper and looked at the text on the top of the fourth page.

OFFICER DENSON: What did Mr. Hinkle say to you?

SALLY BADWATER: It was about that brother of his. Frank. The murderer.

OFFICER DENSON: Do you remember exactly what he said?

SALLY BADWATER: Yeah, I remember. He was real intense. Got up in my face. He said, 'Tell my brother to meet me at the quarry.'

OFFICE DENSON: The quarry? Does that mean anything to you?

SALLY BADWATER: No, of course not. He was talking nonsense.

"What did he mean by 'the quarry'?" Ms. Raymond asked.

Frank thought for a long moment. There was no quarry in Rook Mountain. "So that's it, huh? Decipher my brother's cryptic message for you and I can walk free?"

Ms. Raymond nodded.

Frank paused. This was the most power he'd had in nine years. He couldn't waste it. "I think I'd like a lawyer."

"Jesus, Hinkle." The voice came from behind him. Rodgers. Frank had forgotten the guard was in the room.

A cold smile crossed Ms. Raymond's face. "The whole point of a lawyer is to get you a better deal. I'm offering you the ability to walk out of prison today. You think a lawyer is going to get you something better than that?"

Frank licked his lips, trying to decide how far to push

this. "No lawyer means no paperwork. No paperwork means maybe you don't hold up your end of the deal."

The woman shrugged. Her face was unreadable. "I understand your concern. Your choice. If you want to go back to your cell, ask for a lawyer again. If you want to get out of prison today, answer the question. What's the quarry?"

Frank weighed the options and then answered. "You're right. I couldn't ask for anything more than what you're offering. The thing is...I have no idea what Jake was talking about. I've never heard of any quarry around Rook Mountain."

Ms. Raymond sighed. Then she did something unexpected. She reached out and she took one of Frank's hands. For a moment, he felt the old familiar shame at their sweatiness, but then she looked into his eyes. And when she did, all other thoughts slipped away. Her gaze had a force to it, a weight. There was nothing intimate about it; in fact it was the opposite. Her stare was cold and clinical. She looked into him like he was a math problem. He felt her gaze squirming into him. It was a feeling he had felt only once before.

After an endless moment, she released his hand. She didn't look away, but her stare lost its weighty intensity. She had an odd look on her face, a surprised look.

"I believe you," she said, and she stood up. "Thanks, warden."

"Wait," Frank said. This was it. His freedom was about to walk out of the room, and he was about to go back to the world of the Newg and mentally drifting and shower stabbings. "Maybe I can still help you."

"I don't think so. But I appreciate your willingness to try."

Frank's mind was spinning. He had to say something. He had to find the right words to stop her from leaving. Jake needed him. Christine needed him. "Jake wants to see me, right? That's what he told Sally. He can't do that in here. But if I were out there maybe he would make contact."

Ms. Raymond picked up her briefcase from the table and put it under her arm.

"And in the meantime, I could do some digging. I've lived here all my life. I know everybody and they'll talk to me. And I know these mountains. I know them as well as Jake does. If anyone can find him, it's me."

Ms. Raymond paused for a long moment, then looked at him. "Thirty days."

Frank's heart almost stopped as he waited for her to finish.

"You have thirty days to find him. If you do, you're free. If you don't, you come back here and serve out your sentence."

Frank felt himself nodding.

"You meet with me each week to discuss your progress. You don't leave town. And if I even suspect you aren't following through, your little leave of absence ends."

She reached into her briefcase and pulled out an envelope. She slapped it onto the table in front of him. "This is enough money to get you some clothes and a week of food. I assume you can find somewhere to stay?"

Frank nodded again. He looked at the envelope. She'd had it ready.

"Okay," she said. She looked at the warden. "Get him released. He has work to do." The warden looked as shell shocked as Frank felt. He nodded to Rodgers.

"Ma'am," Frank said. "How do I find you? For the weekly meetings."

Ms. Raymond smiled. "You don't. I'll find you."

Rodgers moved back into Frank's field of vision and unhooked the cuffs. Frank felt a smile growing on his face, and he was powerless to stop it. He had a feeling it would be there for a long while.

Ms. Raymond turned to the warden. "He's carrying a weapon. Tell the guards to overlook it."

Warden Cade nodded. "Ms. Raymond, I'm not sure how to do the paperwork on this thing."

"Jesus, Cade. Figure it out. Do it fast. If he's not a free man in the next sixty minutes, I will not be happy."

As Rodgers led Frank out of the room, Frank heard the warden say, "Shouldn't we tell him?"

Ms. Raymond said, "No. Let's see how he does. He'll either figure it out or he won't."

4.

The walk down to the boulder took much longer than it should have. The boys were quieter, and they walked behind the men. There was an energy in the air, part nervousness, part anticipation. The things the boys had been taught in school, the things they had been trained to do in the Scouts, the stories they heard the men telling, usually after a few drinks, they were about to see them up close. They were about to carry out their duty. They would soon take down a Regulation breaker.

Will leaned close to Henry. "You bring a gun up here?"

Henry nodded and patted the pocket of his thick jacket.

"I got mine too," Will said.

"I've got plenty of rope. Enough to tie him up and also tie a lead around his waist for bringing him to town."

The men had spent almost an hour talking to the boys on the summit of Rook Mountain. They had talked about the boys' responsibilities in capturing the Regulation breaker. They had told them to stay out of the hiker's reach and to stay alert. It was all review, stuff they had heard a thousand times before in the classroom, but the boys had listened with focus. There hadn't been any laughter or side conversations. Not this time.

Will held up a hand to stop the group before a curve in the road. He waived the boys in close. "The boulder is about a hundred yards ahead. From here on out, we are silent. Stay as quiet as you can and follow me and Mr. Strauss. Stay behind us and don't do anything different than what we discussed. Nod if you understand."

Will looked around the group, making eye contact with each boy. They all nodded when he looked at them, a silent vow that they understood, that they would perform their duties.

Will reached into the front pocket of his backpack and pulled out the pistol. It was a 9mm Glock. It had been a couple years since he had fired the thing at the range, but that was okay. He didn't intend to use it today. He just wanted to have it ready in case things turned bad. There were six boys here to think about after all.

Will slung the pack onto his back and began creeping down the road, the gun held loosely in his right hand. He stepped lightly, but he knew any effort to be silent would have been futile. A group of eight was sure to be noticeable. They walked down the center of the road to minimize the noise, but bits of gravel still crunched under their feet.

It didn't matter. Will could see the boulder. Most likely, there would be no one there. The backpack could have been abandoned, or its owner might have left it for the day while he went foraging for food. They would probably find nothing, the Scouts would file a report when they got back to town, and that would be that.

The lump of ice in Will's stomach told him there was another possibility. There was a possibility that someone would be there, and it would fall to Will to take the lead. Scout leader or not, Henry had already shown that he didn't have it in him. Try as he might, Will couldn't help but hate Henry a little for that. The way things were, there was a burden that had to be borne. For every person like Henry, too squeamish or indecisive to do their part, there had to be someone like Will to pick up the slack. It wasn't meanness on Will's part; it was just the way it was.

Will was fifty feet from the boulder. Henry was a few steps behind him, and the rest of the group hovered back a bit farther. Will reached down and shifted the pistol to a two hand grip. He looked at Henry one more time to make sure the man was ready. Henry nodded.

"Step out from behind the rock," Will said. He spoke in the calmest, most authoritative voice he could manage.

He was met with silence.

He tried again. "Come on out. We don't mean you any harm."

Another long moment of silence.

Henry spoke softly. "I don't think—"

Will held up his hand to quiet him.

Will said, "I take your non-response as hostility. We are moving in."

"Wait!" The voice came from behind the rock. It was a hoarse, throaty voice, but it was also higher pitched than Will had expected.

"Step out onto the road," Will said.

A shadow moved at the edge of the boulder, then it grew

until it revealed feet, legs, a body. The figure moved into the sunlight. Will heard a boy behind him gasp.

"Don't shoot!" the woman said. Her eyes were glued to Will's pistol. Her hair was a tangle of blonde and black. Her t-shirt featured the faded logo of the band Phish.

Will kept his gun trained on her. He concentrated on keeping it steady.

"Ma'am, you have broken Regulation 11. We need to escort you back to town."

The woman's voice trembled when she spoke. "Please. I haven't hurt anyone. I just want to be left alone."

"Jesus," Henry said. "That's Jessie Cooper."

Will felt a surge of anger rising up. The last thing he needed was Henry complicating matters.

"Jessie Cooper," Henry repeated. "She works at the Food City. And before...she was my accountant."

"Henry Strauss?" the woman asked, squinting into the sun.

"I don't care what she was in the Before," Will said. "Get out your rope and tie her hands. Boys, go collect her things."

Henry paused only a moment before reaching into his pack and pulling out a coil of nylon rope. He moved toward the woman.

Will kept his gun trained on her while Henry bound her hands.

"Mr. Osmond! Come here!" The voice came from one of the boys behind the boulder.

Will looked at Henry. "You got her?"

Henry nodded. "Go."

Will pocketed his gun and trotted around the boulder. On the other side, he saw the boys huddled around something on the ground. They parted as he approached, and he saw the oversized piece of paper that held their attention.

It was a map. And not just a map of Rook Mountain. It was a map of the county. A red line had been drawn straight north from the town of Rook Mountain to Elizabethton.

Russ said, "Mr. Osmond, was she planning a route to leave town?"

Will didn't respond. He stood up with a grunt and then took a deep breath. This was not good. He tried to steel himself for what was next. What had to be next.

Will walked back around the boulder. Henry stood a few feet away from the woman. Her head was down, and her shoulders were slumped.

"Ms. Cooper," Will said. "Are you familiar with Regulation 1?"

She raised her head. Her face was a bitter mask of contempt. "Yes, I think I've heard of it."

"Were you planning to leave Rook Mountain?"

She kept her eyes on him, but she did not speak.

"Ms. Cooper, were you trying to leave town?"

"It's not fair what they've done to us," she said. "It isn't right and I'm done with it. Done with all of them!"

"Jessie, are you leaving Rook Mountain?" Will asked.

"Yeah," she said. "I'm leaving. Now let me go."

Will fired, and the sound echoed off the side of the mountain. The bullet hit Jessie Cooper in the chest, and she staggered backwards. She made it three wobbly steps before collapsing. She landed with a thud.

Will walked toward her, not rushing, but careful not to hesitate either. He couldn't lose his nerve. He stood over her, staring into her vacant eyes. A sick wheeze came from her chest as the breath leaked out of her.

Will fired again, this time hitting her near the center of the forehead. There was no mistake now—the woman was dead.

He turned and saw the group staring at him. He looked from one to another, making eye contact with each of them just as he had done before they approached the boulder. He saw looks of shock, horror, revulsion, and terror. There was even a look of awe from Carl Strauss. But they were all present behind their eyes. Whatever feelings they had about what had just happened, none of them were going to lose it. At least not now.

Will spoke softly and calmly, as if his tone could counteract the violence. "We did what we had to do. This woman was a Regulation breaker. Not only that, she was a Regulation 1 breaker. She was going to leave Rook Mountain and go elsewhere. At best, she would have been killed by the Unfeathered. At worst, she would have led them back to Rook Mountain."

The boys remained still.

"There was no shame in what we did here," Will continued. "We protected ourselves. We protected our families. We did our duty, no more and no less. Everyone understand?"

The boys all nodded, some more enthusiastically than others. Things would be different now, for Trevor and for all of them.

"Don't touch anything," Will said. "Leave her things where they lay. When we get to town, we will report what happened. The police will come up here to investigate. They'll want to ask you all some questions. As long as you answer honestly and tell them exactly what happened, everything will be fine."

Will looked at Henry and waited for the man to say something. If Henry took charge, it would go a long way toward getting things back to normal. But Henry said nothing.

"We want to get to the ranger station before sundown," Will said. "Let's get moving."

As Will turned, he heard Carl say, "Hinkle, your dad is a badass."

"Don't call him that," Trevor said.

"Sorry," Carl said. "Step-dad. Whatever. He's still a badass."

"Yeah," Trevor said. "I guess he kind of is."

Will angled his way through the group until he stood next to Trevor. He put his arm around his stepson's shoulders and started down the mountain.

IN THE BEFORE (PART 1)

The first time Will met the Hinkles, Jake was sitting on the porch drinking beer and Christine was wielding a chainsaw. Over the years, Will often thought back to that day and considered it the perfect introduction to both their personalities.

Will was fresh out of college and in the state of Tennessee for the first time. He had grown up in the plains of central Illinois and driving a car, let alone a U-Haul, through the mountains was an adventure to him. He had been skiing a few times out west where the mountains were tall, jagged things that jutted proudly into the sky and dared you to summit them. They were mountains for extreme sports, ski lifts, and feeling on top of the world.

The Appalachian Mountains of Eastern Tennessee were different. They were much smaller, yes, but they were also sneakier creatures. They were round and tree covered. There would be no skiing down them. They clung too close to the Earth, and they wore a coat of dense forest. They were mountains where you could imagine Daniel Boone blazing a trail, and you could understand why it would have been such a big deal.

They looked like mountains that held secrets.

Will made it through the Cumberland Gap and the twisty ups and downs of Kentucky and Virginia, clutching the steering wheel of his U-Haul in a death grip for hours on end. He made it past the giant, illuminated roadside crosses of Bristol and into the beautiful valley that cradled Elizabethton. After surviving a winding state highway and passing countless roadside stands selling boiled peanuts and South Carolina peaches, he made it to Rook Mountain.

He pulled off the highway and onto the first side road. A man in an old Subaru passed him going the other direction and waved. Will hesitated, then waved back. You didn't get much waving at other drivers in Illinois. Unless the wave featured only one finger.

After ten minutes on the country road, he saw the sign, 'Hinkle Resort.'

He heard the distinctive buzz of a chainsaw as he drove down the driveway. A chainsaw wasn't the most comforting sound that could have greeted Will on his first visit to the Tennessee mountains, but he pressed on nonetheless.

A few hundred feet down the driveway he saw her. A woman in a sleeveless t-shirt cutting into a pine log. A pickup truck was parked behind her just off the driveway. Will figured there was room for the U-Haul to get by if he drove tight against the trees on the opposite side of the path, but just barely.

Will pulled up alongside her and rolled down the window. She didn't seem to notice. Up ahead, the driveway forked into four smaller paths. Will had no idea which way to go.

The woman shut off the chainsaw. Her long chestnut

hair was pulled back in a loose ponytail. The look suited her. "You Osmond?"

Will nodded. "Are you Christine?"

She returned his nod. "Welcome to Rook Mountain." She set down the chainsaw and marched over. Christine looked to be in her late twenties. She moved gracefully and with purpose. Will's heart skipped a beat as she gave him the slightest hint of a smile and held her hand up to his open window. He took the gloved hand and shook it.

She pointed to the fork in the driveway. "Your place is on the right. My husband Jake is up there now. I'm sure he'll be glad to help you unload." She turned and walked back to the waiting chainsaw.

Will felt like he should say something else. "Have fun."

She looked at him, gave a half smile, and fired up the chainsaw.

Will eased the U-Haul to the left, taking it as far off the gravel as he dared. He didn't want to knock off the side view mirror of his new landlord's truck, but he didn't want to get stuck, either. After a bit of finagling, Will got the U-Haul past the truck, turned onto the right-hand fork, and caught sight of his new home.

What he saw surprised him.

Christine had accurately described the cabin over the phone. She told him that it was nothing fancy, that it was old but roomy and solidly built. He liked the look of it. The large and numerous windows. The stubby chimney shyly poking out above the roof. The large porch which stretched the length of the house.

What surprised him was the man sitting on the steps leading up to the porch. He was leaning back on the stairs and looking up at the sky, surrounded by a half dozen empty beer bottles. An oversized portable cooler stood behind him. The man sat up as the moving truck approached, gave Will a casual wave, and wobbled to his feet.

"You're from Indiana or something, right? That's a long drive in this scrap," Jake Hinkle said.

"Nice to meet you. Illinois, actually. But yeah, it was a long drive."

Jake was maybe twenty-five years old, at least a few years younger than Christine. He was average height and bulky without being either fat or too muscular. He was solid, the kind of physique that comes from heavy labor rather than hours spent in the gym. His most distinctive feature was his shaggy blonde hair. If this had been a coastal town, Will would have taken him for a surfer type.

"Want a beer?" Jake asked.

Will paused for a moment, then looked at the U-Haul and considered the work that lay ahead of him.

"Truck ain't going nowhere." Jake smiled and nodded toward the cooler. "Help yourself."

Will grabbed a beer and took a long satisfying drink. It tasted mighty fine.

"So, listen," Jake said. "I don't want you to get the wrong idea."

Will took another drink before answering. "About what?"

"You see a man sitting around drinking while his wife is hard at work, you might not think too highly of him. I want you to understand this is a special circumstance." Jake gave Will a crooked smile. "I lost a bet."

"Oh," Will said. He took another drink and noticed the bottle was half empty.

Jake snorted and shook his head. "Dude, seriously? I tell you my wife is cutting down trees because I lost a bet and you're not going to ask about it?"

Will shrugged. "Didn't think it was any of my business."

Jake roared with laughter. "Man, you see that house over there?" He pointed to another cabin just past a thin line of trees. "Me and Christine live there. Your business and my business are bound to get tangled up from time to time. Might as well start now."

Will smiled. "What was the bet?"

"Christine's dad, Clark, used to own this place. He'd rent these cabins out a week at a time to vacation people. Demand was so high that he'd occasionally rent out his own place and sleep in the tool shed out back. We bought it from him when we got married. 'Course, he couldn't help but share his thoughts on the way we run the place. He lives in the cabin on the end. He didn't much like it when Christine and I moved in as it meant there were only two left to rent out. Then we let my brother Frank move into the third cabin. He really didn't like that. When we decided to rent this cabin out monthly rather than weekly, he had some thoughts on that as well. Needless to say, Clark and I have some communication problems."

"So what was the bet?"

"That brother I mentioned? Frank? Christine has a couple issues with him. We knew they'd both be gone today, so we had ourselves a little bet. We shot darts. And I lost."

Will heard the gravel crunch and looked at the road just in time to see Christine's truck roll by, dragging a large log behind it.

"So if you lost, why is she cutting wood while you drink?"

Jake smiled again. "That's her fifth trip. See, we had the bright idea that it might be fun to build a little blockade across either Clark's or Frank's driveway. She won the bet. God, she was on fire last night."

"So when Frank comes home tonight..."

"He's going to find his driveway blocked with at least five logs. My guess is that it will be more like ten before the girl runs out of steam."

Will couldn't help but laugh. "Remind me to never piss off Christine."

Jake held up his bottle. "Cheers to that."

Will raised his beer, and the two bottles clinked together.

"Welcome to Rook Mountain, Mr. Osmond, where we make our own fun. The great thing about this place is that nothing crazy ever happens." He met Will's eyes and that crooked smile reappeared. "The downside is that nothing crazy ever happens."

SAME OLD TOWN

I.

"If I had to guess the cause of death, I'd go with the two bullets," Christine Osmond said.

The deceased woman, positively identified as Jessie Cooper, lay on the medical examiner's table. She was stuffed into a black body bag, unzipped at the top. Her head and torso poked out like a candy bar from a peeled-back wrapper.

"Seriously, Doc?" the man in the police uniform asked. "That's all you got?"

Christine sighed. "Sullivan, she's been unzipped for about thirty seconds. Come back in an hour and I might have something a little more in-depth."

Sullivan nodded. "I was hoping to get home tonight."

"Very subtle." She looked up at him. "So you don't have any concerns with me doing the medical examination?"

Sullivan shrugged. "It's not ideal. In the Before, we probably would have had to find someone else. But now... who else are we going to ask?"

Christine nodded. She'd grown used to that refrain over

the last eight years. She was one of only two medical doctors in Rook Mountain, and the other one had just celebrated his eighty-fifth birthday. In the Before, most people had gone to Elizabethton for their medical needs.

In the old days, Christine had been a podiatrist. She had worked in a small but progressive hospital in Elizabethton, a tight-knit workplace high on results and comparatively low on drama. They were even starting to get some national recognition. A medical journal had written up their unique approach to cross-disciplinary teamwork. There had been talk of awards. Grant money.

It had been a good life. Work hard all day and sometimes all night at a job she was passionate about. Sure, it was stressful, but it was a good stress, an invigorating stress. When work was done, she drove to her beautiful home in the mountains and her amazing family.

Then the Bad Things had happened. The Unfeathered. Regulation Day. Jake's disappearance. Now she might as well be one of two doctors alive.

"Anyway," Sullivan said, "I don't guess you'll find anything unexpected. This couldn't be any more straightforward. Ms. Cooper here was a Regulation breaker. Will took care of her, protected the town, and taught all those boys a thing or two at the same time. You should be proud of your husband."

Christine smiled. "I am. Always." Ever since she had married Will she'd never once been anything but proud of him. It was different than her marriage to Jake had been in many ways. She supposed no two marriages were exactly alike. She and Will had their ups and downs, but her trust in the man never wavered. The best part was that she knew he felt the same way about her.

"Man alive, I wish Peyton had been in that group,"

Sullivan said. "His Scout leader hasn't even taught him to start a proper fire. And he's fourteen in September."

Christine pulled on a pair of latex gloves. She reached up and hit 'record' on the video camera pointed at the table. Who the hell would ever watch this thing, she didn't know. But procedure was procedure. Christine made a point of following the rules. Trust was a must.

"I'll leave you to it then." Sullivan turned and sauntered out of the room, letting the heavy metal door slam shut behind him.

Christine dragged the zipper of the body bag down until the rest of the corpse was exposed. In spite of what she had told Sullivan, she didn't want to be there all night, either. She wanted to get home to her family. She wanted to be with Will. And Trevor too. It wasn't the first death that either of them had seen, and it probably wouldn't be the last. But they both had to be going through some things.

Christine sighed and took a deep breath. She couldn't think about any of that now. There was a dead woman in front of her who deserved the courtesy of a thorough examination. Like Sullivan, Christine doubted there was anything to find, but that didn't mean she wouldn't try.

Christine pulled the body bag away from the woman's arms and legs. Jessie Cooper was forty-two years old, or so her records said. It was a little hard to tell on visuals alone with the distracting hole in her forehead. It was clear from her clothing that she had been out in the wild for some time. The denim of her jeans was hard with dirt. Her hair was tangled and uneven. Christine tried to picture the way she might have looked before she went into the wild.

Christine started with the hands. They were bound with rope but appeared uninjured. Her wrists showed no signs that she had struggled against the rope. Most likely it had been quick and her suffering had been minimal.

Where to go next? She could start from the bottom and work her way up. The feet would be in terrible shape, Christine knew. It was difficult to take care of your feet when spending any significant time in the wilderness. Christine had seen it on countless hikers in the Before, men and women passing through Rook Mountain on the Appalachian Trail who had finally given in to their screaming feet and come in for a checkup. The feet were always the first sign of a life hard lived, long before the teeth or the hands.

Not that the head was much prettier in this particular case.

The shot, Christine had to admit, was impressive. Dead center of the forehead. From the way Sullivan had told it to her, the woman had been lying on the ground with Will standing above her. Shooting down was more difficult than it might seem. It wasn't the way a weapon was meant to be fired and not the way anyone practiced shooting. It would have been easy for Will to take off the top of her skull, but his shot had been true. Steady hand, that one.

Not as steady as hers, of course, but she was a doctor.

Christine could have stopped there. But she felt it was her responsibility to check for any other possible injuries prior to death. That was when she noticed the necklace.

Jessie Cooper wasn't wearing any rings, earrings, or bracelets, but she did have a thin gold chain around her neck. Christine slid a probing tool under the chain and lifted it, pulling it from underneath the woman's shirt.

On the end of the chain, there was a key.

Christine took a sharp breath. It couldn't be. Not on this random woman who had spent the last month hiding in the woods and planning her escape to Elizabethton. Christine unhooked the chain and held it up so the key dangled in front of her eyes.

It was an old-fashioned key, a long cylinder with dramatic teeth jutting out at the end. There was a symbol on the head of the key, and that symbol was what held Christine's attention. It showed the face of a clock with a jagged crack running down its center.

Christine had seen the symbol before. She had spent much of the last eight years searching for something, anything, with the symbol. She'd searched until she had run out of places to look. No, that wasn't accurate. There were still plenty of stones unturned in this little town. She had run out of something else. There was a word for it... Hope? Motivation? Some combination of those things.

Christine peeled the latex glove off one hand and reached for the key. She closed her hand tight around it, feeling the coolness of the metal against her skin. Then she opened her hand and traced the symbol of the clock's face with her thumb.

It was real. She had found it.

Christine took a deep breath and tried to clear her mind. Keeping this key—keeping anything with the broken clock symbol—was a violation of Regulation 2. The rule was clear —she was supposed to turn the object over to the police immediately. Breaking the Regulation didn't bother her, she had broken this one before, but it did complicate things. It put her and her family in danger.

She switched off the video camera. Then she took out the Mini-DV tape and put it in her pocket. Thank God for the old school video camera in the medical examiner's room. She would burn the tape later. It wasn't ideal, she knew, especially since Sullivan had seen her turn the camera on. Couldn't exactly say she had forgotten. And since the shooting involved her husband, it was plausible that someone might review the tape to make sure she wasn't covering anything up. It wasn't likely in Rook Mountain, but it was plausible.

Christine, by her very nature, didn't like dealing with this level of uncertainty.

Still, there was nothing she could do. She couldn't risk someone reviewing the tape and seeing the key. If the wrong people saw it, things could take a very bad turn.

She would put another tape into the video camera, hit 'record,' and take the examination from the top. She would be thorough. Even though she desperately wanted to run home and show the key to Will, to celebrate the good news with him, she would force herself to complete the job. When Sullivan came back in forty-five minutes or so, she would tell him about the results of the examination. She would have an unhurried, casual conversation with him for as long as she could stomach. Only after all that would she go home. There was too much at stake for her to be anything but meticulous.

She slipped the necklace into her pocket and went to find another tape for the video camera.

2.

Frank sat on a park bench in downtown Rook Mountain. He was eating a vanilla ice cream cone with sprinkles. It was the first time he'd tasted ice cream in over nine years. He was a free man.

The release from prison had been a whirlwind. Usually, the hours leading up to a prisoner's release were an exciting but stressful time. Often the prisoner was given little information on the exact time of their release. But the main reason for the tension was the fear that something would go wrong. Maybe there had been a paperwork snafu. Maybe someone in some government office somewhere would review your file and have a change of heart. It was unlikely to happen, but that didn't stop the fears from coming in those final prison hours.

Frank had been spared all of that.

After the meeting with Ms. Raymond and the warden, Frank had been taken to another office area and asked to sign a few pieces of paper. Rodgers then led him to a large room where he was given a set of clothes he'd never seen before, an envelope of cash, and a hearty handshake. With that, Rodgers had called for a prison transport van and sent Frank on his way.

Of course, Rodgers hadn't been able to leave it at that. As Frank boarded the van, he heard Rodgers calling to him. "Maybe I'll see you on the outside."

Frank had no idea if that was a threat or the guard's awkward way of saying that he considered Frank a human being again. Frank didn't much care. He turned and gave Rodgers a tooth-baring smile that probably could have been interpreted as menacing. "Yeah," Frank said. "Maybe you will."

Frank asked the van driver to drop him off in downtown Rook Mountain. He wasn't ready to head out to the cabin just yet. He wandered a few blocks, enjoying the freedom of not having his next move dictated to him. He didn't have anywhere to be, and no one would yell at him if he wasn't walking fast enough or on a straight enough line. He passed a few people on the street that he recognized. Some of them looked at his face for a little too long, as if trying to place him, but no one said anything. Thank God for that. He wasn't ready for small talk. To say he was out of practice would have been a severe understatement. And he had no idea how he would explain his release from prison.

He spotted Grumpy's Creamery. It had been one of his favorite places when he was a kid. He'd spent many happy hours there back in the days before he knew anything bad could happen. Before he knew how dark life could get. Back when the future was something to look forward to rather than something to dread.

So he took the envelope out of his pocket, peeled off a twenty, and walked inside.

After he got the ice cream cone, he wandered for a few more blocks, licking at it when it started to drip. He sat down on a bench in front of a small playground. It was only after he sat that he realized where he was.

It couldn't be a coincidence. It had to be his subconscious that had led him there. Perhaps it had been leading him there all along.

Right there, right next to the swing set, was where he had killed Brett Miller almost ten years ago. It looked almost exactly the same as it had on that day. Frank could almost see Brett's blood splattered across the ground and dripping from the park sign.

He looked hard and didn't try to force the remembered blood out of his mind. He'd had a lot of time to think about that night, and he didn't run from it anymore. The thought of it still made the guilt bubble up inside him, overwhelming all his senses, but he didn't try to push it down. He had done something terrible. As the prison counselors would say, it was an event that defined his past, but it did not have to define his future.

So what did the future hold? Frank inspected his waffle cone, and then licked a drip running down the side. He bit into the cone, and it cracked with a sweet crunch. It tasted as good as he remembered.

There wasn't much in this world Frank was good at. He'd messed up his life about as bad as was possible. Even before he became a killer, he'd been fired from about every reputable employer in Rook Mountain. Frank had never known his father very well, and his mother had died still worried about how her younger son would turn out. But there were three things Frank knew. He knew locks, he knew the people of Rook Mountain, and he knew his brother Jake.

The police had been searching for Jake for years, but that didn't mean much to Frank. The cops never did really understand the Hinkle boys. Frank could do it. He could find his brother. And what would happen when he found him? Frank didn't have it in him to turn in his own brother. But Jake needed him. And maybe he needed Jake.

"Hello, Frank."

Frank whipped his head toward the figure on the bench next to him. Damn it, he had been doing it again. Drifting.

The first thing he noticed about the man sitting next to him was the uniform. Then he saw the face. For a moment, Frank flashed back to the morning he killed Brett. He saw himself hitting Brett with the tire iron. He saw two police officers tackling him to the ground. Now, in the same spot ten years later, one of those officers was sitting next to him.

"Hello, Sean."

Sean Lee was one year younger than Frank. In their elementary school days, Sean had often come over to the Hinkle's house to play basketball in the driveway. The kid had shot the ball pretty well and hit the boards with enthusiasm on offense, but his defining basketball characteristic was his complete lack of interest in playing defense. He just stood around and waited for his team to take possession of the ball again.

"You doing okay?" Sean asked.

Frank wasn't sure how to answer that question. How was he doing? He was ecstatic. He was confused. He was angry. "It's been an odd day."

Sean said, "You really put me through my paces in the last couple of hours. You know how many calls we've had to the station about you? Go ahead and guess."

"I really don't know."

"Seven. We've had seven calls, and they were all pretty much the same. The murderer has broken out of jail. The Hinkle boy is out on the street. For some reason, even though they say your brother killed three people, you are the Hinkle everyone seems most afraid of."

Frank sighed. "I thought maybe no one recognized me."

Sean laughed. "You're famous, buddy. Rook Mountain famous anyway. I called the prison and they confirmed that your release was legit. I told the next six people who called. It should be making its way around the gossip circuits. By midday tomorrow everyone will know. Then maybe people will start being a little friendlier. You got lucky today, though."

"How do you mean?"

"You're lucky people called us about you. Things have changed in Rook Mountain since you went inside."

"So I keep hearing."

"Yeah, well, it's true. When folks see someone doing something illegal, they don't always tip off the law. A lot of times they decide to take care of it themselves."

That didn't sound all that new to Frank.

"I'm not saying it's going to happen," continued Sean, "but if anybody starts harassing you, you come to me, understand? Or someone else in the department. Don't try to resolve it yourself. Things can turn ugly fast that way."

Another image flashed into Frank's mind: the tire iron slamming into Brett Miller's head, the head bending and then caving in. And Frank pulling back the tire iron, slick with blood and coated with chunks of what had been Brett.

"That I do know," Frank said.

Sean frowned. "Yeah, I guess you do. What I'm trying to say is...well, you remember that nickname Jake had for me?"

Frank couldn't help but smile. "Yeah. No D. Lee."

Sean's ears turned a shade of pink. "That's the one. I never agreed with it. I played some top notch defense in your driveway. Still do every Wednesday morning down at the Y."

"Sure. I remember your great defense. It involved a lot of standing behind your opponent and waiting for him to score, right?" It felt good to talk to an old friend, and it was surprising how quickly he fell back into the old pattern of giving Sean a hard time. It was like the last nine years had suddenly fallen away.

"Now's the time for you to play some serious defense. Don't get in anyone's face. Go with the flow. It will take you some time to get used to things, but you'll get there. Did they tell you not to leave town?"

Frank nodded. "Yeah, they made a big deal about that."

"That's the most important thing. As long as you don't leave town, and you don't start any trouble, you'll get along fine."

"Thanks," Frank said. "Hey, can I ask you about something that's been bugging me?"

Sean looked away. "Frank, I'm sure you've got lots of questions. But I'm not really the guy to answer them."

"Just one. It's about the cars."

Sean paused for a long moment, then nodded.

"I bought a new Ford F-150 a couple months before the thing went down with Brett. I'd wanted one my whole life, and things were going well with the lock business, so I finally pulled the trigger. I thought about that truck a lot in prison. About how unfair it was that I'd finally gotten it and then had it taken away from me. Anyway, I can picture that truck almost perfectly in my mind."

"So what's the question?" Sean asked.

"I was walking down the street a little while ago and I saw an F-150 drive by. And it looked exactly like mine. Same color, same detailing, same new truck shine on it."

Sean smiled. "That's a popular truck, Frank. Yours wasn't exactly one of a kind."

"That's not what I mean. The F-150 I saw had to be almost brand new, and it looked exactly like mine. Sean, I went to prison in 2013. Are you telling me Ford hasn't changed one detail of the F-150 in the last nine years?"

The smile fell from Sean's face.

"So then I started looking around at other cars. And you know what I noticed? They all look like they did in 2013. There weren't any changes to the models I remember, and there weren't any new models."

"You're right," Sean said. He spoke slowly and carefully. "At least not in Rook Mountain."

"What the hell does that mean?" Frank asked.

"When I said that you need to go with the flow, this is the type of thing I was talking about. This is one of the hundreds of tiny things you are going to notice in the next few weeks. Like I said, things have changed here. I don't feel very comfortable talking about it, especially in public and even more so while I'm on duty."

"That's a pretty weird thing to lay on me and not explain, Sean."

"I know. And I'm sorry about that." He patted Frank on the shoulder and smiled. "Still, beats the hell out of prison, right?"

Frank nodded.

"Listen, if you still want to chat about this stuff, why don't you come over tomorrow night? I'll throw a couple of steaks on the grill and we'll drink some beer. I won't promise to answer all your questions, but with a couple beers in me I'll be more likely to answer some of them."

"Yeah, that sounds great," Frank said. And did it ever. Steak. Beer. And to think, he'd been excited about the ice cream cone.

"Awesome. Come by around sixish. I'm still over on Maple Street." Sean stood up.

"Thanks, man. I really appreciate it."

"I'm glad to see you, Frank. I've missed you. Welcome home."

Frank felt a lump growing in his throat. When was the last time someone had spoken a sincere kind word to him? He couldn't remember. "Thank you."

"Hey, you got a place to stay?"

"I was going to head out to my cabin. See if the place is still standing."

Sean looked away again, the same as he had when Frank asked about the cars. "Yeah, of course. Cool." Something in his voice made Frank think Sean did not consider it cool at all. "Just make sure you don't sleep in the park or something. We've got these...regulations against that. We're pretty strict about them."

Frank nodded. "See you tomorrow night."

3.

Will stood in front of the open refrigerator for a few minutes, and then he shut it and wandered back to the living room. He couldn't sit still. He couldn't stop pacing, snapping his fingers, stretching. Anything to keep moving. He had too much nervous energy.

Up on Rook Mountain, killing Jessie Cooper had seemed necessary. Now he wasn't so sure. He had taken the life of a woman who only wanted to be free of this town. He had added another name to the ever-lengthening list of Regulation casualties. And for what? Had it been worth it?

After the shooting, Will had led the boys down the mountain and joked with them a little bit, but not so much that it disregarded what had happened. At the police station, he had calmly given his statement. He hadn't left anything out or held anything back. He had told the truth to the best of his recollection. After an hour and a half of questioning, the police had given him instructions to stay home tonight in case they had further questions and released him.

When he got home, Will had tried to talk to Trevor, but he wasn't sure how much got through to the kid. No, Trevor wasn't upset. No, he did not want to talk about it. Yes, he understood why it had to happen. Yes, he knew that he could talk to Will about anything. Will ended the conversation feeling ineffective and out of touch. The way his own dad had once seemed to him.

The pacing started after the conversation with Trevor. Will felt odd. Tired and hyper at the same time, and a little sick to his stomach. He felt like a hypocrite. He was still pacing almost an hour later when Christine walked through the door.

She stepped toward him and gave him a tight hug. "Are you okay?"

"I feel weird. It's probably the adrenaline. I'm okay."

She sighed. "Tell me what happened."

"I thought the woman was camping, so I talked Henry into going after her. I figured it would look good to bring in a minor Regulation breaker, you know? As soon as we saw her map, every kid in the troop knew she was headed out of town. I couldn't see any way out of it, so..."

He took a deep breath and continued. "Henry wasn't going to pull the trigger. If we hadn't executed her, the board of selectmen would have started an investigation. They would have looked into our lives more deeply than they have since right after Jake disappeared."

"Honey, you did the right thing. You know that, right? We knew something like this could happen."

Will nodded. Her hair tickled his face.

She pulled away from him and gripped his upper arms. "Will. I found something on the body."

"They made you examine it? I thought they would have had someone else do it." He noticed the intensity on her face, and stopped talking.

"It was hanging from her necklace. She was wearing it like a charm."

She put her hand into her pocket, pulled it out, and slowly opened her hand.

Will's breath caught in his throat. "Is it really one of them?"

Christine smiled. "It has to be, right?"

Will nodded. "Why would she have it? Where'd she get it?"

"I don't know," Christine said. "Here." She placed the key in his open hand and closed his fingers around it.

Will shut his eyes and concentrated on the key in his

hand. All the nervous energy drained away, and he enjoyed a moment of peace.

Will said, "This...this is huge. We have to be careful. We've waited this long. We have to make sure we don't rush into anything."

Christine looked at Will. Her eyes were shining. "I know we're not there yet, but we're getting close to the finish line. If we can stay strong a little longer."

Will nodded. Her excitement was infectious. He leaned toward her. His lips were almost touching hers when the doorbell rang.

4.

Trevor lay on his bed, his earbuds in his ears, staring at the letter.

He still wore his clothes from the trip, and he stunk of sweat and campfire smoke. He needed to change and do it soon. Will had been too distracted to notice, but he would have no such luck when Mom got home. She could discuss the dangers of dirty clothes on a clean bed at great length and with deep passion. He should probably take a shower too, to be on the safe side.

Come to think of it, a hot shower sounded pretty good.

But he couldn't stop looking at the letter. No one knew about it, no one but him, and that was part of what made it special. He would have to tell Will and Mom soon, probably that night. Tomorrow at the latest. He wanted to savor the secret for a little longer first.

What would Will and Mom say? Would they force him to accept? Would they say he was too young? Would they leave the decision up to him?

He read the letter again, probably for the hundredth time.

September 13th, 2022

Trevor Hinkle

1407 Riley Dr.

Dear Trevor:

Congratulations! I am pleased to inform you of your acceptance to the Rook Mountain Beyond Academy for the Fall Semester of 2022. Your acceptance is evidence of our Board of Directors' confidence in your potential as demonstrated by your academic achievements, your standardized test scores, and your unique personal qualities. You are now part of a select few, and you will be a part of the fifth graduating class in the Academy's history.

RMBA is dedicated to providing the best education for our students. Our faculty strives to find new and innovative ways to prepare students for the challenge of leading our community. While some of our students will go on to careers in Resource Expansion, we expect others will follow other paths such as Law Enforcement, Medicine, and Business Administration.

Whatever path you choose to follow, we look forward to you starting it with us.

Sincerely,

Janet Miller

Dean of Students

At the bottom of the letter was a handwritten note:

Trevor, we are all very proud of you. You have overcome a lot in your life and we believe you can be successful here at RMBA. See you in October! —Janet

The board of selectmen had launched the Rook Mountain Beyond Academy three years earlier as a school for advanced students. They didn't accept a set number of students each year, nor did they disqualify students based on age. They accepted eight students the first year, the second year only three. Most of the students were between fifteen and twenty years old. The youngest person ever accepted was thirteen. A full year older than Trevor.

Trevor would be the youngest ever. But would his folks allow him to go?

He felt anger building up inside him at the very thought that they might object. Trevor knew Will's feelings on the school. The man wasn't usually outspoken, especially when his thoughts went against the official stance of the Rook Mountain board of selectmen. But he couldn't hold his tongue about the RMBA. He thought it was elitist. He thought it created an unnecessary class system. Most importantly, Will thought it unfairly bypassed the town's Certification and Mentorship programs, programs which he happened to run.

Trevor knew that Will had applied to teach at RMBA and been rejected. Janet Miller had told Will he had the book learning but not enough real world experience.

It didn't matter. His step-dad couldn't tell him what to do. Sure, about little stuff. But something big like this? Something that affected his future? No way. Will Osmond had no say in that.

There was a lot to love about the RMBA. Some of Rook Mountain High's best teachers taught exclusively at the RMBA. There were certain freedoms allowed to Academy students, certain Regulations they didn't need to follow. They were all little things, sure, but it was the town's nod of respect to its best students.

Those weren't the reasons Trevor so desperately wanted to join the Academy. The real reason was that the Academy gave him his best chance, probably his only chance, of becoming a Resource Expansion Specialist. And RESpys were allowed to leave town. They hunted down citizens who ran. They gathered supplies for the town. They explored the unknown territories.

Carl thought Will was a badass. And for what? Shooting a defenseless woman who was sleeping in the woods? Compared with what the RESpys did every day, that was nothing. RESpys faced down the nightmares that wanted to eat the world, and they fought them back.

Trevor would be a RESpy someday. He knew it. He would leave this town. He would see the plains. Maybe even see the ocean.

Then he would find his father.

5.

Frank walked the edges of the road, staying close to the tree line. Cars driving down the tiny road in the middle of nowhere didn't expect to see pedestrians, and they drove accordingly. It wasn't just the thought of cars that pushed him to the side of the road—his desire to be near the trees pulled him toward their shade. He had grown up playing in these woods. He'd climbed many of these trees and fallen out of a few of them. He'd camped out here. Played hide and seek. Drank his first beer and taken his first shot of moonshine. These woods were a constant presence in his life, and after so long away he wanted to be close to them. The crunch of pine needles beneath his feet and the rich scent of the woods in his nose just felt right.

Frank was walking home, walking toward the cabin he had lived in for six years before his incarceration. He had never owned the place, Jake and Christine had owned all four cabins on the property, but he had lived there long enough that he felt a sense of ownership. After Jake and

Christine had moved into town to be closer to the schools for little Trevor, Frank had taken care of the property. And he had taken care of Clark, Christine's father, until the old man had gotten too sick and spent the last two months of his life at Elizabethton Memorial.

In some ways, that had been the best year of Frank's life. His lock business had been growing steadily, and there was plenty to do around the cabins when he wasn't working. He'd been dating Wendy, and things had been getting pretty serious. He and Christine had patched up their differences —most of them anyway. He had the land to take care of, and he took great pleasure in doing so.

Frank grimaced as he rounded the bend and saw the driveway. Weeds as high as Frank's knee sprouted through the gravel. He would have thought Christine would have kept the place up, or at least hired somebody to do so. He walked up the driveway, grabbing randomly at weeds and pulling them out as he passed. He knew he wasn't doing any good. He wasn't pulling up the root. But it still made him feel a little better.

He came to the four-way fork in the drive and took the one on the left that led to the cabin that had served as his workshop after Clark died.

Frank walked the remaining weedy stretch of the driveway slowly, taking in the sights and the sounds of the place. He climbed up the porch and looked out over the view. He had spent many a pleasant evening on this porch, sometimes strumming his guitar, sometimes sipping Tennessee whiskey, sometimes simply thinking. Or had he really been thinking? He remembered many hours spent out here, sure, but he couldn't remember what he might have been thinking about so hard. Maybe he had been drifting a little, even back then.

Frank turned and pulled the keys out of his pocket. They had been in his possession when he was incarcerated, so they were given back to him when he was released. He paused before inserting the key, and took a look at the place. Not bad for nine years of neglect, he decided. The paint wasn't exactly flake-free, but it wasn't falling off the door either. Part of the benefit of a log cabin—the age didn't show as quickly. If it wasn't for the weeds growing in the driveway, you might not even know it was abandoned.

Frank reached out and gave the doorknob a wiggle. It turned freely in his hand. Damn, that wasn't good. Not good at all.

He had left instructions with Jake and Christine. He had asked them to lock the cabin and leave his things untouched. That was all he had wanted from them. Jake had nodded, and even though he had been furious about what had happened between Frank and Brett Miller, it seemed like he had understood and that he would take care of it.

There was another possibility. Maybe Jake had followed through and left the place locked tight. Maybe someone had found their own way in. Maybe that someone was still there.

Frank wished he had thought to bring some sort of weapon. A gun would be ideal, but anything would do. A knife. A hammer. Anything but a tire iron.

Frank took a deep breath and pushed on the door. It was only open an inch when he heard a voice behind him say, "Don't move. Put your hands in the air, please."

Frank released the doorknob and raised his hands. He squeezed his eyes shut tight, as tight as he could, to clear his mind. Then he opened them. The man hadn't said he had a gun, but he didn't need to. In these parts, a man might not have a legal home, but he wouldn't be caught without a gun.

Frank gritted his teeth in frustration. He hadn't survived

nine years in NTCC to get shot by a squatter the day he got out. He began turning toward the voice.

"I said don't move!"

Frank froze. "Okay. Sorry. And I'm sorry if I frightened you. I'm—"

"Yeah, you're gonna be sorry," the man said. "You better tell me what you're doing here, and tell me quick."

Frank took a deep breath. "I...I used to live here. I've been away for a while."

"Away? What the hell do you mean, away? You expect me to believe you're a RESpy?"

"RESpy?" Frank asked. Sean's words came back to him. Go with the flow. "No, I'm not a RESpy."

"Okay, then I guess you're a Reg Breaker. That means I could shoot you dead and be a hero. They might even give me these cabins legally. Put them in my name as a way of saying thanks."

Frank's jaw ached with tension. No way in hell was this asshole getting the cabins. He wasn't about to say that now, though. "I don't know anything about that. I've been in prison. Up at NTCC. Got out today."

"Holy shit. You're that Hinkle boy, ain't you?"

Frank nodded slowly. "Yeah. I am."

"Ha. I thought you looked familiar. It's Gus Hansen. From 3rd Street Baptist."

Gus Hansen. It took Frank a moment, but he finally placed the man. He had been an usher at church. Always sucking on mints. The man had always had a mischievous little smirk on his face. Frank had never really understood what the man did for a living, but he'd had the impression it was not exactly legal.

Frank lowered his hands. "Gus. Yeah, of course."

"Keep them up!" shouted Gus. "The fact that I knew you in the Before don't mean nothing."

Frank put his hands back up. "Okay. Sorry."

There was a long silence. So long that Frank began to wonder if the older man had nodded off or something.

Finally Gus said, "Frank, you've put me in a bit of a pickle here. I don't want to hurt you, and I know you didn't come out here with any ill will toward me and mine. You're just a man enjoying his freedom."

"That's right," Frank said. "I don't mean you any harm."

"At the same time, here you are, mucking up a nice situation for me. See, I lost my house in one of those goddamn property regulations. Thankfully, we found this place and made ourselves a nice little arrangement with the owner. Part of that arrangement is we don't let people go snooping around on the property."

The door in front of Frank swung open and Frank suddenly remembered the other important thing about Gus Hansen: his sons.

Ty and Kurt Hansen had been the scourge of Rook Mountain during Frank's high school days. The brothers were both in the neighborhood of six foot seven and built like brick walls. In high school, they had helped put the Rook Mountain High football team on the map. By the time Frank was a teenager, the Hansens had graduated from high school and had moved on to bar fighting and general hell-raising.

Every time Jake and Frank Hinkle got into trouble, which was frequently, folks would say, "Well, at least they aren't the Hansen boys."

The Newg had run with the Hansen boys back in the day, so Frank had heard plenty of stories about them during his time in prison. Enough stories that he hoped he'd never again cross paths with either of them.

One of those Hansen boys was standing in front of Frank now, filling the open doorway so thoroughly that only a sliver of light managed to eke in around his edges. The man was as big and solid as Frank remembered. He grimaced at Frank, and then looked past him and noticed his father. Frank kept his hands in the air and waited.

"Dad, what's going on here?"

"This here's Frank Hinkle," Gus said. "He's a little confused. Ain't that right?"

Frank nodded slowly. "You Ty or Kurt?"

The man in the doorway scowled.

"This is Ty," Gus said. "And I think it's time for you to be moving on, Hinkle."

Frank started to go, but then stopped. Maybe he could still get something out of the long walk out here. Maybe he could get the one thing that mattered. "I don't care about you living here. I'm going to be staying in town. And I don't care about my stuff. You can have it for all I care. I only want my guitar case."

There was a long pause. Gus asked, "Your guitar case? The locked one?"

Frank nodded.

Another long pause. "Boy, you don't know how long I've spent trying to get that case open. My fingers have been itching to play that thing for years. I found those keys in the kitchen, but they didn't work. I take it there's a trick to it?"

"There is," Frank said.

Gus sighed. "Been driving me crazy trying to figure it out. I could have smashed the hinges off and opened it that way. I came close to doing just that a few times. But I kept thinking some night it would come to me. I thought I would beat the thing somehow."

Another long pause. Gus said, "Whoever heard of a guitar case with a puzzle for a lock? I take it you can open it? You remember how?"

Frank said, "Let me have the case and I'll show you how to open it."

Gus was quiet for a long moment, and then he said, "You used to make those, right? Trick locks?"

Frank couldn't help but correct him. "Puzzle locks."

"And people paid you for that?"

Frank nodded. It was a small market, but the customers paid well. He had spent years creating thirty original designs. And they were all in the guitar case. His life's work was in that guitar case.

"So wait a minute," Ty said. "You know so much about locks, how come you never broke out of that prison?"

Frank smiled. "They put pretty solid locks on prison doors. Besides, the guards kind of frown on lock picking. They knew I was a locksmith, so they watched me pretty close."

Gus sighed. "Well, as much as I'd like the trick to opening that case, it ain't gonna happen. Like I said, we got an arrangement with the owner. Ty?"

Ty smiled like he had been given the green light.

He moved fast for a big man. His fist hit Frank in the gut like a sledgehammer, driving the air from Frank's lungs. Frank hit the ground with a thud.

He lay on the ground, gasping, his mind reeling. He had spent the past nine years successfully avoiding fights, and he had let his guard down the moment he got out. Stupid.

Ty grabbed a handful of Frank's hair and pulled him up to his knees. He leaned close and whispered into Frank's ear.

"Don't come back here. This place is off limits. You come back here, and I'll have to get rough."

6.

It took Frank an hour to walk to the section of town where Christine lived. The sun was down now and he felt a slight sting of worry. Sean had said not to sleep in the park, but what about walking down the street at night? Was he asking for more trouble? And what if Christine wasn't home? Or if for some reason she refused to let him stay with her? What would he do then?

He turned onto Riley Drive and slowed his pace. He hadn't thought much about what he would say to Christine; he had only considered getting there. How much would he tell her? Would he admit he had been released to find her missing husband?

He paused for a minute in front of the tan, ranch-style home. It looked bigger than he remembered. More intimidating. The bushes were carefully manicured and the lawn was nicely hedged. No weeds growing in this driveway. Frank reached for the knob, then stopped and pressed the doorbell instead.

After a long moment, the door opened. The man on the inside squinted out into the darkness, trying to see Frank. Frank should have said something, but he was too surprised. Why was Will Osmond answering the door at Christine and Trevor's house?

Will fumbled for the porch light and finally flipped it on. It was his turn to be shocked.

"Frank?" Will asked. "Frank, is that you?"

"Yeah. Hi, Will. I got out today and I was...well, is Christine here?"

Will's mouth hung open in an expression that was half surprise and half confusion. Christine appeared, pushing past Will. "Frank?" She laughed and the sound was a balm to Frank's soul. She looked older, but the years sat well on her. To Frank's eyes, she looked prettier than she had a decade ago. "What are you doing here?"

She stumbled forward without waiting for an answer and threw her arms around him. He returned the hug, maybe a little too tightly. He wasn't accustomed to physical human contact these days—it was going to take some getting used to.

"I was wondering if I could stay here for a while." The words felt awkward and dumb coming out of his mouth. What had he been thinking, showing up here after all these years? That he could sleep on the couch like some teenager crashing at a friend's house? Maybe he should have stayed at Sean's place.

"Of course you are staying here," Christine said. "You're welcome to stay as long as you like, right Will?"

"Yes, of course," Will said. "We wouldn't have it any other way."

Frank looked at Will and then back at Christine. "Does he...live here too?"

Christine smiled. "I'm sorry. I forgot you didn't know. So many things have happened. Yes, he lives here. Will and I are married."

"Oh. Well, congratulations. Is this...recent?"

"Almost seven years," Will said.

Frank blinked hard, trying to remember when Becky Raymond had said Jake had disappeared. Eight years ago? He wasn't sure.

As if reading his mind Christine said, "We have so much to talk about. Please, come inside."

Christine stepped back to allow him to enter. She was beaming. The look on Will's face was less easy to read. He was smiling, but there was something else, something troubling behind that smile. Frank took one last look over his shoulder onto the emptiness of Riley Drive, and stepped across the threshold and into the house.

IN THE BEFORE (PART 2)

"Should we have brought wine? I feel like we should have brought wine." Frank sighed. Why was he so nervous? He'd shared a bedroom with Jake for sixteen years. And he had lived next door to Jake and Christine for the last five. He walked into their house without knocking. He'd walked into their old house without knocking, anyway. This new place on Riley Drive, he wasn't so sure.

Wendy reached across the car and squeezed his hand. "You'll be fine. Stop stressing. You brought something." She held up a package slightly smaller than a shoebox.

"I don't know," Frank said. "Maybe the gift wasn't such a good idea."

"Oh come on. I'll bet all Christine's doctor friends brought wine. I guarantee no one else brought one of these."

"You're right. Let's go."

Frank had to admit, Wendy looked great tonight. He might feel self-conscious around Jake and Christine's friends, but one look at Wendy set things right.

They walked together toward the door, hand in hand. Frank had never been a big hand holder, but something about Wendy made it feel different. Even after almost a year together, he still wanted to touch her as much as possible.

Frank paused at the door and then tapped his knuckles against it. He heard laughter from inside the house. Sounded like the party was well underway. A woman he didn't know opened the door and showed them inside.

The place was crowded. There must have been a dozen people crammed in living room with at least half a dozen more in the kitchen, and Frank recognized only a precious few of them. Frank was relieved to see that Will was there. Will was standing across the room engaged in conversation with an intense-looking pudgy little man. Frank nodded to Will, and Will motioned him over with the insistence of a man stuck with a conversational partner he is desperate to pass off to another unsuspecting victim.

Frank smiled, shook his head, and walked in the other direction. Will's eyes shot daggers at him.

Frank looked around and saw Wendy was gone. How had he lost her already? It wasn't surprising really. She was a great social mingler. He heard her distinctive laugh across the room, a lower pitched version of a schoolgirl's squeal—all the delight but none of the ear-splitting.

He walked toward the group, the largest in the room. They all seemed to be listening to a story. As he approached he was surprised to find he knew the storyteller. It was Sean Lee, his childhood neighbor.

The group burst out in another fit of laughter. Jake spotted Frank from the bowels of the group. "Hey, man!"

"Hey! Nice party," Frank said.

Wendy grabbed his arm. "Frank, you've got to hear this. You know that naked guy who was wandering around downtown yesterday? Sean was the one who arrested him."

Sean nodded. "Yeah, it was pretty wild." Sean turned

back to address the group. "So Wes and I are still on the way downtown when we get the third message from dispatch. Seems he's near the Post Office now."

A woman Frank had never met before asked, "And did the dispatcher mention how, um, large the naked man was again?"

Sean laughed. "Indeed she did. In fact she seemed so obsessed with this central point that Wes offered to snap a couple of cell phone pictures for her. She shut up pretty quick after that."

The group roared with laughter again.

"So we finally turn onto Main Street, and we see him standing there in front of the Post Office. He's looking all around, up in the sky, down the street, not a care in the world. We get a little closer, and we see the guy a little more clearly. More clearly than either of us wanted to, I'll tell you that."

"So was he as big as everyone was saying?" Wendy asked.

Sean grinned. "He was, and not just the way you all are thinking but are too polite to say. He had to be six foot four or six foot five and he was completely bald. Pretty ripped, too. So Wes and I park the car and approach the guy. We start calling to him, saying, 'Sir, we need you to come with us,' stuff like that. But he doesn't respond. He keeps looking around like he's never seen a city street before. And he's got something in his left hand."

Frank glanced at Jake and Christine sitting together on the couch. Little Trevor slept in Christine's arms with the kind of slumber that only babies know, the kind that occurs independent of location, body position, or the noise level around them. They looked happy, this little Hinkle family. Peaceful.

Frank didn't know if he'd ever have anything like that. He wouldn't mind settling down with Wendy, but sometimes he got the feeling she didn't feel the same way. Sometimes he felt like she was passing the time with him, waiting for something better to come along.

"So we keep walking toward him," continued Sean, "yelling to him the whole time. And he continues to ignore us. Finally, we're right up next to him, and he is still in his own little world. Wes and I look at each other, trying to figure out how to proceed. So I decide, what the hell, and I reach out and put my hand on his shoulder. And as soon as I touch him, he gives me this look, and I'll tell you what. In that moment I saw pure crazy. He looked like he wanted to eat me for dinner."

A wise guy sitting in a recliner in the corner grinned. "I ate his liver with some fava beans, Clarice."

"Something like that. He definitely gave off a Hannibal Lector vibe for a moment there. But then he smiled and said, 'I like your town. I think this will do just fine. I think I'll live here for a while.'"

"Oh my God," Wendy said. "'This will do just fine'?"

Sean shrugged. "We cuffed him and put a blanket around him. I didn't want his naked ass sitting in my backseat, so we put another blanket down under him. We took him down to the station, and that was about the end of it."

"Wow," the smart ass in the recliner said. "So what was in his hand?"

"It was an old-fashioned pocket watch. The only time he got lippy with us was when we tried to take it away."

"He still down at the jail?" someone else asked.

"No, they took him to the psych ward at Elizabethton Memorial. Makes you wonder what he was doing though.

We tried to question him, but we never got farther than his first name. Zed."

Wendy put a hand on Sean's arm. "It could have been worse. At least you didn't have to frisk him."

The group burst out in laughter at that.

"Hey, thanks for your help back there." The voice came from Frank's right, close to his ear. He looked over and saw Will grinning at him.

"No problem. Least I could do."

Will sighed. "The guy invented some new type of stucco or something. He talked about it for twenty minutes and I still don't understand."

"Poor communication skills," Frank said. "I blame the educational system."

"I blame the fact that the guy was a self-centered prick."

Jake sidled up next to them. "Glad to see you two are branching out. You're really mingling. Meeting new people."

"Hey, we haven't talked in like twelve hours," Will said. "Lots of catching up to do."

"That reminds me." Frank handed the gift to Jake. "Happy house warming."

"Aw, thanks, man. Christine, Frank brought us a gift."

"Thanks, Frank," Christine said. "Jake, can you open it? I'm kinda of tied up." She gestured to the sleeping baby in her arms.

Jake nodded and tore into the purple wrapping paper. Frank felt a slight twinge of unease. The whole group was watching Jake open the present. Frank wished he had waited and given it to them privately.

Jake pulled off the last of the wrapping paper and lifted the lid off the box. "Huh," he said. There was a perplexed grin on his face.

"What is it?" Christine asked.

"It's a doorknob." Jake lifted the brass assembly out of the box and held it up. It looked like an ordinary doorknob except for an ornate letter H engraved on the top of both knobs.

The group stared at the door knob. A few people nodded politely.

"That's more practical than the traditional bottle of wine," the man in the recliner said.

"I'm guessing that's not an ordinary door knob, Frank?" Christine asked.

Frank smiled. "Yeah, I, uh, made some modifications." He held out his hand, and Jake gave him the door knob. "You know how Jake is always losing things? His wallet, his keys, stuff like that?"

"Games of darts with his wife," Christine said. The group laughed.

"This door knob will help with that. It'll keep him from getting locked out. See, it works like a regular lock." Frank turned the lock, and then reached into the box and pulled out a set of keys. He inserted one of the keys into the keyhole and twisted. The lock popped open.

Frank continued. "Let's say you forgot your keys and you need to get inside to get Trevor's diapers. With this you won't have to call your wife at work and interrupt her in the middle of some foot-saving surgery or something. If you know the secret, you can open it without the key." Frank turned the lock again and set the keys down. He grabbed the doorknob, twisted it a quarter turn to the left, putting pressure on a specific spot, and then he turned it hard to the right. The lock opened.

The group murmured and Frank felt his ears redden.

"Is that safe?" the man in the recliner asked. "With a

baby in the house and all? Couldn't someone just mess with the door knob a little and come right in?"

"Trust me," Frank said. "You'd have better luck picking the lock than opening the door knob without knowing the secret." He looked at Jake and Christine. "I'll show you two how to open it later."

"Thanks, Frank," Christine said. "That's sweet."

Jake slapped him on the back. "That's really thoughtful, man."

Frank smiled. "I wanted to make sure you three are safe. Will and I sit around and worry day and night about you crazy kids."

"I'll bet you find time to fit a few beers in there somewhere," Christine said.

Will laughed. "Occasionally. It gets lonely. All we have is each other."

Jake and Christine exchanged a look. Jake turned to the other two men.

"Yeah, about that." Jake spoke softly so the rest of the group couldn't hear. "I've been meaning to talk to you two. We, uh, we rented out the other cabin."

Frank tried not to let his disappointment show on his face. He was surprised at how hard the news hit him. He had always assumed that Jake and Christine would keep the cabin empty and use it themselves from time to time. Maybe move back out there full time when they got sick of life in town. It was a ridiculous notion.

"That's great. Anybody I know?" Frank asked.

Jake shook his head. "It's a guy Christine works with. Nice dude. We've gone out to dinner with him a few times and been to a couple cookouts at his house. He's going through a rough divorce and he needs a new place."

"Cool. We could use another bachelor," Will said.

Jake waved to the guy on the recliner.

"Hey, I was telling Frank and Will that you're going to be their new neighbor."

The man eased himself out of the chair and ambled over. He smiled and held out his hand to Frank. "Hey, nice to meet you, man. I'm Brett Miller."

CERTIFIED

I.

Wendy Caulfield missed the Internet. It had been eight years and it seemed like she should be over it by now. And most of the time she was. She agreed with Zed and the others. It was better to have a world with more personal connections and less virtual ones. It was better to have a world where families talked during dinner rather than glancing at their iPhones every thirty seconds. A world where cyber-bullying and cyber-crime and online pornography were things of the past.

Still, she couldn't help but miss it sometimes. Facebook. Twitter. Blogs. YouTube. Podcasts. The collected knowledge of human history a few keystrokes away. Sure, there was a lot of bad stuff and misinformation out there, but plenty of good stuff came along with it. She missed being able to take a five-minute break from working and hop over to CNN.com. And, okay, maybe Vulture.com too. Now she was left staring at Word and PowerPoint.

It was a better world the people of Rook Mountain had

created for themselves, but that didn't mean she couldn't indulge in a little nostalgia now and then.

She sighed and pushed those thoughts away. She had to concentrate on this syllabus.

Wendy was just getting back into the groove when there was a rap on her classroom door.

"Come in," she said. If this was Grace Harris asking for help with Excel again, Wendy was going to punch her in the face.

The door opened, and Becky Raymond stepped into the classroom. The city manager moved elegantly, sliding through the barely open doorway and easing the door shut behind her.

"Hi Wendy," Becky said. "Do you have time to chat for a moment?"

"Becky, of course." Wendy started to stand up, but Becky held up a hand.

"Please, don't get up for me. I know you're busy. I won't take much of your time." Becky walked to the student desk nearest Wendy and sat down. "How's the prep going? Ready for another year?"

Wendy smiled. "I'm getting there. It'll be a challenge with the restructuring, but we'll make it work."

"I appreciate that, and Zed does too. I know we threw you for a loop with the reduced classroom hours this year, but we feel that the students of the Beyond Academy are better served by having more time in the field."

Wendy nodded. "I understand. I hope you know that reduced class time means we have less time to spend with the students who are struggling. It also probably means lower Certification scores."

The smile was still frozen on Becky's face, but her eyes went a shade colder. "The Board knows that we have the best teachers here. We ask a lot, but I think you'll agree that we reward you well for your results. The Beyond Academy has a history of one hundred percent Certification of our graduates, and that can't change. Otherwise, what are we doing here? We might as well send the students to one of Will Osmond's night classes."

"I agree. I'm not saying they won't pass certification. I'm just saying you have to expect this to have some impact."

"We understand that. And we are confident that you and the other teachers will find a way to mitigate those impacts. But I'm sorry to get off topic. I didn't come here to discuss the schedule changes. I came to talk to you about one of your new students."

"Oh? Which student is that?" Wendy knew which student, but she felt it polite to ask.

"Trevor Hinkle."

Wendy rubbed her arms. "Okay, sure. Trevor's a bright kid. I've seen his test scores and his essay work is strong. Seems mature enough. I'm not expecting any problems due to the age difference."

"The age difference isn't my main concern. His family is."

Wendy sighed. "Is it his mother the doctor that's worrying you? Or his step-father who runs Zed's certification program?"

Becky drummed her manicured fingernails on the desktop. "There's no need to be a smart ass, Wendy. You spent a lot of time with his family in the Before. What do you think?"

Wendy fought to remain calm. This woman was technically her boss, one of them anyway. Becky wasn't being rude exactly—she was interested in a situation into which Wendy had special insight. But Wendy had long ago grown tired of talking about her ex-boyfriend and his family.

"Yes, I spent time with the Hinkles. Christine and I were good friends. But that was all in the Before. Trevor was a baby. I'm not sure how I can help you."

"I know. It's not fair of me to ask. I guess I'm a little nervous. Here's this kid whose father threw that little temper-tantrum after Regulation Day. His uncle has been in prison for most of the kid's life. How will a kid like that will hold up under the strain of the Academy?"

"We've had kids from tough backgrounds before. You remember Marcus Yates? There were three Regulation Breakers in his immediate family. He managed to turn his life around in here."

Becky smiled. "Thanks for saying that. I needed to be reminded of something positive today." She tilted her head at Wendy and lowered her voice a little. "Can I bounce something off you?"

"Of course."

"Zed's considering fast-tracking Trevor. He thinks maybe if he takes Trevor outside early in the semester, it might help get the kid in the right mental state. What do you think?"

Wendy sat up in her chair a little straighter. "You mean take him on a trek out of Rook Mountain?"

Becky nodded.

Students didn't usually make their first trek until their second year at the earliest. Had a freshman ever been allowed outside? But there was only one answer Wendy could give. She spoke slowly. "Kids are different when they come back from their first time. Some of them have a hard time dealing with it. If Zed thinks Trevor is ready for that, I trust him."

Becky smiled, showing her impossibly perfect teeth.

"Good. I appreciate your honesty. One more thing I wanted to mention while I'm here. Frank is out of prison. Got out yesterday."

Wendy suddenly felt numb all over. "How is that possible? He had years and years left on his sentence."

"I oversaw the release myself. The Board thought he might be able to help us find his brother."

"But—why now? After all this time?"

The smile fell from Becky's face. "That's Board business. I just wanted to let you know in case he contacts you."

Wendy sat for a few long moments, trying to think of something to say. Nothing came to mind.

Becky stood up. "Thanks for the chat. Please let me know how things go with Trevor." The city manager stood and walked out of the classroom. She did not shut the door behind her.

Wendy closed her book and rubbed her eyes. She wouldn't get any more work done today. Frank was back and he was looking for Jake. Well, good luck to him. Wendy was the one person who knew exactly what had happened to Jake, and she wasn't talking.

2.

In another classroom across town from the Rook Mountain Beyond Academy, Will stood in front of a class of bored and vacant-eyed teenagers. They all aspired to part-time jobs in the Rook Mountain food service industry, but before they could take their proud places in the checkout lines or in front of the fry cooker they needed to pass the Rook Mountain Food Handling Certification Test. Will's job was to get them ready.

"Okay," Will said. "Renee and Brad, you role play the

scenario. Renee, you are a customer breaking Regulation 14 at a grocery store, and Brad is the Food Service Professional who is going to stop you. Got it?"

Brad and Renee looked at each other for a moment and then nodded, signaling their mutual readiness. Renee took a deep breath and then began.

"Oh, man, you know what my family totally loves? Pepsi." She spoke in a loud, theatrical voice. "The store sure has a lot of Pepsi this week. But what if they don't have any next week? You know what I'll do? I'll buy, like, fourteen cases of the stuff today to be safe."

A twitter of laughter made its way through the classroom.

"Okay," Will said. "Good, Renee. Brad, she's bringing her fourteen cases of Pepsi to the checkout counter. What do you say?"

Brad cleared his throat. "Excuse me, ma'am. May I ask you how many people are in your household, please?"

Renee put her hand to her chest and put on a shocked expression. She was in full-on drama club mode. "Oh, certainly, young man. It's me, my super rich and handsome husband Jacques, and our three lovely girls."

The class laughed again.

"Ma'am," Brad said. "I notice that you have fourteen cases of Pepsi. That is over the weekly limit for a family of five. Can you please put twelve of them back?"

"Nicely done," Will said.

Renee pretended to choke up. She wiped a mock tear away from her eye. Will really wanted a drink, and not Pepsi. "But what if you don't have any Pepsi next week? My Jacques would be so disappointed in me!"

Brad held up a hand. "Ma'am, the Rook Mountain Resource Expansion team is hard at work even as we speak, gathering supplies for next week's groceries. They won't rest until we all have what we need. You have to trust them. Trust is a must."

Will rubbed his eyes and reminded himself that he only had two more classes today.

"This is unbelievable!" shouted Renee. "How dare you deny me my rights! This is America. I'll buy as much Pepsi as I want, and you can't stop me, you fascist pig!"

"Okay, we probably don't need the name calling," Will said. "That was good, though, both of you. A round of applause for Renee and Brad?" The other students clapped half-heartedly. "At this point, Brad would call for his manager to assist with the situation. And Renee would probably be looking at a nice fine after all that fascist talk. Any volunteers to go next?"

Will loved asking that question. More to the point, he loved the silence that followed, the absolute peace in the classroom while every student tried to sit still and not be noticed. Back in college, they had taught Will to wait a full seven seconds after asking a question. At first, that had seemed like an eternity. Now he preferred to stretch it to fourteen. It gave him a moment to collect his thoughts. And this morning he needed all the moments he could get.

Last night had been rough and he hadn't gotten much sleep. With the shooting yesterday and Christine finding the key, there would have been more than enough excitement. And then Frank showed up.

It was worrisome, Frank showing up the same day they found the key. It was too much of a coincidence, and Will didn't believe in coincidences, not these days. How much did Frank know? And why had they let him out of prison? What had he promised them? Will trusted Frank, the old Frank, but who knew how nine years in prison could change a man? Frank hadn't been there on Regulation Day. He hadn't been there for what happened to Jake.

Will suspected that he and Christine had changed as much as Frank had over the last nine years. The old Will certainly wouldn't have shot a defenseless human being on top of Rook Mountain for the purpose of keeping up appearances.

Last night Christine, Will, and Frank had kept the conversation light. They didn't talk about Frank's time in prison, or why he had been released. They didn't discuss the shooting earlier in the day or the key Christine had found. They hadn't mentioned the Regulations. They avoided these topics by unspoken, mutual consent. They had talked about old times. Frank had marveled at how old Trevor looked and had asked a lot of questions about the boy. It had been nice.

But they wouldn't be able to avoid the difficult conversations forever. They would have to face them soon—probably tonight.

Will noticed a hand raised near the front of the class. "Yes, Jen? What is it?"

"I will," the girl said.

"You'll what?"

Jen looked confused. "I'll volunteer. For the role play."

"Oh," Will said. "Right, sorry." Will focused on the class. He couldn't let his attention waver, not now. The last thing he needed was a student mentioning to the wrong person that Mr. Osmond seemed weird today.

"Who else?" Will asked. He suspected a few of the boys would be more apt to volunteer now that Jen Durant had.

The last ten minutes of class went by without incident. Will took a long drink of his room-temperature coffee as the class filed out. He didn't mind the temperature or the harsh, bitter taste. He'd need all the caffeine he could get for this next class.

Rook Mountain offered twenty-five Certification tests on topics ranging from heavy equipment operation to law enforcement, and Will taught prep classes for every one of them. He had little input into the tests themselves—the board of selectmen put those together. He just prepared the students. It was a job the old Will, the Will from the Before, would have hated. It was the very definition of 'teaching to the test.' Old Will would have complained about the instructional philosophy behind a system so test heavy. The present day Will drank his bad coffee and tried to make it through the day without breaking any Regulations.

Of all the Certification courses he taught, this next one was his least favorite. It was also the most popular. Resource Expansion Certification. The only Certification that gave the ability to leave Rook Mountain. Will had trained this class to over four hundred people. Four hundred in a town with a population of four thousand. Young and old, it seemed like everyone wanted to venture beyond the borders of the little town. None of his students had ever passed.

And none of the students at the Rook Mountain Beyond Academy had ever failed.

It was a source of constant frustration for Will. Unlike the other Certification tests, Will was not allowed to see the Resource Expansion test. He had only a vague idea of the topics the test covered. As the teacher, he was barred from taking it himself, and others who had taken the test were barred from discussing it lest they face jail time under Regulation 17. The Beyond Academy had three years to prepare their students for the test, and Will was sure the teachers over there knew what was on it. The deck was stacked against Will and his students. Those not selected for Beyond Academy weren't meant to pass the test, and they never did.

Will actively discouraged folks from signing up for this Certification course, but most of them could not be deterred. They kept signing up, month after month, and Will kept teaching the curriculum designed by the board of selectmen, despite its zero success rate.

Will looked out at the class. It was the first day of this course, and they were eager. Hopeful. They'd all heard the stories about how difficult the test was, but they all thought they would beat the odds. It made Will sad to look at them. He wanted to tell them to go home, that it wasn't going to happen for them.

Instead, he put on a smile, stepped to the front of the class and said, "Okay. Ready to begin?"

3.

Frank hesitated at the bottom of the porch steps for as long as he dared, then trotted up to the front door of the house. The steps bent and groaned under his feet. The porch was badly in need of a paint job. A single artificial plant stood in a moldy planter near the door.

Frank knocked and waited. There was no answer, but he saw the living room curtains flutter.

He knocked again. He saw a dark, indistinct shape through the door's frosted glass window.

"Sally," he said. "Sally, are you there?"

Again there was no answer, but the shape in the window grew a bit larger.

"Sally, it's Frank Hinkle. I need to talk to you for a minute. It's about my brother."

He heard a series of clicks as deadbolts were released and locks were turned. The door opened three inches.

"Did they let you out of prison, or did you escape?" The voice coming from behind the door was low and raspy, but definitely female.

"They let me out, fair and square. I'm actually on assignment from Becky Raymond. That's what I wanted to talk to you about."

The door eased open halfway, and Frank saw Sally Badwater for the first time. Her face was sickly thin and her hair clung to her head in stringy, greasy clumps. Though she was close to Frank's age she looked at least ten years older.

"Damn Hinkle boys," she said, looking Frank up and down. "I want to be left alone to do my business and you all keep bothering me. The devil take both of you."

Frank cleared his throat and gritted his teeth. "What business are you in?"

Her eyes narrowed. "I'm curious why you're so interested. You never gave me the time of day back in high school."

"I apologize for that," Frank said. He shrugged. "I don't have any excuse except that I was a dumb kid, and that's no excuse at all."

She stepped out onto the porch and leaned against the door frame. "I suppose we all were. You asked about my business. It's photography. I do the usual weddings, senior pictures, and the like. The occasional boudoir type thing for an anniversary." She winked at him. "I've been known to capture some other stuff too though. Scary stuff from you-know-where. Figure it'll make me rich if we are ever allowed to travel again."

Frank had no idea where 'you know where' was, but he nodded. He was still trying to assess Sally Badwater's sanity.

She frowned at him. "I trust you won't share what I just said with Becky Raymond? It might technically be against the rules." Frank shook his head. "Good. They got lots of rules here now. They tell you about those?"

"Some of them. I hear we're not supposed to leave town. Or sleep in the parks."

She snorted out a laugh. "Yeah buddy, and that's only the start. You want to do something, they probably got a rule for it." She squinted at him again. "'Course, I'm sure they've got their reasons. Trust is a must and all that. What did you say you were doing here again?"

"I wanted to talk to you about Jake. About the day he spoke to you. Would it be all right if we went inside?"

She crossed her arms and glared at him. "No. Out here's fine. And I already told the police all about what Jake said to me."

"Yeah," Frank said. "I read the report. I'm wondering if there could be anything else you might have forgotten to tell the police. Between us."

"I didn't forget anything and I didn't leave anything out on purpose neither. Jake kept it short and sweet. It was over in ten seconds. And I'm not dumb enough to hold back info about Rook Mountain's most wanted. Even if I did make out with him at some party in tenth grade."

Frank sighed. "Okay. Of all the people in town, why did he pick you?"

Sally shrugged. "How the hell should I know? I hadn't spoken to the man in years."

"Have you thought any more about what he said? Does that thing about the quarry make any more sense to you now?"

"No," Sally said. She pulled at the neck of her sweater as if it were choking her, although it looked two sizes too large. "Trust me, I've thought about all this. Why me? Why did he say what he said in the way he said it? I can't make heads or tails though. How about you? Did it make any sense to you?"

Frank shook his head. "I have no idea what the quarry is or when he wants me to meet him."

"What about the thing with the lock?" she asked.

Frank's head snapped up. "What?"

"The lock. What he said about the Cassandra lock. Did that make sense?"

"Sorry, I'm not sure what you mean."

She snorted again, this time with frustration. "I thought you read the report."

"I did," Frank said. "But the copy I saw didn't say anything about the Cassandra lock."

Her face softened a little. "Guess they're lying to you too. That makes me feel a little better about you as a person."

"Sally, what did he say? Tell me exactly." Frank felt the breath catching in his throat as he spoke. He had considered that this woman might be insane, that she hadn't spoken with Jake at all. There were a million inside jokes and stories Jake could have used in a message that only Frank would understand. Why would he pass along one that Frank couldn't? But this, the Cassandra lock... Sally had spoken to Jake. There was no doubt in Frank's mind.

She licked her lips and spoke slowly. "He said, 'Tell my brother to meet me at the quarry.' Then he turned and I thought he was gonna leave. But he stopped like he had remembered something and he turned back. He said, 'And if Frank comes, tell him to bring the Cassandra lock.' That part mean anything to you?"

"No. Not a thing." The lie came to his lips automatically and without thought. His mind was a million miles away.

"And the way he disappeared. I could tell the cops didn't believe me, but I swear it's the truth. He was there one second and gone the next. He didn't run away. He just... vanished."

Frank needed to get away. He needed to think things through. "Listen, I should go. I've bothered you enough. Thanks for your help."

He turned and scurried down the steps before she had a chance to respond.

4.

Christine read the letter for the fourth time.

"When were you going to tell us about this?" she asked.

Trevor sat across the dining room table from her. He looked miserable and frightened. Sometimes Christine could have sworn he was a grown man. He'd get that determined, mischievous look in his eyes, and he was the spitting image of his father. But right now he looked like a scared little boy.

"I'm telling you now," he said.

"Yes, you are. Less than a week before the start of school."

He squirmed in his chair. She let him sit in uncomfortable silence while she read the letter one more time.

"So there's no registration paperwork I need to fill out?" she asked. "Or some kind of parental consent form or something? 'Cause I'm guessing we missed the deadline for all that stuff."

Trevor shook his head. He looked relieved to have been asked a question for which he could give a solid answer.

"No, Mr. Thorpe explained all that to me. The Academy is technically part of the Rook Mountain school system, so they pull all your paperwork from there. He said no one has ever declined an invitation to the Academy, so you don't need to accept or anything. They assume everybody who got in is coming."

"Well," Christine said, her eyes still on the letter. "There's a first time for everything."

Trevor got quiet again.

"May I ask why you waited so long? Were you afraid we would say no?"

Trevor shrugged.

"I can't help but notice that you waited until Will was at work before you brought this up," Christine said. Trevor stared straight ahead. She reached across the table and took his hand. "What do you want to do?"

He looked up slowly, that shaggy hair he refused to cut hanging in his eyes. "I want to go."

"Okay," she said. "Tell me why."

"I want to get out of this town someday. I want to see what's out there."

"Honey, you know what's out there."

"Yeah," he said, "but beyond that. Out farther. Out of this state. Maybe even across the ocean, you know?"

Christine raised her eyebrow. "You know they don't let Resource Expansion workers do that, right? They go as far as they need to in order to get what we need. Then they come back."

"Maybe someday they will. You always said I should go after my dreams, right?"

Christine looked back down at the letter. "What about supplies? Dress code? There's not a lot of information here, Trev."

"Mr. Thorpe said they'll cover all of that during orientation."

"Did Mr. Thorpe say why they picked you? Was it your test scores?"

"Yeah, I guess that was part of it. Zed selects every student himself. He came to the school a couple of weeks after we took the tests. We had an assembly and he talked for a while and looked every student in the eye. It kinda creeped me out. But then the next day Mr. Thorpe gave me the letter."

A chill ran through Christine. Zed had looked her son in the eye and liked what he had seen there. She let the silence linger for a moment. Then she said, "Youngest person ever accepted, huh?"

He nodded.

Christine smiled. "I'm very proud of you. I'll talk to Will. And we will all discuss it as a family, okay?"

"Think he'll be mad?" Trevor asked.

"No, of course not." Will wouldn't be mad at the thought of Trevor going to the Beyond Academy. He'd be terrified.

Christine reached into her pocket and touched the key she had taken from Jessie Cooper. She knew she would let Trevor attend the Academy. It would look too odd if she didn't. No one had ever declined an acceptance before. She had no choice. It was a terrible risk, putting Trevor in that place, but Christine couldn't think of a way to avoid it.

Things were changing, accelerating around her. The key. Frank showing up to stay with them. And now this. They would have to move up their timeline. They'd been taking it slow and playing it safe for too long. Trevor might start Beyond Academy, but there was no way in hell he was going to graduate from it. If things went as planned, this would all be over long before that.

5.

Frank dragged the knife across the steak, sawing off a tiny piece. He wanted to savor every morsel of the rib-eye. He slid it into his mouth and closed his eyes. Without a doubt, this was the best thing he had tasted in nine years.

"Dang, dude," Frank said. "This steak is outrageous."

Sean smiled. "Thanks. I dry brine them. That's the key. People think it's the way you cook it, but it's actually the preparation that makes the difference. You like the beer?"

Frank set down his fork and took a sip from the frosty glass. His eyes widened again.

"I know, right? That's Dogfish Head 90 Minute IPA. My personal favorite."

"Man, what did I ever do to deserve all this?"

Sean laughed. "It's your welcome home. What did you expect? I'm sure Will and Christine will have something at the house sooner or later, but I wanted to be the first."

"Thanks, man," Frank said. "So do you see Will and Christine much?"

Sean shrugged. "Not as much as I'd like, but we get together every once in a while."

"How about Todd? You still tight with him?"

Sean set down his silverware. "Frank, I'm sorry to tell you this, but Todd's dead. He died about eight years ago."

"What? No. What happened?" Todd had been a friend. He'd been closer to Jake than to Frank, but it was still a shock to hear he had died.

"He was shot. They say Jake did it."

A chill ran through Frank. "No way. I don't buy that for a second."

Sean furrowed his brow. They both took a few more bites of steak.

"Did Christine and Will talk to you last night?" Sean asked. "Did they give you the run down on, you know, the Regulations and everything?"

Frank shook his head and answered mid-bite. "No. We kept it pretty light."

Sean sighed. "Well, as the first to officially welcome you home, I guess it falls to me to give you the lay of the land."

Franked nodded. He had been dying for someone to come right out and give him some answers rather than hinting around everything. He had intended to ask Will and Christine last night, but things had been too awkward. "Thank God. Start at the beginning."

"The beginning, huh?" Sean took another sip of his beer. "Well, you were here in the beginning. You remember Zed showing up in town, right? And the way people started going to listen to him talk in the park."

"You kidding? My ex started following the guy around."

Sean grinned. "That was pretty funny."

"I remember him showing up on my doorstep too. Showing up on everybody's doorsteps. What's he got to do with what happened?"

"Maybe nothing." Sean paused for a long moment. "Maybe everything. It's not something people talk about, and honestly it's not something I even like to think about. All I know is that when the bad things happened, Zed and his disciples got organized mighty quickly."

"What bad things? You're being vague again."

"Yeah, sorry. I've never had to explain it before. It's just something everyone knows."

Frank let the silence linger. He wanted to give Sean the time he needed to find the right words.

"March 27th, 2014, we went to bed and everything was normal. We woke up on the 28th and everything had changed."

"Changed how?" Frank asked.

"People were dead. Lots of people. There had been attacks during the night. I went on duty that morning and the dispatchers were already overwhelmed. We tried to contact Elizabethton to send some support units, and that was when we realized something was really wrong."

"People were dead? What people?"

Sean took a deep breath. "Okay, it's like this. Sometime during the night of March 27th, every person on the streets of Rook Mountain was killed. Torn apart. We didn't know who did it and we didn't know why, but fourteen people were ripped to shreds. Took awhile for us to even ID the victims. It was Christine who finally cracked that nut. We found what was left of the bodies in the streets. It looked like it had been done by wild animals. The meat had been stripped from their bodies."

Sean glanced down at Frank's steak. "Sorry. Maybe this isn't the time."

Frank set down his fork, his appetite shrinking. "No. Keep going."

"You remember Kurt Hansen? Ty's brother?"

Frank nodded. "Ty and I got reacquainted yesterday."

"Kurt was one of the people they killed that first night. We found him on top of a squad car outside the station. Anyway, when I got to work it was chaos. Someone finally thought to call for help from an outside department, and that was when people started to lose it."

"What do you mean?" Frank asked.

"Well, we tried calling Elizabethton and the call didn't go through. That's not exactly right. The call went through, but there was no answer on the other end. No voice mail either. It just kept ringing. We tried a dozen other departments and they were all the same. Our cell phones were down, and all we had were the landlines. Some of the cops at the station tried calling out of town friends and relatives, and there was no answer from any of them."

Frank's mouth felt dry. It had been filled with the savory taste of steak a few minutes ago, but that was forgotten now. "It sounds like some kind of coordinated attack or something. Like someone was trying to isolate the town."

"Maybe," Sean said. "As the day went on it started to feel like we were the last people left on Earth. The Internet didn't work. All we could get on the TV was static—even the over the air local stations were gone. People started gathering around the police station and City Hall. They wanted answers and we didn't have any to give."

Frank wiped the back of his hand across his mouth. "So you're telling me that a bunch of people were brutally murdered in the middle of the night, and the next day Rook Mountain was cut off from the outside world?"

Sean smiled. "It sounds even weirder when you say it out loud. Don't get me wrong, it seemed crazy that day too, but I was busy. I kind of took it in stride. I guess most people did. We eventually got everyone to go home for the night. That turned out to be a pretty good move. There were eight more murders that night. Again, it was all people who were outside. Four of them were cops. One was my partner Wes Dinsmore. He'd volunteered to pick up an extra shift."

"I'm sorry, Sean."

Sean nodded. "Thanks. The next day, as you might imagine, the group of people in front of City Hall was even larger. They wanted someone to explain what the hell was going on. No one could. Then he showed up."

"He?" Frank asked.

"Zed. By that time, everyone in town knew him. He'd knocked on almost every front door in town. Most people thought he was a harmless nutcase, but he had a dozen or so loyal followers by then. Most of them were people in their early twenties. A lot of them came from rough backgrounds and were looking for something, you know?"

"So what does that wacko have to do with any of this?" Frank asked.

"He gets up in front of the crowd and starts talking about how he foresaw this. Saying that he warned the town."

"Warned the town? How?"

Sean raised an eyebrow. "You said he came to your door, right? Do you remember what he said?"

Frank thought for a long moment. Then he remembered. "Holy shit. Are you saying that this dude actually saw this coming?"

Sean shrugged. "I'm just telling you what happened. I don't know if he told the future or if he caused his prophecy to come true or if it was all a weird coincidence. But when he stood up in front of the town and said he had warned them, every person in the crowd knew exactly what he meant."

Sean poured the rest of his beer down his throat. "There was a moment," he said, "when it could have gone either way. For a split second, it seemed like the crowd might turn on him, blame him for what was happening. If it would have played out that way, I don't know how it would have ended. Maybe we all would have lynched him or something. But it didn't happen that way. Because, at exactly the right moment, Zed told us he knew how to fix it."

Frank tilted his head. "He said he could set things back to normal?"

"No. He was very clear on that. He said life would never be the same, and there was nothing he or anyone else could do to change that. But he said he could stop the killings. He could protect us."

"Did he say what he was protecting you from?"

Sean paused and looked away for a long moment before speaking again. "He didn't have to. Many of us had seen the creatures by then. The rest had heard about them. It's hard to describe, but I can tell you that he spoke with authority. I fully believed he knew what he was talking about, and so did everyone else. And then he pulled out this long sheet of paper and tacked it to the City Hall door."

"What was it?"

"It was eighteen Regulations."

"Huh," Frank said. "So that's how the Regulations started?"

Sean nodded. "Zed said that he could stop the killings for good, but that the town needed to agree to live by these Regulations. He didn't ask for any elected office or any sort of title. He just wanted the vow of the people."

"And the people agreed?"

"Yeah, they agreed. Wait, I'm trying to be honest here, so let me restate that. We agreed. I voted too. But, think about it, what was the harm? If Zed couldn't protect us like he said, we were under no obligation to follow his rules. If he could protect us, well, maybe he knew what he was talking about and we should listen to him anyway."

Frank whistled through his teeth. He wasn't sure how much of this to believe. Twenty-two people dead in two nights? "What did these Regulations say?"

"They were well thought out, that's for sure. Basically, they were the rules for sustaining a society in isolation. Stuff like how much food was allowed per person per day. How specialty fields like medicine and plumbing would be managed and sustained. How to go about getting gas for your vehicles and what to do if your vehicle broke down. But the most important Regulation was that no one was to leave town. Regulation 18 set up a plan for certifications."

"Certifications for what?"

"They call them certifications, but most of them are more like exceptions. If you're certified for a certain Regulation, that means you're allowed to break it. Will runs that program, by the way."

Frank ran his hand through his hair. He always did that when he was nervous. "And the people agreed to follow these rules?"

"Yeah," Sean said. "They... we did. It seemed like a long shot, but we didn't have many options at that point. So we voted to approve the Regulations. As soon as we did, one of Zed's weird disciples came out of the crowd and handed him this little box. Zed said he needed a room with some privacy, so me and a couple other cops showed him to an empty office in City Hall. A few hours later, Zed came out and said everything was all set. He said no one is to go in that room and he asked us to lock the door."

"So what happened after that?"

Sean smiled. "Nothing. Nothing at all. There were no killings that night. Or the night after that. Or in the eight years since. At least not in Rook Mountain city limits. Regulation breakers haven't always been so lucky."

"So who killed those people?"

"It wasn't a who. It was a what. The killings were done by these...animals."

"What kind of animals?" Frank asked.

"We'll get to that," Sean said. "But to understand that you have to understand a little more about what's happened to the town. With the killings stopped, the Regulations took on this holy significance. We started enforcing them even though they had never officially been passed into law. Regulation 18 says that anyone who knowingly fails to report a Regulation breaker is just as guilty as the one who committed the crimes. There were these in-depth investigations into who knew about which crimes and when they knew it."

"That's why you told me to be on the defensive?"

Sean nodded and then continued. "Zed's disciples started getting elected into public office. It's gotten to the point where no one outside of his inner circle has a prayer of being elected to the board of selectmen. Officially, Zed runs nothing. In reality, he runs everything."

"People like Becky Raymond?"

Sean smiled. "Yeah. She's got ambition, that's for sure."

"And my brother?" Frank asked. "What do you know about what happened to him?"

Sean shrugged. "On that, I'm not much of an expert. I only know what I'm told. He killed three people. Two police officers and Todd. Then he disappeared." Sean tilted his head at Frank. "Wait a minute, is that why they let you out? Is it about your brother? Is it because of the thing with Sally Badwater?"

"Yeah. They want me to find him. If I do, I get to stay out of jail." Frank took a long pull on his beer. "But I'll tell you something. I know Jake, and there is no way he stuck around the scene of the crime. Maybe he did duck back into town to give Sally his cryptic message, but he is holed up somewhere else. If I am going to find him, I need to leave Rook Mountain."

Sean held up his hand. "Whoa, Frank. That's a really bad idea."

Frank felt his face flush with anger. "It's the only one I've got. I'm going to find my brother. He needs my help. And I'll tell you something else. I wasn't around to get brainwashed by Zed and his weirdo disciples. I never agreed to his Regulations and I don't see why I should have to follow them. Jake's hiding outside of town somewhere, and I'm going out there to find him."

Sean sighed and shook his head. He grabbed the phone and punched in a number. Ice filled Frank's chest. Had he misjudged his friend? Was Sean turning him in? Was he about to be sent back to jail?

Then Sean spoke. "Hi Christine, this is Sean. Listen, does your neighbor still sell rabbits? Could Will pick one up for me and bring it to the edge of town over on Dennis Cove Road? Frank needs a little demonstration." There was a long pause where Sean did not meet Frank's eyes. Then finally, "We're finishing up our dinner. Can he meet us in twenty minutes? Perfect. Goodbye."

Sean took a bite of his steak and then motioned to Frank's. "Eat up, my friend. We have somewhere to be."

6.

It was full dark when they pulled over to the side of Dennis Cove Road in Sean's Subaru Forester. Will was already there. He was parked perpendicular to the road, the headlights of his sedan pointing into the woods fifty yards off the road. Sean eased his vehicle onto the gravel alongside Will's. With the headlights of both vehicles pointed toward the grassy area off the road, it was lit up like day.

A wire-mesh cage sat on the ground next to Will's feet. In the glow of the headlights, Will looked grim and uncomfortable.

Frank opened his door and stepped out before Sean had come to a complete stop. He raised a hand in greeting to Will. "Hey, roomie."

Will nodded back to him. "So I take it Sean's been telling you about the Regulations?"

"Yeah," Frank said. "I'm not sure how much to believe, but he's been telling me."

"Good," Will said. "Look, Christine and I should have been the ones to give you the rundown. I'm sorry. Things last night were a little..."

"Weird," Frank said. "I know."

Will nodded. "Yeah. Sorry about that. We'll do better tonight."

Sean stepped up beside Frank and patted him hard on the shoulder. "Will, your boy here has been taking this whole thing in stride. He hasn't freaked out on me once."

"Night's not over yet," Will said.

"That's for damn sure," Sean said. "But really, Frank, I'm proud of you. You seem to be taking this better than I ever would."

"Thanks," Frank said. "It's all a bunch of crazy-talk of course, but bits and pieces of it make sense. This whole Regulation thing happened about the same time they stopped letting us prisoners have any contact with the outside world. Guess now I know why."

Will pointed at something on the pavement. "You see that white line going across the road? That's the town line. We are on the Rook Mountain side. Whatever happens next, do not cross that line, you hear me?"

Frank nodded. He heard a little chirping-like sound coming from the cage, and he bent down for a closer look at the rabbit inside. It was a fat little thing with long floppy ears hanging down on either side of its face. It huddled in the corner of the cage farthest from Frank.

"Cute little bugger," Frank said.

"Don't get attached," Will said.

Sean patted Will on the back. "Thanks for coming out, man. Frank was talking about maybe leaving town. He said he wasn't sure that the Regulations applied to him. I didn't know how to explain. I thought maybe we needed to show him."

"I figured it was something like that," Will said.

Frank crossed his arms. He couldn't help but smile at his two friends and their clandestine plan. "I'm game. This is the first time I've been outside after dark in years. Just seeing the stars is enough of a demonstration for me. Ain't nothing better than freedom on a warm autumn evening."

Sean grinned at Will. "He thinks he's free now. Isn't that cute?"

Will lifted the wire-mesh cage and walked toward the town line. "It's like the old saying, I guess. Out of the frying pan and into the fire." Will set the cage down on the white line. He put his foot on the back of the cage and slowly pushed it forward until it was completely on the other side of the line.

"Okay," Frank said. "What's supposed to happen?"

Sean put a hand on his arm. "Shhh. Listen."

Frank watched the cage and tried to listen. He didn't hear anything besides the oscillating whine of the cicadas. He stood like that for about thirty seconds, listening, but wasn't sure what he should be listening for. Then, under the cicadas, there was something else.

"Here it comes," whispered Sean.

At first it was just one sound, like a man singing a wordless melody in the distance. Then it was joined by another. And then another. It vaguely reminded Frank of a Gregorian monk's chant, except this tone was aggressive instead of worshipful. The pitch of each of the voices was different, but the notes of the song fit together into an unsettling and beautiful harmony. More voices joined the throng and the clamor grew louder. Frank tried to count how many distinct voices he heard, but he quickly lost track. He became aware of something else under the sound of the many-tuned song. It was a sharp snapping sound, a fluttering sound. It was the sound of wings.

Quick as a flicker of light, a shape appeared in front of the cage. Frank could see it all too clearly in the beam of the headlights. The creature was about four feet tall, and it was bone thin. It had a face of a bird and a large curved beak. Its bat-like wings reached from its shoulders to the ground. It had no feathers, and its skin, its beak, and even its eyes were all the purest white. Its beak was wide open and pointed toward the sky as it sang its song. Others of its kind soon joined it.

Frank stepped back and felt himself taking sharp, quick breaths. The creatures were less than five feet in front of him.

Will put a hand on his shoulder. "You're safe. They won't cross the town line."

Frank forced himself to stand with the other men though his every instinct told him to run. He reminded himself that he was the stranger here and he didn't know the rules. Will and Sean did. If they were confident in their safety, Frank should be too, right? He clenched his fists and stood fast, but his heart thumped so loudly in his chest that he felt sure the creatures would hear it and attack.

"What the hell are they?" Frank asked, his voice betraying his fear.

"Zed and his crew called them the Unfeathered," Will said, "which I always thought sounded sort of lame. Most people call them the Birdies."

"Both pretty good band names," Sean said.

There were eight of them gathered in a semicircle around the cage. They were crowded in tight. The backside of the cage was flush against the town line, the line the creatures appeared unable to cross, so Frank had a clear view of both the cage and the Birdies.

The creatures stood stone still, their heads raised, singing their terrible song. All the beauty Frank had heard in it before was gone now. It sounded as much like a cacophony of screams as it did music. It grew louder by the moment, filling Frank's ears and worming its way under his skin, making him feel unclean.

Frank turned to Will. "I thought you said things weren't going to be as weird tonight." He had to speak loudly to be heard over the singing. He heard the quiver in his own voice as he spoke.

"I guess weird is a relative term," Will said. "I've seen a fair amount of these guys in the last nine years. I ain't seen you once."

Frank nodded, conceding the point.

As if by some undetectable signal, the creatures all stopped singing at the exact same moment. Silence ruled the night. Even the cicadas had gone silent.

Then, as one, they struck.

Their heads snapped into the cage, tearing into the mesh wire like it was wrapping paper. The rabbit huddled near the back of the cage, shaking violently. Soon the creatures had torn open a hole big enough to allow their beaks access to the back of the cage.

The creatures slowed then. The mad hunt for food was

over and it was time to enjoy their meal. Their beaks still moved with an uncanny quickness, but they paused between each thrust, as if savoring the moments before the kill.

The one in the middle shot forward, its beak too quick for Frank's eyes to follow. Just as fast, its head was back outside the cage, a strip of furred flesh dangling from its beak. The others quickly followed, tearing off flesh, then muscle, until the panicked rabbit was finally silent. Less than a minute later the rabbit was nothing more than bones on the bottom of the cage.

One of the creatures took a last half-hearted lunge at the carcass. The Birdie in the middle straightened up, shook itself off with a shudder, and launched into the air, cutting a graceful arch into the sky and back into the forest beyond the clearing. The others each gave an identical shudder, and then followed their brother into the night sky.

None of the men spoke for a long while.

Finally, Frank said, "Those are the things that killed all those people in town?"

"Yeah," Sean said.

"They do that to anything that leaves town? Animal or human?" Frank asked.

Will said, "They come out quicker in the nighttime, but they'll attack during the day too, albeit a bit more slowly."

"There's no way past them?"

Will and Sean exchanged a look. "There's a way," Will said. "Zed and his Resource Expansion team are able to venture out."

"How do they do that?" Frank asked.

"We don't know," Sean said.

Frank thought for another moment. "Are all the other

towns like this too? Are these things gathered around Elizabethton and Bristol and, hell, Washington, DC?"

"We don't know," Sean said.

"Why don't they cross the town line?" Frank asked. "What exactly did Zed do to keep them away?"

"We don't know," Sean said.

"But we're hoping you can help us figure it out," Will added.

IN THE BEFORE (PART 3)

A pounding noise woke Frank. It was as loud as a church bell, and he could feel it in his brain, his teeth, and his balls. He pulled the pillow over his head and tried to ignore it, but the noise didn't stop. If anything, it grew louder.

Frank didn't want to open his eyes. He knew the pain would be worse when he did. He wanted to drift back to sleep. He had been dreaming of the Cassandra lock. In the dream, he had finally figured it out. He'd discovered how to make it work.

But now he was awake, and he knew that the solution had been nothing more than a dream. The Cassandra lock was still a fantasy. He knew it would be perfect, but he couldn't visualize it quite well enough to make it a reality.

It had been a rough night filled with liquor store moonshine, the stuff they produced for the tourists. It wasn't only his raging headache that made him want to stay curled up under the covers. Getting up would mean coming into contact with three items he would rather not deal with: his text messages, his outgoing calls list, and his email. Wendy had broken up with him four days ago. He didn't remember the events of last night too clearly, but he was certain he would see Wendy's name on at least two of those three lists.

The pounding continued, and now a voice joined it. "Frank! You in there? You awake, buddy?"

Frank sighed. It was Brett.

It wasn't that Frank didn't like Brett. He enjoyed hanging out with him most of the time. There was something kind of cool about having three bachelors living in the cabins. There were many late nights of poker, whiskey, and non-judgmental slothfulness. Frank had never been to college, but he imagined this was what dorm life would have been like. It was the perfect environment for a recently dumped guy like Frank.

But Brett had boundary issues. He came over at all hours, and he never took the hint. He simply kept knocking and shouting until Frank opened the door. It had been that way even when Frank and Wendy were together. He had been meaning to talk to Brett about it, about how it killed the vibe a bit when Brett came knocking on the door wanting to play Madden when Wendy was over. But, Frank supposed, there was little need now. His nights could use a little filling, even if it was playing Madden with his socially clueless neighbor.

Frank tried to shift his mind to something more positive. Every morning he tried to think one or two positive thoughts before getting out of bed. Lately, it was getting harder and harder. This morning all he could think of was the Cassandra lock. He had the whole day in front of him without any plans. That meant he had the whole day to spend in the vacant cabin that served as his workshop. He was getting so close. A few more days and he would have it finished, he was sure of it.

Frank sighed and got out of bed. He glanced at the t-shirt and running shorts on the floor and then decided against them. If Brett wanted to talk to him so bad this early, he would get Frank in boxers.

Frank shuffled his way to the door and opened it, squinting into the sharp morning light.

"Hey man," Brett said. "You up?"

Frank blinked hard. "Yeah. I'm up. What's going on?"

Brett looked anything but remorseful. His face was straight, but a gleeful grin was beginning to peek through. "I wanted to make sure you were up. He's here."

"Well, mission accomplished—wait, who's here?"

Brett's grin widened. He was no longer attempting to hide it. "You know. That guy Zed."

"Zed? The naked guy Zed?"

"The very same. I knew our turn was coming, I just didn't know it would be so soon."

Frank stepped back from the door and gave Brett a nod. Brett scurried inside.

"Okay," Frank said, shutting the door. "Talk."

Brett moved to the couch and sank into it. "About twenty minutes ago, there was a knock on my door. I figured it was you or Will. 'Course I heard you playing guitar and singing at the top of your lungs pretty late last night, so I figured it probably wasn't you."

Frank rubbed his eyes, trying to keep up with Brett. "Yeah, sorry about that. I was celebrating freedom."

Brett waved him off. "No, it's cool man. Anyway, I open the door, and there he is. He's so tall that I have to crane my neck to look him in the eye. I'm not used to that. And he's dressed in a long sleeve shirt, buttoned all the way up to the top. The shirt is one of those heavy wool jobs. He looks cool as a cucumber, though, I'll tell you that. A man wearing that shirt on a day like today, and he isn't sweating even a little? I'm not sure what to think of a guy like that."

Frank walked to the bedroom and pulled on his shorts and t-shirt. "What did he want?" Frank called back over his shoulder.

"It's like everybody's been saying. He says he wants to introduce himself, but then he starts talking all weird, about blood in the streets and I don't know what else. Guy's a real loony, I'll tell you that. He's talking to Will right now, poor guy."

Frank didn't know if Brett meant Will or Zed, but he didn't care enough to ask. He walked back into the living room and saw Brett fiddling with one of the locks he had left lying on the coffee table. Frank felt his face flush with anger.

"Dude. How many times do I have to tell you?"

Brett grinned at Frank. "What? I'm not hurting anything. I'm trying to figure out the trick."

Frank took a deep breath. Every time it was the same. No matter how often he asked him not to, Brett always messed with his locks. His livelihood. And when Frank called him on it, it was always the same argument.

"They are not tricks. They are puzzles. And the ones I leave sitting out are the ones I'm working on. Which means they are not ready. You could twist something the wrong way and snap a tiny component as easily as snapping your fingers, and that would create hours of work for me."

"Yeah," Brett said, setting the lock on the table. "Sorry."

Frank glanced up at the window and saw a large man in a black wool shirt walking toward his cabin. "Well, here he is. You staying for this?"

Brett chuckled. "No sir. I've had enough crazy talk for one morning. In fact, I think I'll slip out the back."

Frank waited until Zed knocked on the door. Then he

waited a little longer. After a few moments, he shuffled over and opened the door.

"Good morning," the big man said. His voice was soft and had a boyish quality.

"Hi," Frank said. "Can I help you?"

The man smiled. "I am new in town and I'd like to introduce myself. My name is Zed."

"Zed what?" Frank asked. Zed tilted his head at Frank questioningly. "What's your last name?"

Zed waved his hand. "No need to be formal. You can call me Zed."

"Okay, Zed. I'm Frank Hinkle. Pleased to meet you."

Zed's smile widened. "And I as well am pleased. Thank you for your warm greeting."

"I'm just glad you're wearing pants."

Zed's smile didn't waver. "Ah, you heard about my little episode. Not the way one wants to be introduced to one's hometown. But what's done is done, and now I am going around making my proper introductions."

Frank leaned against the door frame and crossed his arms. "Can I ask you something, Zed?" Zed nodded. "Do you think it's a little strange that you're knocking on every door in town and introducing yourself?"

"No," Zed said. "I think we live in a strange time in which common courtesy is perceived as odd."

"Well, you call it courtesy. Some folks might call it a nuisance. In my experience, strangers who come knocking on doors are selling magazines, cookies, or religion. Which one are you peddling?"

Zed spread his hands out at his sides. "I am selling only myself. Rook Mountain is my new home. I want to know her, and I want her to know me."

"Yeah." Frank put his hand on the door. "Well, now we know each other."

"There is a time coming, Frank, when you will need me. The world will spit out this town like a watermelon seed, and we will be alone. Death will come, first by night and later by day. That is when I will save this town."

Frank squinted at the big man. "You're going door to door spouting this nonsense? Scaring kids and old ladies with this?"

"Fear is sometimes a temporary side effect of truth."

Frank had heard enough. "Okay. Good luck with your introductions. You're really making a great impression."

He moved to shut the door, but Zed looked him in the eye before he could. The smile was gone from Zed's face. That stare held him like a vice. It was like a physical force, the way the man looked into him. He felt Zed's gaze worming its way past his eyes and into the darkest corners of his mind. It was an invasion, and Frank's stomach turned. He was powerless to look away.

Then Zed blinked and the spell was broken.

Frank staggered backwards, struggling to keep his balance. "What was that? What did you do?"

Zed smiled again. "It was very nice to meet you, mister Frank Hinkle." He turned and walked away.

4

CASES

I.

Christine held her hand out the window as she drove. Her fingers didn't quite brush the pine needles on the trees along the side of the road, but it was close. She had all the windows down, enjoying the autumn breeze blowing through the car and the pleasant, rich smells of the forest around her. When she'd lived here, she'd driven this route two or more times each day. It had been a commute no different than any other. Now that she rarely made this trip, she noticed its beauty.

She drove up the driveway and stopped in front of the second cabin. The one Frank had lived in.

Frank. She hadn't figured out what to tell him about why these people were living in his former home and why he couldn't have it back. She hadn't had to; he'd been so shell-shocked from the things he had learned about Rook Mountain in the past week that he hadn't been asking too many questions. But the time was coming when she would have to make a decision: trust him and tell him everything, or don't and tell him nothing. She wanted to trust him, but after nine years in that prison and an unexpected release, she'd be a fool to take anything he said at face value.

She parked the car and pulled out her roller bag filled with medical supplies. Gus Hansen stood on the porch, leaning against the railing, making no effort to hide the way his eyes were glued to her.

As she reached the steps, Gus said, "Doc, Candace is going to be glad to see you. She's worried sick about that boy."

Christine sighed. Gus was a proud man, too proud to say thank you straight out and too proud to admit his concern for his own son.

"Hi, Gus. How long has he had the fever?"

Gus looked away. "Oh, a day or so, I guess."

Christine knew he was also too proud to call a doctor unless he was really scared. "Maybe it's been a little longer than that?" she asked.

Gus nodded. "Yeah, maybe a little. Maybe three days, I guess."

Christine frowned. "Okay. Can I take a look?"

Gus led her into the house. She'd been in here a dozen times since the Hansens had taken up residence, but it never failed to catch her off guard. She always expected it to look the way it had when Frank lived here. When she had spent three nights a week here, drinking, playing games, and acting like a fool with the guys, and whatever girlfriends Will and Frank had at that moment. Those had been good times. She had felt so alive. She had felt like she and her three boys could take on the world. Nowadays she could barely get through the day.

Frank would have had an aneurysm to see the old place like this. The Hansens may not have had the nicest clothing, but there sure was a lot of it. It lay around the house in piles

Christine swore hadn't been touched since the last time she'd been out here eight months ago. Frank had plenty of faults in those days, but he sure kept a damn neat house. His work with tiny and delicate parts for locks necessitated a certain level of orderliness, but Frank had taken it to the next level. The place had been spotless. That was probably why they had hung out in this cabin so much –no matter how badly they treated it in the night, it always seemed to be ready for the white glove test by the time she saw it the next day.

Gus led her to the back bedroom where little Hal lay on the bed covered to the neck with a thin sheet. His hair was matted to his head with sweat and his complexion was pale and drawn.

His mother sat in a chair across the room from him. "Oh, thank God," she said.

Christine shuffled her way to the bed. "Hello, Hal."

The boy gave her a weak smile. "Hi, Doctor Christine."

"Hi," she said. "I understand you aren't feeling well."

He shook his head. "My throat feels bad. And I keep having the weirdest dreams."

"Can I sit down?" she asked.

He nodded, and she sat on the bed next to him. She spent five minutes examining him—taking his temperature and blood pressure, listening to his heart and lungs, and looking in his throat and ears.

She turned to his parents. "I don't suppose you would let me take him to my office?"

Gus and Candace exchanged a glance. Candace said, "By your office, you mean the clinic. And no. Gus and I agree that he needs to stay here with his family. Just tell us what's wrong with him."

Christine took a deep breath and tried to summon the

courage to avoid the same old debate she'd had with the Hansens a dozen times. They didn't trust anyone in town and they wouldn't come to the clinic even for their son's benefit. For once, Christine forced herself to steer clear of that line of conversation. She pulled a rapid strep test kit out of her bag.

Ten minutes and one throat swab later, she had a diagnosis.

"Hal has strep."

Candace sighed with relief. Gus smiled. "Shit, is that all it is? Give him some of that pink stuff and let's call it a day."

"Strep is nothing to smile about," Christine said. "Especially not these days. In the Before, it was a little simpler, but now we have to be careful. There is less we can do if things escalate. Having a fever this high for so long isn't good, especially for someone Hal's age. You need to call me sooner next time."

"Okay," Gus said. "Sermon delivered. Can you help him or not?"

Christine pressed her lips together, hoping to mask her scowl of frustration. She unzipped her roller bag and sorted through the contents until she found what she was looking for. She pulled out the translucent red bottle and held it out to Gus.

"Here," she said. "One pill twice daily."

Gus grabbed the bottle, but Christine didn't release it. She looked him in the eyes. "Have him keep taking it until the bottle is empty. Don't stop when the fever goes away. You hear me?"

Gus nodded and gave her a grin that displayed a wide expanse of yellow teeth. "Yes, ma'am."

"Good." She released the bottle. "I'm going to need to spend a little time out in the shed before I go."

Gus nodded. "I figured you would. You never miss the opportunity when you're out here."

Christine squeezed Hal's hand. "You take your medicine and you'll feel better tomorrow, okay?"

"Yes, doctor," the boy said.

She nodded farewell to Candace and walked out. Gus followed her.

"How's Ty?" Christine asked.

"He's okay." They had reached the porch. "Did we do the right thing last week? When Frank came calling?"

Christine thought for a moment. She didn't even know what the right thing was herself. How was she supposed to tell Gus? She said, "I told you not to let anyone on the property except for me and Will. Yeah, you did good."

She started to walk away, and Gus called after her. "What if Frank comes out here again? Do I let him on the property or do the normal rules apply?"

Christine paused but didn't turn. "No one but me and Will."

Gus whistled through his teeth. "You're a tough woman."

Christine smiled, glad her back was turned so he couldn't see it. There weren't many people that Gus considered tough. "I am," she said. "And you'd better remember that."

She heard the screen door bang shut behind her as Gus went back in the cabin. She started toward the driveway but veered off onto a dirt path leading away from the road. Thirty yards down the path stood an old shed. Christine pulled out her keys and unlocked the padlock. The door let out a high pitched squeal as she slid it open. She stepped inside and flipped on the light. She slid the door shut behind her.

The shed was filled with the usual items. Tools, shovels,

the chainsaw she had used to play that prank on Frank so many years ago. There were a few half-empty paint cans and a couple bags of fertilizer. Frank's old guitar case sat in the corner. And in the back of the shed there was an old freezer.

Christine put her hand on the lid of the freezer and felt it humming. She breathed a sigh of relief. Sometimes she woke up in the middle of the night in a cold sweat, sure that the freezer had broken down. Still, no matter how much she worried and obsessed about it, she didn't allow herself to come out here more than twice a year. There was always the chance, however small, that someone would wonder why she was coming out here so often when everyone else in town was staying away. And maybe that person would mention it to a friend in passing, and maybe the wrong person would overhear.

She couldn't risk that. She had given up far too much. She simply didn't come out unless the Hansens needed her for something.

Christine reached back into her roller bag, unzipped an inner compartment, and pulled out a single key. Though the key looked mundane, she didn't keep this one on her key chain. She put the key into the lock, turned the key halfway, pressed the hidden button on the lock, and turned the key the other direction. The lock popped open.

The lock was one of Frank's creations of course. Another reason to keep him away from here. Even with the key, only Christine, Will, and Frank knew how to open this particular lock. And Jake, she reminded herself. If indeed he was still alive.

Christine took the chain off her neck and lowered it into the freezer. Another key dangled from the chain—the key she had found on Jessie Cooper.

She quickly surveyed the contents of the freezer to make

sure it was all there. There was the large pocket knife, the kind that folded. There was a mirror. There was the lighter, wrapped in cloth and sealed in a Ziploc bag. A three-foot long cane lay wedged in diagonally across the bottom of the freezer. The cane was a rich mahogany. The knife, the cane, the mirror, and the lighter all featured the same broken clock symbol as the key.

The final item in the freezer was the severed head. It was a light shade of blue, and tiny icicles grew from the eye sockets.

A knife, a lighter, a cane, a key, a mirror, and a head. Would they be enough when the time came? Would they be any help at all? Christine had no idea, and not knowing weighed on her heart. There was no way to know, not until it was too late to make a difference. When the time came, they would work and save her, or they wouldn't and she would die.

2.

"Uncle Frank? Uncle Frank?"

Frank looked up and saw the cereal bowl on the table in front of him. It had happened again. He had been drifting. He blinked hard to clear his mind of the cobwebs.

"Uncle Frank!"

Trevor stood near the table. The boy was dressed in only blue jeans, and he held two shirts, one in each hand.

"Yeah, man, what's up?" Frank asked.

"What do you think? The red shirt or the blue?"

Frank stared blankly at both shirts for a moment. "They, uh, they both look great to me."

Will chuckled from across the table. "Your uncle has been a little out of the fashion scene for a few years, Trev."

"I'm only looking for, like, a second opinion," Trevor said.

"The blue," Frank said. "Definitely the blue."

Trevor grinned. "Yeah, that's what I thought." With that, he ran back toward his room.

"Trevor loves you, dude," Will said. "He hardly talks to me anymore. You gotta tell me your secret. I guess he missed you."

Was that even possible? Frank wondered. The kid had been three years old when Frank went away. "I missed him too."

Christine walked into the kitchen and began making herself a bowl of oatmeal. "So what's on the docket for today, Frank?"

Frank shoveled a spoonful of cereal into his mouth to give himself a moment. That was an excellent question. What was on the docket? He had been out a full week, but— aside from talking to Sally Badwater on his second day of freedom—he hadn't accomplished much. The last few days he had seldom left the house. He was still shaken by the things Will and Sean had shown him at the edge of town.

But it was more than that. The whole town seemed to have gone crazy. Crazy/naked Zed was a hero? Will was in charge of some certification program? And now Trevor was going to go to some weird school where they trained kids to pass a test to leave town?

He had known finding Jake would be challenging, but he had no idea where to go from here. After talking to Sally, he had hit a dead end. Jake said he wanted Frank to bring him the Cassandra lock, but the Cassandra lock didn't exist. Frank had never finished it.

Finally, he swallowed his cereal and said, "I'm thinking I might get out a bit today. Maybe go for a hike."

"On the mountain?" Will asked.

Frank nodded.

"Good for you," Christine said. "It'll do you good." She took a seat across from Frank and dug into her oatmeal. "Make sure you drop by City Hall first. You need a permit. Not a big deal to get one, but you don't want to be caught without it."

Frank felt a little guilty looking at Christine. She had let him into her home and asked only the most basic of questions. She wasn't pushing him to talk about anything before he was ready, and for that he was grateful. Yet, he still hadn't told her that he was here to find Jake. He had told her he was here as part of a temporary release program. He would be out for a month, and if he could prove he was ready he might get to stay out longer. It wasn't a lie exactly, but it certainly wasn't the full truth. She had taken his story at face value.

Trevor came back into the kitchen wearing the blue shirt. "Ready to go, Mom?"

"In a minute," Christine said.

Will squinted at Trevor. "Did you use gel in your hair?"

Trevor blushed. "So?"

Will shrugged, trying to hide the grin on his face. "I've never seen you use anything in your hair."

Trevor's shade of red deepened.

Christine gave Will a stern look, but she was grinning too.

"I understand," Will said. "New school. New girls. Wait, do they have girls at this school?"

Trevor smiled. "They definitely have girls."

The morning routine always baffled Frank. The whole thing seemed hectic but well-orchestrated. The three of them flowed in and out of the kitchen, the bathroom, and bedrooms in a blur of constant motion. The schedule never seemed quite the same, but there was never any discussion about whose turn it was in the single bathroom. They never got in each others' ways. Frank, on the other hand, couldn't seem to get in sync with them. He was always standing in the wrong place, blocking someone's access to the bananas or the lunchboxes.

The exit happened the same way. This morning Frank barely had to time shout, "Good luck on your first day," to Trevor before they were gone.

Frank enjoyed the silence for a moment. Of all the things he loved about freedom, silence had to be near the top of the list. Prison was a loud place. He had almost forgotten what it was like to sit in silence with your own thoughts. He sat for a long time, staring into his empty cereal bowl. Almost drifting.

Then he heard a knock at the door. He considered not answering. It was his choice, after all, to answer or not. Such options were the luxury of free men. He pushed himself to his feet, drifted to the door, and opened it to find Becky Raymond standing there. She was staring at the door knob; the one Frank had made for Jake and Christine so many years ago.

She looked up at him and smiled. "Hi, Frank. You didn't forget about our weekly meeting, did you?"

"No, of course not," he lied. "You want to come in?"

She glanced down at the doorknob again and then shook her head. "Walk with me. I have an errand to run."

"I'd rather not. Can we talk here?"

"Come on," she said as if she hadn't heard him. She spun on her heel and marched toward the sidewalk.

Frank took a deep breath and forced himself to unclench

his fists. He stepped outside and followed her down the sidewalk.

"Let's talk," she said. "How is the search for your brother going?"

Frank looked at her. "I haven't found him yet, Becky."

She arched her eyebrows. "It's Becky now, is it? What happened to Ms. Raymond? You were much more polite at the prison."

"When you appear in my home and bully me into going for a walk, you are Becky."

"Well this isn't your home, is it? Your home is Northern Tennessee Correctional Complex. At least until I say it isn't. So I'll ask you again: how is the search for your brother going?"

The woman made him uncomfortable, but he had to keep a grip on his emotions. She was right. She held all the cards here.

"I'll be honest. I haven't opened up too many leads yet."

Becky frowned. "You said you knew places where he hung out. That you knew the land. That you knew where he'd go."

Frank nodded. "Yeah, that's all true. It's taking me some time to acclimate to... how things are."

"That's understandable." Her gaze softened. "Let's take a step back from the facts. What's your gut feeling? Based on what you know about Rook Mountain and what you know about Jake, do you think he's in town?"

Frank scratched his chin. It felt strange, talking to her about Jake. Working with the people who were trying to track Jake down. He told himself he wouldn't turn over any information that would hurt Jake. If he found Jake he would warn him —maybe they could even escape Rook Mountain together.

Speculating couldn't hurt, though.

"The way I see it, there are two possibilities," Frank said. "Either he's in town and he's been in town the whole time, or he found a way to survive outside of town without those crazy bird things eating him."

"And which of those options seems more likely to you?"

"I'd say he's in town. If he really knew a way to get past those things on the outside, it seems like he would have taken his family and gone somewhere else." Frank shrugged. "Either way, he is close enough that he can at least slip into town to pass a cryptic message to Sally Badwater."

The woman smiled. "Let me ask you something, Frank. Was Jake close to his son?"

"Yeah, of course. After the kid was born, it was all he wanted to talk about. It bordered on annoying."

"That's what I thought." She leaned toward him. "Can you imagine any scenario where Jake has access to Rook Mountain and doesn't at least keep tabs on his son?"

Frank thought about that for a moment. Becky was right. Frank couldn't imagine a scenario where Jake wouldn't be in touch with Trevor.

When he was about to answer, Becky said, "This is my errand. It's an interesting case. Follow me." She turned up the sidewalk leading to the next house. Frank glanced up at it, a ranch-style home not much different than any of the dozen or so other houses they had passed on their walk. Frank stayed two steps behind Becky.

When she reached the door, Becky knocked, waited about two seconds, and then opened the door and walked inside.

"Hello!" she said.

Frank followed her in. The man sitting on the couch

sprang to his feet. He was short and slightly overweight, but his most distinctive characteristic was the scar on his left cheek. It was shaped like the number eight.

"Hello, Ms. Raymond," the man said. "I wasn't expecting you."

Becky smiled at the man. "That's sort of the point of surprise inspections, Phillip. Anything I should know before I look around?"

"No, ma'am. Everything in this house is in keeping with the Regulations."

"Good," Becky said. She wandered out of the room as she spoke. "Frank here just got out of prison. He's learning about the Regulations. Why don't you tell him about your crime while I look around?"

The man cleared his throat and looked at Frank. "I'm a Regulation breaker." He pointed to his cheek. "Regulation 8."

Becky called from the other room. "He doesn't know what that is, Philip. Explain."

"I uh, there was this family. They broke a Regulation, and their punishment was no rations for two weeks. I shared mine with them."

"Rations?" Frank asked. "You mean food?" Philip looked at Frank like he was trying to determine whether or not Frank was an idiot, then he nodded and looked away. "Yeah. I aided Regulation breakers. Not my finest hour. I'm paying my debt to society, though. Part of that means surprise inspections from time to time."

"Really? From the city manager?"

Philip shrugged. "No, this is a first. Usually it's a couple of cops."

Becky returned to the room. "Well Philip, I don't see any evidence of Regulation breaking." He smiled and nodded.

"Thank you, ma'am. It's an honor to have you handle this personally."

Becky smiled back at him. "You're proof that the system works. Hey, why don't you tell Frank about your scar?"

He looked at Frank. "It's part of the punishment for Regulation 8 breakers. So people know not to trust me."

"And tell him who gave it to you."

Philip took a deep breath. His smile wavered for only a moment. "It was my wife. She found out about my crimes, and she drugged me and took care of it. She's a good woman."

"She sure is," the city manager said.

Back out on the street, Frank asked, "So what was the point of that little show?"

Becky Raymond shrugged. "I'm continuing your education. I want you to know the score. Family is important, but Rook Mountain comes first."

"I'm not sure I agree with that."

"It doesn't matter what you believe. It's what the town believes. All I'm saying is to stay vigilant. You are out there grilling Sally Badwater and visiting your old haunts, and at the same time you are living with the town doctor and the head of the Certification program."

Frank took a deep breath and tried to stay calm. He spoke softly, but he still heard the anger in his own voice. "Listen to me. I agreed to look for Jake, and I am doing that. I will find him. You leave them the hell out of it."

"Of course," Becky said. "I want you to know that we are watching. Always. Zed has eyes everywhere. You are never out of his sight, not in Rook Mountain."

Frank nodded. "I'll find Jake, but I'm not bringing Christine and Trevor into this thing."

The woman smiled. "Frank. They live in Rook Mountain. They're already in this thing." They stopped in front of the Osmond's house. "There's something else. Something I didn't tell you before."

Frank waited for her to continue.

"Since Regulation Day, odd items have been appearing in Rook Mountain. They look like everyday objects. A mirror, a lighter, things like that. But they are extremely dangerous. We believe that Jake was interested in these items. Obsessed with them, really. We know he had at least one of them. He may have hidden it before he went away. If you find any of these objects in your search for Jake, you let me know right away. Understand?"

"If they look like everyday objects, how am I supposed to find them?"

"They have a symbol carved into them. It's a broken clock."

Frank froze. He struggled to keep any reaction off his face. He had seen that symbol once. He'd seen it on the worst day of his life.

"You find something with that symbol, you bring it to me." Becky Raymond turned away from him and toward the street. "You've had your week to acclimate. Next week I expect to hear some results. If not, well, I'm sure CO Rodgers is keeping a bunk empty for you."

Becky Raymond gave him a curt nod and turned back up the sidewalk.

Frank stood on the threshold of his former sister-in-law's home, taking long slow breaths, trying to figure out his next move. He didn't notice Will standing in the front yard, watching Becky Raymond walk away.

3.

Trevor followed the signs pointing toward the auditorium and tried not to make eye contact with the other students.

Everyone had been polite so far, but when they looked at him he saw it in their eyes. They were all wondering how the son of a terrorist had gotten into the Beyond Academy.

At his old school, it had been much more overt. Kids would make comments, ask Trevor if his dad had taught him how to make pipe bombs, ask when Trevor was going to blow up the school. It bothered him, of course, but most of the time he had been able to laugh it off. As Mom always reminded him, these kids didn't know his dad. Yes, Dad had gone crazy for a little while there at the end, but that didn't define him as a person. Trevor remembered other things about his dad. He remembered Dad reading him stories, and wrestling with him on the floor, and taking him for hikes in the mountains.

But today, even though no one was saying anything, it was different. It was probably just the stress of starting a new school, but Trevor had a terrible feeling that someone would realize the error and expel him at any moment.

He wished Carl had been accepted. Then at least he would have someone to walk with in the halls.

"Trevor!" a female voice called.

He looked around, bewildered for a moment, then saw a woman in a blue dress. She wore glasses and her black hair fell in loose curls around her shoulders. She was hot, but she was also clearly a teacher.

"Trevor, hi." The woman walked over to him. "You probably don't remember me. I'm Wendy Caulfield. Your uncle Frank and I used to babysit you when you were little."

Her statement was so unexpected that Trevor had no idea how to respond. "Hi, Ms. Caulfield."

She smiled. "I teach History and Civics. You'll have me for fourth period this semester."

He nodded dumbly.

"Anyway, I just wanted to say hello." She turned to go, then stopped and nodded toward the auditorium. "Trevor, remember, however weird this place seems, and whatever you hear in there, this is still a school. We're here to help you learn. And you can talk to us –to me—if you need anything. Okay?"

Trevor nodded again. "Okay. Thanks."

She turned the other direction, and Trevor stepped into the auditorium.

To call it an auditorium was a bit of an overstatement in Trevor's opinion. Like the rest of the school, the room was clean and state-of-the-art. Every surface said quality. But it was more of a classroom with stadium seating than it was an auditorium. The school only had forty students. Trevor guessed this room could hold maybe seventy-five total. He eyed the back rows, looking for a block of empty seats where he could squeeze in without having to sit next to anyone. Fancy genius academy or not, this was still high school. Who you sat with mattered, and Trevor wanted to get the lay of the land before pigeon-holing himself into any particular clique. He found a likely spot in the second row from the back and hustled toward it.

He had barely sat down before the lights flicked once, and a voice over the PA system asked them to rise for the national anthem. Trevor rose with the rest and turned toward the American flag on the left side of the stage. Pre-recorded music filled the room at a surprisingly loud volume. As the first verse began everyone's voice rose to match the level of the music. Trevor looked around as he sang and saw most of his fellow students for the first time.

What he saw didn't remind him of the first day of school. They weren't slouching or giggling, and there were no annoyed frowns. Every pupil stood ramrod straight and sang loudly, their eyes glued to the flag. There was a quality about them that it took Trevor a few moments to identify. Then it came to him. The students weren't just glad to be starting the school year, they were proud to be here. It was pride he saw on the faces of his fellow students.

The "Star-Spangled Banner" built to its crescendo. The pre-recorded music cut off a moment too soon, jarring Trevor out of his thoughts. Everyone sank back into their seats. Trevor did the same, his eyes on the still-empty stage.

The voice on the PA returned. "To open the 2022-2023 school year, please welcome back guest speaker and friend of the Rook Mountain Beyond Academy, Zed!"

The students erupted with applause, and a tall bald man jogged up the steps to the stage. He wore a green, long-sleeved t-shirt and khaki pants. He stood there with an easy smile on his face waiting for the applause to die down.

Trevor had heard a lot about Zed, of course, but he had only seen him up close once before. Trevor knew Zed had saved the town. They told that story every year on the anniversary of Regulation Day. He knew Zed lived in the big house downtown. He also knew that his father had gone crazy and tried to blow up Zed, killing three innocent people in the process.

Zed was a legend in a town that had far too few of them. Everyone talked about him with respect and admiration. Everyone seemed to love him. In a lot of ways, he was the complete opposite of Trevor's father.

When the applause stopped, Zed held out his hands, palms up. He was wearing one of those headset microphones, and his deep voice filled the room when he spoke.

"Thank you. You know, it's really an honor to be asked back again to open the school year. Sometimes I feel like a broken record. I've said the same thing every year for the past four years, and I'm about to say it again. Some of you returning students might be sick of hearing it—"

"No way, Zed!" called a male voice from the crowd. The kids all laughed.

Zed pointed toward the student. "Thanks for humoring an old man, son. Some of you may be sick of hearing it, but what I have to say was true last year and it is still true today. Here it goes. This year is going to be the most important year of your lives."

Zed paused, his eyes moving back and forth across the faces in the crowd. The laughter was gone now, and the room was filled with a reverent silence. "I believe that with all my heart. Think about it for a moment. This year is going to be the most important year of your lives." He paused again, this time looking down at his own feet as he gave the students a moment.

He looked up and spoke again. "Let me ask you something. How many of you have traveled outside the United States? In the Before, I mean."

A few hands rose.

Zed nodded. "How many of you have traveled outside Tennessee?"

This time, over half the hands in the crowd went up, including Trevor's. He didn't remember it well, but he knew his family had taken a vacation to Florida when he was three.

"How many of your parents talk about their travels? About what life was like outside Rook Mountain in the Before?"

Every hand went up. Zed nodded. "Thanks. You can put

your hands down. For those of you attending the Beyond Academy for the first time this year, today is an important day. Today is the day that you stop listening to your parents' stories about the world outside. Because I'm going to tell you something important: your parents' stories don't mean shit."

He held up his hands as if calming the crowd, though not one student had voiced an objection. "Don't get me wrong! Those stories have their place. Just like stories of George Washington or stories of the Roman Empire. But I know every one of your parents at least a little, and I can say with confidence that they do not understand the world outside of Rook Mountain. Not anymore. Very shortly, you will. The days of your parents are over. Your day has begun."

He looked out over the crowd again. "A person can survive somewhere between three and six weeks without food. We have some food stored in town, but how long do you think Rook Mountain would survive without our brave Resource Specialists?" He let the question hang in the air, then continued. "But it's not about survival. It's about what you want the future to be. I know that many of you will choose to become Resource Specialists when you leave this school, but some of you will pursue different paths. That's perfectly fine. As long as you work hard to get whatever it is you want out of life, this school has done its job.

"I don't work for the school. I am just a guy who cares deeply about Rook Mountain. Your parents have obviously done things right since you've all made it this far. But in the coming days and weeks and months you will see things that your parents will have no way to understand. Sometime during the next couple years, you will be allowed to go on a trip outside of town with some Resource Specialists. Depending on the expedition you are assigned to, you might see Elizabethton, or Kingsport, or Johnson City. You might even go somewhere farther if your Resource Specialist needs to fulfill a more exotic request."

He held up a finger for emphasis. "When you go, you will see how the world on the outside really is, and then you will start to understand why Rook Mountain is so special and why we must do everything possible to protect it."

Trevor couldn't help but imagine the places he would go as the man talked.

"The things you see will change you," Zed continued. "And you might need someone to talk to. Someone who understands. I want to tell you—and I mean this from the bottom of my heart—that from this moment on, I consider each person in this room family. Anytime you need to talk, day or night, you call me. Even if it's something silly, something you don't think is worth bothering me for, you call me. And, I promise, I will do everything I can to help you. You might need a listening ear, a place to stay, or even protection from your own parents. Doesn't matter. I will help you.

"Like I said, I love Rook Mountain, and I believe you are her future and her brightest hope. It doesn't matter what you were before today, what your dreams are, or—" he looked at Trevor, "—what your parents might have done. You are the future, and the future starts today."

Zed smiled and put his hands on his hips. "Ready to get started?"

4.

Frank walked in the door a few minutes before six o'clock. He had spent most of the day wandering the town. He'd walked past his childhood home and his elementary school. He'd gone by Sean's house and knocked on the door, but there had been no answer. He'd even walked past Wendy's place, though he knew she would be at school. People had to work for a living.

The hours of walking had left his feet sore but his head clear. Becky Raymond had been wrong to suggest he should be suspicious of Christine and Will, but she did have a point. It was odd the way they weren't asking him any questions, and the way they steered clear of certain topics. The way they hadn't told him anything about the Regulations, and the way Will had only shown him those things on the outside of town after Sean had called him and asked.

Frank had come to a conclusion on his long walk through town: either Christine and Will were hiding something, or they didn't trust him and thought he was hiding something. Possibly both.

Of course, if they thought that he was hiding something, they were correct. He hadn't told them why he had been released from prison. He'd had to sort through his own feelings first. But now was the time. He had to have an honest talk with them tonight. Everybody needed to put their cards on the table. Enough with the secrets already.

The front door was locked, but that was no problem. The door knob was still the same one he had given Jake and Christine as a housewarming present so many years ago. Frank twisted it a quarter turn, pulled, twisted it a full turn the other direction, gave it a push at just the right angle, and the lock popped open.

Will and Christine were sitting at the dining room table.

"Hey," Frank said. "You all have a good day?"

Will and Christine exchanged a glance.

"It was fine," Christine said. "Frank, could you sit down for a minute? We need to talk."

"Yeah, of course." This was it, Frank knew. The chance for everyone to come clean.

Frank sat down. He felt a little like a child with mommy and daddy sitting at the ends of the table.

"Where's Trevor?" Frank asked. "I wanted to ask him about his first day."

"He's at Carl's," Will said. His hands were squeezed into tight fists. "What was Becky Raymond doing at our house this morning?"

Frank shifted in his seat a little. The question caught him off guard. He wanted to discuss that, but he had hoped to be the one to get the ball rolling. "How'd you know about that?"

"I forgot my coffee this morning. I came back to get it and I saw her leaving. The two of you were chatting like old buddies." Will's ears were bright red. Will was a calm man, able to hide his emotions better than most, but Frank had played enough poker with him over the years that he could see what was wriggling beneath his cool exterior. Will was furious.

"Will," Christine said, "let him explain." She spoke in an uncharacteristic staccato. Her eyes were troubled.

"Okay," Frank said. "She was here to check on my progress."

"Your progress on what?" Will asked.

"Finding Jake."

"Excuse me?" Will raised up out of his chair and leaned forward, palms on the table.

Frank met Will's eyes. He felt himself getting a little heated too. There was no reason he should be under attack.

"I'm sorry I didn't tell you sooner," Frank said. "I was trying to get my bearings before we had this discussion."

"Time's up," Christine said. "Talk to us."

Frank nodded. He took a deep breath. "Becky Raymond came to see me in prison last week. She offered me a deal. If I agreed to help find Jake, I would be released."

Will shook his head. "I don't understand. Why would they think you could help?"

"Jake made an appearance last week. He talked to Sally Badwater."

"That's impossible." Christine's voice quivered as she spoke. "Sally Badwater's making it up. She's batshit crazy, and she's telling stories."

"No," Frank said. "Jake told her something. Something only he would know. I believe her." Frank didn't want to explain the Cassandra lock. Not now, anyway.

Will stood up straight and pointed a shaky finger at Frank. "There is no way Jake's in town. You think he'd go see Sally Badwater and not visit Christine and Trevor?"

Frank shrugged. "I only know what I know. It seems crazy to me, too. Maybe he's trying to protect you guys."

Christine rubbed her eyes with the back of her hands. "Okay, say it is true. Why did Becky Raymond come to you?"

"Jake told Sally that he needed to see me. So they let me out. Becky said I had one month to find him. And I had to agree to weekly meetings to discuss my progress. That was what you saw today."

"This is incredible," Christine said.

Will took a step back from the table. His balled up fists were at his side. "You know what's incredible to me? After we took you in, no questions asked, you didn't think to mention that Jake, Christine's ex-husband, Trevor's father —" he gritted his teeth, but Frank saw the tears in his eyes, "—my best friend. You didn't mention that he was out there. They're hunting him right now and he might need our help."

"Will," Christine said. "You're wrong."

"Thank you," Frank said. "If we could all take a minute—"

"You're wrong to say that they're hunting Jake." She nodded toward Frank. "Frank is the one hunting Jake."

"Whoa, Christine, please. Let me explain."

"Explain what?" Her eyes were filled with fury. "You agreed to track down Jake in exchange for your freedom! Explain to me what kind of a person does that."

"It's not like that. I'm trying to find Jake, yeah, but I'm gonna warn him. I wouldn't turn him in."

"Then why the secrecy?" Will asked.

"It's not like you've been super forthcoming, either. Listen, maybe we need to work together. We can find Jake. Isn't that what you want? Becky Raymond mentioned these objects. They have a broken clock symbol on them. She said Jake was obsessed with them. Have you seen anything like that?"

Will's lips pressed together into a tight line. He said, "I've never seen anything like that."

Frank knew Will was lying. He knew it as sure as he knew his own name. "Okay. How about the cabins? Did you clear them out before the Hansens moved in? Maybe we can look around out there. If Jake had to hide something, that's where he'd stash it."

"We moved everything out," Christine said. "There's nothing there."

"What about my guitar case? The one with my locks in it."

"We put all your stuff in a storage unit. We can go down there tomorrow if you want."

Frank shook his head. "Gus Hansen said he had the guitar case. If you missed that, there might be other things out there too. Some of Jake's things maybe. I should go take a look."

There was a long moment of silence. "Damn it," Will said. "I know you are fresh out of prison and don't know any better, but there are things going on in this town that even your buddy Sean doesn't know about. Bringing the city manager here could have really screwed us. I love you like a brother, and Christine does too. But if you put my family in danger—"

"What?" Frank asked. His voice was loud, almost a shout. He felt himself slipping, starting to lose control of his emotions. "What will you do, Will?"

Christine spoke softly. "You're not the only killer in this house, Frank."

Frank stopped, mid-breath. "What are you saying?"

"Will and I have done things, terrible things, to protect this family and to make sure Trevor has a future. We've sacrificed so much. We've hurt people, and we will do it again if we have to."

Frank looked back and forth between Christine and Will, two of his closest friends in the world. All he saw in their eyes was ice. He believed Christine.

He pushed back his chair. "I'm sorry if I put you in danger. That is the last thing in the world I'd ever want to do. Maybe I should clear out of here for a while."

Christine and Will were silent.

Frank paused, hoping they would say something. Maybe ask him not to leave. At least say goodbye. But they didn't. Frank walked out the front door and headed into the darkening streets of Rook Mountain.

IN THE BEFORE (PART 4)

"Frank," Brett said. "You ever feel like maybe you need a change of scenery?"

Frank shrugged. "You want to get out of Rook Mountain?"

Brett strummed a lazy D7 chord. "I don't know. I guess. I've lived in these mountains all my life. I still think they're pretty, but there's something stifling about them too, you know? The trees are so thick it's like they want to squeeze you. Not like the Rockies. Those mountains give a man a little room to think. Or the ocean. I could really spread out near the ocean."

"You've got some weird ideas, dude."

The two men were playing guitar on Frank's porch, strumming old country tunes and 90's grunge songs. Brett did a mean Billy Corgan imitation on "Bullet with Butterfly Wings." It was the odd night when Will wasn't around. He had some PTA function or something, so the three amigos were dos tonight. On nights like these, they often pulled out the guitars and jammed. Will was learning to play, but his limited chord vocabulary held them back a bit. Sometimes

Todd came by with his perpetually out of tune ukulele. But on the nights when it was just Frank and Brett, they could get lost in the music and really jam.

They made an odd pairing. Brett was always talking as if he couldn't stand the silence. He'd talk about anything, from the sad state of popular music to his grandfather's rare coin collection. He was the type of guy who would start calling friends to chat anytime he had a drive longer than ten minutes. It didn't even matter who—he would keep working his way through his contacts list until someone answered. Frank, on the other hand, cherished the silence.

It was understandable, Frank supposed. Brett was used to a houseful of kids and a wife who talked his ear off. His recent divorce had left him lonely. At first, he had a hard time understanding Frank's quiet nature, but he came to accept it over time.

Frank was about to launch into "Interstate Love Song" when Brett said, "You know what I saw today?"

Frank reached for his beer. "I really don't."

"I was walking down by Gravel Park and I saw this little crowd gathered around. There were maybe ten people. I figured it might have been some kind of class or something, so I wandered over to see what was up. And guess what I saw?"

"I still have no idea."

Brett leaned his guitar against the porch railing to free up his hands. He was a big hand talker. "Okay, so all the people are sitting on the ground in a semicircle around this rock. And guess who's sitting on the rock like he's Buddha or something? That Zed guy."

Frank snorted out a laugh. "Naked Zed?"

"Yeah. I mean, he was wearing clothes but that's the guy. I didn't recognize some of the people, but I did know a few of them. There was Nate Grayson. And that girl Will took to that Strange Brood concert in Asheville—"

"Mary Gunderson."

"Yeah. And Becky from the gas station on the corner of Dennis Cove Road."

"Becky Raymond."

"Yeah. So I stood back a little ways and watched. I wasn't close enough to hear what he was saying, so I was kind of watching their body language. And, man, they were hanging on his every word. He was going on and on like he was giving a sermon or something. And they were eating it up. It was like Jesus with the 'Blessed are the meek' stuff."

"The Beatitudes."

"What?"

"The 'Blessed are the meek' stuff. That's from the Beatitudes. It's part of the Sermon on the Mount."

"Anyway, I'm standing there watching, and all of a sudden Zed looks right at me and nods toward me. And all his little groupies turn their heads. Then one of the guys, this dude I've never seen before, stands up and walks over."

"No way."

"So I stand there, trying to figure out if this guy is going to get aggressive, trying to decide what to do if he does. Fight or flight and all that. But then I see he's smiling. He walks up and says, 'Brett, Zed would like you to join us.' Keep in mind, I've never met this dude."

Frank laughed. "What did you say?"

"I didn't know what to say! I just kind of shook my head and walked away. I'm telling you, Frank, this Zed guy is up to no good. We've got a real David Koresh situation building here. You met him. Can you imagine sitting there listening to him talk for twenty minutes? Voluntarily?"

Frank shook his head. "I could barely stand him for five minutes."

"Weak minds, I guess." Brett took a drink of his beer. "So how's the workshop fund coming?"

Frank sighed. "It's coming. I got a big payment in yesterday. I'm still eighteen months away from being able to get a real shop set up, though. That's if I'm lucky."

Brett smiled. "Man, when you start mass producing your locks, I'm going to be bugging you for a job."

"I didn't realize you were a qualified locksmith."

Brett shrugged. "I'll do whatever. Sweep floors. Help with the books. As long as I make enough to tell my current boss to suck it. I don't need much. Just enough for rent on one of these cabins, a little food money—"

"Child support," Frank said.

"Yeah." Brett frowned. "That too. How much are your locks going for these days?"

"Anywhere from fifty bucks for the standard models up to a few hundred for the custom jobs. But it's not like the money's going to be rolling in the minute I get the shop set up. I'll still be a one man operation. I'll be able to work a little faster, that's all. I'll build it up slowly. Maybe bring on another locksmith in a few years so I can concentrate on designs."

Brett wagged a finger at him. "What you need is an investor. You get some capital behind you, I'll bet you could have your locks in every magic shop and hobby store in the country in a couple years."

Frank smiled. "Maybe I should join Zed's cult. Get them to fund me."

Brett let out a full-bellied laugh which quickly devolved into a coughing fit. "Not the worst idea I've ever heard." He stood up. "I gotta take a piss. Mind?"

"Yeah, sure," Frank said. It was a little odd that Brett asked. He wasn't usually averse to walking into Frank's house without asking permission.

It wasn't until almost eleven the next morning that Frank noticed the guitar case was gone.

It was only by chance that Frank had discovered it at all. He had wanted to look at it this morning. Tinker with some of the locks he kept in there. He looked under the bed, but the case wasn't there. He ran over to the cabin next door, the one he used as his workshop, but it wasn't there, either. His guitar case and all the locks inside of it were gone. His life's work. Thirty original lock designs, including ten prototypes not yet for sale. Including the unfinished Cassandra lock.

After some initial panic, a surprising sense of calm settled over him. There had only been one person in his cabin since he had last seen the guitar case. That person had always shown an uncommon interest in the locks Frank left laying around the house. Brett would mess with them for days trying to figure out the trick to opening them until Frank finally took pity and showed him how to do it.

Frank started at Brett's cabin, first knocking on the door and then breaking in through a window when there was no answer. The inside of Brett's place had always been sparse –nothing on the walls and only a few pieces of furniture, as if he expected to move back in with his wife at any moment—but this took it to a whole different level. The furniture was still there, but everything else was gone. The clothes, the bedding, even most of the food. Brett must have packed up his things during the night and headed out.

The room felt ten degrees colder than it had a moment ago. How long had Brett been planning this?

Frank sat down on the old overstuffed recliner in Brett's

living room and pushed the heels of his hands into his eye sockets. The pain brought clarity.

It all made a sick kind of sense. Brett had been wiped out financially and emotionally by the divorce. He had gone from living an upper-middle class lifestyle to barely being able to scrape by. He had been on the edge for a while. It wasn't shocking that he would bolt in the night. But what was he planning to do with Frank's locks?

He took a deep breath and pulled out his cell phone. He needed to call the police. Something held him back, though. If he could get to Brett himself and talk to him, maybe the law didn't have to get involved. And there was one place Frank was almost certain Brett would go before leaving town for good. Frank glanced at his watch and ran for his truck. There was still a chance.

He almost cried with relief when he saw Brett's Chevy Malibu parked in front of the bank downtown. Its back seat was stuffed with clothes and boxes. Frank pulled in next to it and got out. He leaned against the back of Brett's car and waited.

Brett walked out of the bank ten minutes later, carrying a backpack slung over one shoulder. Brett slowed when he saw Frank. The color drained from his face, but he recovered quickly, forced a smile, and kept walking.

"Hey man," Brett said. "A little early for you isn't it?"

Frank put on a smile of his own. "I couldn't sleep. I kept having this weird feeling like there was something I needed to do this morning."

"Cool," Brett said. "We still on for poker tonight? Maybe we can see if Jake and Christine are free?"

"I don't think that's gonna happen, buddy." Frank nodded toward the backpack. "You might have packed up during the night, but I knew you'd have to wait until the bank opened to get those. That was a mistake. What are they worth? Two grand?"

Brett shrugged. The smile was gone. "Sentimental value, I guess." His grandfather's coin collection was one of the few things Brett had been able to keep in the divorce. He was immensely proud of it. He kept it in a safety deposit box at the bank, but he talked about it constantly. Frank knew he wouldn't leave town without it.

Frank stood up straight and crossed his arms. "I only have one question. Was this a spur of the moment thing? Or have you been planning this?"

"I'm not going to lie to you. It was a little of both. I'd been thinking about it for a while and last night I saw my opportunity."

"Damn dude, that's cold. How'd you get the guitar case out?"

"I slipped it out the bedroom window. I came back and got it later after you went to bed."

"What are you gonna do with a bunch of puzzle locks anyway?" Frank asked.

"This dude approached me, and offered me some cash for your locks."

Frank paused. Who would want his locks? A competitor? "How much?"

"They offered me five grand."

Frank stepped forward. He was close to Brett now, only a few feet away. Within arm's reach.

"That's it?" Frank asked. "Five grand? You sold me out for five grand?"

Brett stepped up to Frank. "I was leaving town anyway. I needed a little more cash. But don't act like we're lifelong buddies. We've known each other what, six months? And you've looked down on me the whole time. You've always thought I was pathetic."

"Give me the case and I won't call the police," Frank said. "I'm gonna beat the piss out of you either way, but I won't call the police."

"I'm not giving you the case. I'm getting my money and leaving town."

Frank looked away for a moment and took a deep breath. How many times had Brett been in his home? How long had he been planning to betray Frank? "You don't understand what's happening here. I caught you. You are not leaving my sight until you give me the case."

Brett chuckled. "No, you don't understand. You want to live your weird little bohemian lifestyle in the mountains making artisan locks or whatever, go right ahead. Live your hippie dreams. I don't want to live like that. I had a great life, and I want to make a new one. I'm leaving, so get out of my way."

He shoved Frank. Frank stumbled back two steps and caught himself on the side view mirror of Brett's car. He straightened himself to his full height and glared at Brett, with his middle age beer gut and that stupid backpack over his shoulder.

Frank lunged forward and drove his fist into Brett's stomach. Brett's breath left him with a whoosh, and he doubled over. The backpack slipped off his shoulder and hit the ground with a thud, and a dozen coins tumbled out of the bag and clinked onto the pavement. One of them fell against Frank's right foot.

Frank glanced down at the coin. He paused, then looked at it a little harder. The coin was different than any currency Frank had ever seen. It didn't feature the face of a historical figure. It didn't display an eagle or the Statue of

Liberty. This coin featured a different symbol—a broken clock.

Frank found it hard to look away from the coin. It held his gaze like a vise. It was suddenly hard to concentrate. Frank felt dizzy.

He heard Brett moan, and the coin's spell was broken. Frank looked up at Brett, and he felt a fury like none he had ever known before. A single punch to the stomach? That wasn't enough punishment for what Brett had done. Not nearly enough.

Frank looked to his left and there in the bed of his truck was his tire iron.

Frank picked up the tire iron, gripping it with both hands. The iron felt cold against his skin and the weight of the thing in his hand was pleasant. He raised the tire iron and brought it down hard on Brett's back.

Brett collapsed, groaning as he wriggled on the ground. After a moment, he rolled onto his side and looked up at Frank, his body rigid with pain.

Frank shifted the tire iron to one hand. He raised it over his head.

"No!" shouted Brett. "Wait! I'll tell you where it is. Just put that thing down!" He twisted onto his back and crab-walked backwards through the parking lot. Frank followed, not hurrying, the tire iron still raised above his head. Brett looked pathetic scooting across the blacktop like that. Frank felt numb and cold.

Brett backed onto the grass next to the parking lot, and kept going until he bumped against a sign. 'Grayson Park: Hours 7am-7pm.' Brett pushed himself up, using the sign for support. He held out of a hand in front of him as if to keep Frank at arm's length.

Frank felt a fresh wave of anger flow through him. He

reached back with the tire iron, then brought it around hard. It crashed into Brett's temple, rocking his head to the side like it was on a hinge. Brett fell to the ground and moaned. After some time—Frank had no idea how long—he noticed the moaning noises had stopped. Brett wasn't moving.

Frank stood over Brett, the tire iron still clutched in his hand, for what felt like hours. Eventually he heard someone scream, and a little while later, he heard a voice yelling at him to drop the weapon, to drop it or they would shoot. He absently wondered what they were talking about, and then he noticed the tire iron in his hand. It was sticky with blood.

With a great effort, Frank uncurled the fingers of his left hand. The tire iron fell to the ground with a clang.

The screaming voices told him to put his hands on his head, and he did. They told him to drop to his knees, and he did that, too. Then they were on top of him, throwing him to the ground. He felt handcuffs click on his wrists and wondered how long it would take him to escape from them if he wanted to. He didn't want to, though. He wanted to lie there and die.

He looked over and saw his old friend Sean. Sean looked upset, and Frank wondered if he was having a bad day.

By the time they put him into the police car, Frank was starting to come back to himself. He didn't fully understand what he had done—not yet—but he couldn't stop hearing the meaty thud of the tire iron hitting Brett's skull, feeling the jar of the impact in his hand, and seeing Brett's dead face.

THE CASSANDRA LOCK

I.

If Frank had any sense, he would have headed to Sean's. Sean lived within walking distance, he lived alone, and—best of all—Sean would take him in no questions asked. But Frank wasn't going to Sean's.

The other option was to head for the edge of town, just step over the town line and let the Unfeathered have him. The board of selectmen weirdos wanted him to find Jake, and he was starting to think maybe that was exactly what happened to his brother. Why not join Jake? But that wasn't where he was going, either.

As he walked, the spaces between homes grew larger and larger until the road was flanked with pine trees and there was not a house in sight. He stepped off the gravel and felt the pleasant crunch of pine needles under his feet. He would approach the cabins from the back and hope for the element of surprise. He didn't know exactly what he was looking for and he didn't know exactly where to look. All he knew was that Will and Christine were hiding something out here. Whatever it was, it had to be important. They had allowed the most feared family in town to live there, which – Frank had to admit – was a pretty ingenious tactic to keep people away. Frank had a terrible, growing suspicion that Will and Christine knew more about Jake's disappearance than they were admitting.

The beginnings a plan were forming in Frank's head. To call it a plan was probably too grand—call it an approach. Combined with a little luck and his reputation as a convicted killer, it might be enough to get him through the night. Frank knew that he would have to take out Ty first. His best bet was to deal with the big man rather than to leave him running around to muck things up later.

Frank paused when he came within sight of the dull light of the cabins. He crouched behind a tree and scanned the yard until he found what he was looking for. A thick dog chain staked to the ground. The chain would serve nicely in the dual role of weapon and potential tool of restraint. The presence of a dog was a little worrisome. The Hansens didn't seem like the type of family who would have a dog that was prone to licking strangers rather than biting them. It hadn't started barking yet, which was a good sign. Frank hoped the dog wasn't in Ty's cabin.

He waited, shrouded in the darkness and security of the familiar pine trees, until the lights clicked off in each of three occupied cabins—first the one on the left, then the right, then the middle. He stayed in his spot for what felt like an hour after that, then made his move.

Frank ran to the chain and unhooked it from the stake. He shuffled to his old cabin and crouched in front of it, his eyes an inch above the level of the porch floorboards. There were two rickety old wooden chairs on the porch, and a small table with a mason jar half full of an unidentified liquid. It might have been tea, whiskey, or tobacco spit—it was too dark to tell.

His approach was a bit juvenile, but he was beyond trying to cook up cool plans. He was flying solely on instinct. He crept up the porch steps and paused at the door. He stood up to his full height and brought the chain to his chest. He took a deep breath and rapped on the door hard three times—rat tat tat. He turned and pressed his back against the wall next to the door.

Frank heard the heavy thud of footsteps inside. A light switched on. Its glow flowed out of the windows into the night, fading a few feet to Frank's left.

Good, thought Frank. Let him ruin his night vision.

The cabin door creaked open, and a huge shadow spilled out onto the porch. Frank stood statue still, trying not to breathe.

"Who's out here?"

Conflicting waves of excitement and terror crashed through Frank. The voice was low, slow, and relatively youthful. It was Ty's voice.

"You hear me? Who's out here?"

The door opened a bit further, and the hulking form appeared in the doorway. Frank saw the big man's hands and grew the tiniest bit calmer. Ty's hands were empty. His uncle and father would have answered the door with a shotgun in hand, but Ty was used to his physical size being enough to dominate most situations.

Moment of truth. Frank gripped the chain in both hands and waited to see what would happen next. Either Ty would step inside and Frank would have to knock again, or Ty would step out a little further. Frank allowed himself a long slow breath. He would need all the oxygen he could get in just a moment.

"I know you're out here." Ty took one step forward. "Better speak up before—"

Frank moved in fast, swinging the chain like a jump rope up and over Ty's head. He pulled both ends as hard as he could, and Ty staggered toward him.

Frank cursed. He had meant for the chain to wrap around Ty's neck, but he had underestimated the size of the man. The chain had caught Ty around the shoulders. Still, Frank had knocked him off balance. Frank kept pulling, and the big man tumbled to the ground with a shout.

Frank pounced on the downed man's back. He pulled both ends of the chain hard, tightening it across Ty's chest. Ty groaned in surprise and pain. Frank held his grip. Ty's hand closed around Frank's ankle and he pulled, sending Frank spinning to the ground. Frank hit the ground hard and lost both his wind and his grip on the chain.

He rolled onto his side and dragged himself to his feet, straining to force enough air into his lungs. Ty rose much faster. The big man was up while Frank still struggled to get his feet under him. Ty grabbed Frank by the collar and slammed his back against the wall of the cabin. The big man held Frank there, Frank's feet dangling off the ground.

Ty squinted at him in the darkness. "Who are you?"

Frank tried to speak, but only a cough escaped. Ty slammed him against the wall again, and the cabin rattled.

"Who are you? Talk!"

"I—I—" Frank tried to speak, but he wasn't having much luck. He wasn't sure what he would have said anyway.

"Do you know who I am?" Ty asked. "Do you have any idea how bad you just screwed up?"

"I—" Frank said, and he slammed his knee into Ty's crotch. The big man released Frank and doubled over. Frank landed and staggered, putting one hand on the wall for balance. Ty raised his head and started to straighten. His face looked an impossible shade of red in the light coming through the cabin window.

Frank threw three quick jabs into Ty's face. He aimed for the nose and connected solidly on two of the three punches. He heard something snap on the last punch. Ty moaned and staggered backwards.

Frank reached down and snatched the chain off the ground. He spun it over his head, getting its speed up until it whistled through the air, then he flicked his wrist and the end of the chain slammed into the side of Ty's head with a crack.

Frank pulled back the chain, once again holding each of the ends in one hand.

Ty raised his bloodied face, let out a howl of fury, and charged. The big man ran on pure rage. His eyes had to be filled with tears from that busted nose. Frank ducked under Ty's outstretched arms, got behind him, and threw the chain over his head. This time, he didn't miss the neck.

He put his knee against Ty's back and pulled on the chain until the big man sank to his knees. Frank eased the pressure on the chain a little. He didn't want Ty to pass out, but he couldn't have him getting loose either.

"Jerry sends his regards," Frank said. "I spent the last few years with him inside. Nice guy. We all called him the Newg. Doesn't like you much, though."

"I'll...rip...your...head..."

Frank tightened the chains, cutting off Ty's words. "Sorry, I didn't catch that. Anyway, I'm here about something else." Frank couldn't help but feel a little sorry for Ty. One minute the guy is asleep in his bed; the next he has a broken nose and is being choked with a chain. Frank couldn't work up too much sympathy, though. According to the Newg, Ty Hansen had done worse than this to less deserving folk. Much worse.

Ty uttered another frustrated groan.

Frank glanced toward the two cabins to the north, wondering if they had heard the fight. He knew from personal experience how well sound carried here, how thin the walls of the cabins were. He had heard more than he wanted to of Christine and Jake carrying on back in the day.

Frank said, "Let's go inside. This is going to be a little awkward, but I think we can do it. Get up."

Frank eased the tension on the chain a little, allowing Ty to stand. Frank's comfort level dropped as Ty straightened to his full height. He was one big guy. Frank was six feet tall, and Ty had a good six inches on him. He was solid too, built like a big NFL linebacker. It was a miracle the guy hadn't crushed him already.

Frank steered Ty, using the chain like a horse's bridle. The big man shuffled forward and awkwardly opened the screen door.

"Easy," Frank said. They walked through the door, and Frank guided him to the kitchen. "Kneel down there. By the radiator."

"You...gonna...kill me?" croaked Ty.

"No, not unless you make me. I have some questions for you. And I can't have you punching me while I'm asking. Put your arms by your side." He took a deep breath and slid the chain off Ty's neck and down around his midsection. He pulled chain tight, pinning Ty's arms to his sides.

Before Frank had gotten into locks, he had been fascinated by knots, and he knew some good ones. He threaded the chain around the radiator and tied a constrictor knot. There was no way Ty would get out of that one. Frank wasn't even sure how he would release Ty when this was over.

With the pressure off his neck, Ty fell forward and coughed violently.

"Take all the time you need," Frank said. "Get some air. Let me know when you're ready." Frank walked over to wall and flipped off the light switch. It was better to do this kind of thing in the dark.

Ty's coughing fit subsided. "You stupid piece of shit. You broke my nose. I'm gonna kill you."

"Not today," Frank said. "Today you are gonna answer my questions, or I'm gonna to beat you even bloodier."

Ty's big silhouette quiver, either with anger or the strain of trying to catch his breath, Frank didn't know which.

"Good answer," Frank said. "I know Christine Hinkle is hiding something out here. What is it?"

Ty smiled. "Osmond."

"What?"

"It's Christine Osmond now. She hooked up with that teacher pretty quick after your brother lit out, didn't she?" Ty spit some blood onto the floor. "Didn't I beat up you and your brother after a football game once?"

"Thanks for reminding me. I was starting to think I might have been too hard on you. Let's get back on topic. What's Christine hiding?"

"Sorry, man. I don't know what you're talking about."

Frank kicked Ty, connecting with the big man's side, and Ty screamed in pain and rage. Frank's eyes flickered toward the window, toward the other cabins. They remained dark.

That kick had probably been a little too hard. He might have done some real damage. Frank was hoping the harder he kicked, the fewer times he would need to do it. That was the theory anyway.

Part of Frank, a distant rational part, was shocked that he was once again hurting someone. But the rest of him, the part that was sick to death of the secrets and the Regulations and Christine and Will dancing around topics, that part was all too happy with what was happening. Maybe he couldn't get his old life back. Maybe he couldn't get his brother back. But he sure as hell was going to try.

"Tell me," Frank said.

"Okay, man, relax. But you can't tell Christine I talked. She lets us stay here for free, but we aren't supposed to ask any questions about what she does out here. And we can't mess with her things."

"What things?"

"In that shed down the path. She's got a freezer chest in there and she keeps it locked. Every time she comes out here she spends some time in that shed. Your guitar case is down there too."

Frank sighed. "Okay. Is the shed locked?"

"Yeah."

"Where's the key?"

"My keys are in a bowl near the door. I don't have a key to the freezer, though, just the shed."

Frank walked to the door and grabbed the keys. "Fantastic," Frank said. He walked into the bedroom and rummaged around in the dark until he found a t-shirt.

"Listen up. I'm going out to the shed. If everything is as you say, I'll come back and untie you in a few minutes. But I can't have you screaming your head off and waking up the family while I'm gone, so I'm going to have to gag you."

Ty didn't say anything, so Frank brought the t-shirt over and wrapped it around his head, stuffing it deep into his mouth. Frank made sure it was tight enough that Ty wouldn't be able to move his tongue much, but not so tight that he wouldn't be able to breathe.

"Look," Frank said, "I know you're not too comfortable,

but we're almost done. Five minutes in the shed and then I'll let you go."

Ty moaned weakly.

Frank walked out the door and headed for the tree line. The path was more overgrown than it had been when he lived here, but even in the dark Frank had no trouble finding the shed. It was locked with a standard-issue hardware store padlock—the cheap kind. Frank clucked with disapproval. Hadn't he told Christine and Will a thousand times how easily one of these could be picked? He pulled out Ty's keys and unlocked the door.

It was pitch black inside the shed. He wished he had thought to bring a flashlight from Ty's cabin. He groped along the wall until his hand found the light switch. With the light on, he quickly slid the door shut.

At the back of the shed, he saw the guitar case leaning in the corner. The breath caught in his throat at the sight of it. He hurried over and ran his hand across the hard plastic exterior. All the trouble his stupid locks had caused. Maybe he should have let Brett take them. Maybe he should have forgotten about locks altogether and done something useful with his life.

He opened the case and saw them, his creations, his babies, his locks. The Yeti, The Horse Collar, The 51st Star, and twenty-seven other models. He loved them all, but it was the one he had never completed that he loved the most. The Cassandra lock didn't look like the rest of them. It was a silver hoop which hooked into a metal square. There was no key hole and there were no perceptible seams on the lock. It was a brilliant design, Frank wasn't afraid to admit. He just couldn't get it to work.

Was this what Jake wanted Frank to bring to their mysterious meeting? Or was he supposed to finish it first? He picked up the unfinished Cassandra lock and put it in his jacket pocket.

Frank saw the freezer in the back of the shed, exactly as Ty had described. The lock on it made Frank smile. Maybe Christine and Will weren't so dumb after all. It was the Gazelle, one of his best models. Opening it required a key and a bit of pressure in the right spot. The freezer would be safe from anyone. Anyone but Frank.

He reached into the guitar case and found the Gazelle master key. He had the lock off in five seconds. He opened the lid of the freezer, and the first thing he saw was a head.

He took an involuntary step backward and put his hand to his mouth. It was one of those things. The Birdies. The Unfeathered. Ice hung from its long beak and its open eyelids. The head was a cool bluish color.

What were Christine and Will into? Had they killed this thing? Why keep the head?

He pushed aside the revulsion and moved back to the freezer. There were other things in there too. A key. A knife. A lighter. A cane. A mirror. Each item had the broken clock symbol. Seeing the symbol again took him back to that day. The day he had killed Brett. A shudder went through him and the familiar feeling of guilt washed over him.

Frank removed the objects, holding each item in his hand for a long moment. This was it. This freezer was Will and Christine's big secret.

Frank had no idea what the items might signify, but he knew they must have some importance. Becky Raymond had called them dangerous. She'd said that Jake had been obsessed with finding them. What was the connection to the coin he had seen on the terrible day so many years ago?

He put the lighter, key, the mirror, and the cane back into the freezer. He picked up the knife, paused, and then slid it into his pocket. He was going to take one of the items with him, and a knife could always come in handy. He picked up the guitar case and left the shed.

When he got back to the cabin, he stopped and stood on the porch, unsure of what to do next. He got what he came for, but what good had it done him? He needed help. He needed to talk to someone who knew the town and might understand the significance of the items in the freezer. He wasn't sure he trusted Christine and Will anymore, and, more importantly, he knew they didn't trust him.

He had to go to the guy with no reason to lie. The guy who had told him the truth about the Regulations. He didn't much like the idea of walking all the way there, though. He reached into his pocket and pulled out Ty's keys.

He opened the door to the cabin and stuck his head inside. Ty's large dark shape was still crouching on the floor next to the radiator.

"Hey man," Frank said. "I'm really sorry, but I'm not going to be able to untie you. I'm gonna need to borrow your truck for a while."

Ty emitted a low groan that he probably had meant to be a scream.

"Yeah, I know the feeling." Frank shut the door and walked out. The truck was parked in the driveway. He got in, took a deep breath, and started the engine.

The lights were on in both of the other two cabins by the time he had pulled out of the driveway.

2.

Frank had been knocking for almost three minutes before a blurry-eyed Sean answered the door. Sean squinted out into the darkness. He turned on the porch light.

"Frank? Is that you?"

"Yeah, sorry to wake you, man. Can I come in?"

Sean blinked hard a few times and then nodded. "Yeah, of course. Come in."

"I'm really sorry, man, but I didn't have anywhere else to go."

"What—what about Will and Christine?"

"We had a bit of a fight."

"Oh."

Sean shut the door and ran a hand through his hair. He wasn't all there yet, Frank could see. Maybe that was for the best. Honesty came easier to the weary mind.

"Well," Sean said. "You're welcome to stay here. The guest bed is all made up. Hasn't been used in about five years, so I guess I'm due."

"Thanks. That's not why I'm here, though."

Sean crossed his arms and stared at Frank like he was looking at a difficult crossword puzzle. "Okay. What's up?"

"I need your help. You ever see anything with a symbol of a broken clock on it?"

Sean's face darkened. He suddenly looked a few degrees more alert. "Where did you see that?"

"I—I can't tell you right now. I take it you've seen it?"

Sean nodded. "Yeah. I've seen it. Frank, if you saw something with that symbol on it, you have to turn it over to the police or board of selectmen."

"Why?"

"That's Regulation 2."

Frank paused. "What does the symbol mean?"

"I'm not sure. But it's tangled up with Zed somehow."

"What do you mean?"

"The first time I met Zed, when he was wandering

around naked, he was holding a pocket watch with that symbol on it."

Frank felt his heart speed up. He reached into his pocket and felt the knife, and he thought about Sean's words. "What's the penalty for breaking Regulation 2?"

Sean looked him square in the eye. "Death." He turned away and sighed. "There's something I need to tell you about your brother."

Frank waited.

"Jake found an object with the broken clock symbol. He showed it to a small group of us. Me, Wendy, Will, Todd, and Christine. Jake believed that we needed to keep these objects away from Zed. That Zed needed them for something. Together we started looking for more of these objects, and we found a few of them. Not long after that, Jake disappeared and they blamed those killings on him. I believe that Zed went after Jake because of the objects we found."

"So why didn't Zed go after the rest of you?" Frank asked.

"We don't know."

"I do," Frank said. "It's because you gave up. You've been living in fear of him. But I'm not afraid."

Frank thought about Will, Christine, and Trevor. He thought about Jake, and his message to Sally Badwater. Frank took the Cassandra lock out of his pocket and looked at it. What could Jake want with a non-functioning lock?

"What's that?" Sean asked.

Frank instinctively closed his hand. "It's a lock I was working on before I went to prison. Never did finish it."

Sean frowned. "I've seen it before."

Frank shook his head. "No. This is the only one."

"I'm sure of it," Sean said. "It was on the box Zed showed the town on Regulation Day. The box he used to keep the Unfeathered outside of town."

Frank's knees felt like water. It wasn't possible. "Sean, that room at City Hall where Zed took the box... I need you to tell me exactly where it is."

Ten minutes later, Frank parked Ty Hansen's truck three blocks away from City Hall. The building was dark, which was a relief to Frank—he had been afraid there might be a night watchman on duty.

Sean had tried to talk Frank out of going, but there had been no chance. Frank had to see that box. He picked the lock on one of the side doors and headed toward the darkness inside.

Frank counted the doors as he passed them. He stopped in front of the sixth door on the left. In the dim hallway, it looked unremarkable, just like all the rest, but this was the door to the room Zed had locked himself in the day he stopped the Unfeathered. This door had been shut later that day and not opened since.

Frank pulled out his lock picking kit. The darkness didn't bother him. This kind of work was mostly done by feel. He gave the doorknob a jiggle and to his surprise it turned freely. His heart was thumping fast, as fast as it had when he was fighting Ty. Something was very wrong. Frank eased the door open.

A small desk lamp illuminated the room with a yellow glow. After the darkness of the hallway, the light hurt Frank's eyes, and he had to squint. The first thing Frank noticed was the wooden box on the desk. The second thing he noticed was the man sitting behind the desk. The man was smiling, and the light from the desk lamp reflected off his teeth and his bald head.

"Hello Frank," Zed said. "Please, come in."

3.

Christine hung up the phone and turned to Will. "Frank's been out at the cabins."

The color drained from Will's face. "The shed?"

Christine nodded. "They don't know if he got in the freezer. If he did he locked it back up before he left."

"If he got in the shed, he got in the freezer."

"Yeah," Christine said.

Will ran a hand through his hair. "Okay, let's think about this. Worst case scenario. Let's say he emptied the freezer and he knows everything he could possibly know. Let's say he's leaping into action. Where would he go?"

"There are only two possibilities," Christine said. "Zed's house or City Hall."

Will stood up from the chair. "We have to find him and stop him. Maybe if we explain things, he'll listen to reason."

"Maybe we should have explained things that very first night."

"The smart thing to do is to split up. I'll take City Hall."

"No, I'll take City Hall. At least if I get caught I have an excuse. I can say I needed to check some medical records."

"I could say I need to get some research materials for a Certification class."

Christine held up her keys. "I have keys. I have a City ID badge. It makes more sense for me to be there."

Will looked at her for a long moment before realizing he wasn't going to win. "Fine. Will you call the Strauss's and ask if Trevor can stay over?"

Christine nodded. "Meet back here at first light?"

Will gave her a quick kiss and turned to go.

"Don't shoot anybody unless you have to," Christine said.

"You either."

Christine drove the three miles to City Hall in about four minutes. She circled the block a few times looking for Ty Hansen's truck, but she didn't see it. The building was dark and none of the doors or windows appeared to have been forced open. Of course, Frank probably would have been able to pick the locks on the doors. Jake used to say that the only reason Frank hadn't broken out of jail was that he was too stubborn to live life as a fugitive.

She parked her car across the street and waited, trying to decide what to do. If Frank wasn't here yet, she would be better off waiting and catching him before he went inside. But if he was already inside he was in trouble and needed her help. She decided to take one look around inside and then come back out to wait.

She grabbed her keys and her purse. She couldn't help but stick her hand in the purse and feel the cold comforting metal of the gun. She left the purse unzipped for easier access.

Christine went into City Hall through the front door. If she was caught it would look better to have gone in as if she had nothing to hide. It reminded her of one of Will's favorite old Lutheran sayings: sin boldly.

The halls were dark and there was no sign that anyone was there. She walked quickly toward her destination, her shoes clicking loudly on the linoleum and echoing through the empty halls. When she reached the sixth door on the left, she froze. For the first time in eight years, the door was open.

4.

Zed gestured to the chair in front of the desk. "Sit down."

"I'll stand," Frank said.

Zed's smile didn't waver. "That's fine. You know, I'm impressed. Your brother killed three people to get to me, and he never made it this far."

Frank thought about pulling the knife out of his pocket. But what would he do with it? Stab the man? Would that even help anyone? "I guess Sean told you I was coming?"

Zed nodded. "He called me the moment you left his house."

Frank imagined introducing Sean to his old friend the tire iron.

"Don't be too hard on him. With your history, and your brother's, can you blame him for erring on the side of law and order?"

"Law and order. Is that what you call it?"

"Yes," Zed said. "What would you call it?"

"I'd call it trapping a whole town. You show up and suddenly we are cut off from the world. You've got your friends out there guarding the town, tearing apart anyone who tries to leave."

"The Unfeathered? They are no friends of mine. I promise you that. I was in town almost a year before they showed up. Besides, correlation does not equal causation. That is a basic principle of science, my friend."

Frank felt his temper rising in a way it hadn't for a long time. "What did you do?"

Zed spread out his hands like a magician before a trick. Nothing up his sleeves. "Didn't you hear? I saved the town!"

"That's not all you did. It was you, wasn't it? You paid Brett to steal my locks."

Zed grimaced. "Come on, you came all the way here to ask me that?"

"What do you know about what happened to Jake? Did

he really kill those people?"

"Okay," Zed said. "I'll make you a deal. If you answer one question for me, I'll answer the one for you."

"What's your question?" Frank asked.

"Where did you see the broken clock symbol?"

Frank thought of Christine. And Will. And Trevor. He said nothing.

"That's what I thought," Zed said.

"How about this?" Frank asked. "Why did you come to Rook Mountain? Were you planning for all this to happen?"

"Ah," Zed said. "That's a better question. And I'll answer it out of respect for the fact that you of all people made it into this room. I'm on vacation."

Frank blinked hard. "What?"

"Haven't you ever had one of those days at work? Well, maybe you haven't, being self-employed and then a guest of the State. But trust me, those of us who work for a living sometimes need to get away. I stumbled across Rook Mountain and thought it might be a good place to relax for a couple of centuries. And if I happen to get a little business done too, all the better."

Frank was trying hard to keep up with the conversation, but something about this room and the way Zed was talking made it hard to concentrate. "Vacation from what?"

Zed sighed. "Do me a favor, Frank. Look into my eyes."

In spite of himself, Frank did.

It was just like the first time, the time when Zed knocked on his door. He felt Zed's gaze claw its way into his mind, into those deepest parts of himself that he kept hidden from the world. It was like being punched in the stomach and standing naked in front of a laughing crowd at the same time.

"Interesting," Zed said. He looked away, and Frank staggered backward, gasping for air even though it had only been a few seconds. "I'll tell you what. I like what I see in you, and what's a vacation without a certain element of spontaneity?"

He grabbed the wooden box in front of him and spun it around so the front faced Frank. Then he waited, watching Frank.

Frank looked at the box for a long moment before realizing what he was seeing. The box was held shut with a metal hoop that passed through a square. It had no discernible seams or openings. The Cassandra lock.

The Cassandra lock had come to him in a dream years ago. Creating it was his ultimate goal as a locksmith. He had tried a dozen times, but he had never gotten it exactly right. It was too technical, too complicated. He'd always felt like his skills were a few steps away from where they needed to be to finish his masterpiece. He'd never even spoken of it to anyone but Jake. Frank always imagined that the Cassandra lock, named after his mother, would be his life's work.

And yet, there was a completed Cassandra lock on the table in front of him. It looked exactly as it had in his dreams.

"How?" Frank asked. "Can you read my mind?"

Zed shifted his head back and forth as if he was unsure how to answer. "Not in the way you're thinking. It's not like reading a book. But when I look into your eyes I do see certain images and feelings. That day at your cabin this lock was right at the front your mind. I got a crystal clear picture. I saw it in ways your conscious mind hadn't. I liked what I saw."

"But how did you build it?"

Zed smiled wide. "I'm a man of many talents, Frank."

Frank felt his breath growing heavy. The back of his t-shirt was wet with sweat. "Why are you showing me this?"

Frank reached for the box, but Zed slid it back, away from him.

"I won't let you open it," Zed said. "This box saved the town, you know. I closed this box and locked it tight, and now the Unfeathered can't come here anymore. It has to stay shut."

Frank's head was spinning, and he felt a wave of nausea. His life's work was sitting on the desk in front of him. "Maybe everything would go back to normal. Maybe those bird creatures would go away and the cell phones would start working again."

Zed ran his finger over the lock. "Or maybe the Unfeathered would come crashing in and kill us all. You'll never know."

Frank reached into his pocket and found the knife.

"It's interesting, though," Zed said. "Only two people in the world know how to open that lock, and they are both in this room."

Frank pulled out the knife and opened it. He held it up toward Zed.

The smile stayed frozen on Zed's face, but the joy left his eyes. Frank saw something frightening in its place.

"You are full of surprises," Zed said.

Frank motioned toward the box with the knife. "Give it to me."

"Where did you get that?"

Frank shook his head. "I'm done answering your questions. Give me the box."

Zed licked his lips. "Give me the knife and I'll give you the box."

Frank looked hard at Zed. He saw something new on Zed's face. "You're scared of this thing, aren't you?"

"It's mine." Zed's voice was low and scratchy like he suddenly had a bad cold. "You could hurt someone with that. It's not a tire iron. It can do some real damage."

Frank took two steps to the right, coming around the edge of the desk. "Give me the box or I will start cutting."

Zed shook his head violently. "It's not right. That isn't yours."

Frank leaned forward, reaching toward Zed with the blade. Suddenly he heard footsteps behind him. He spun around fast, holding out the knife in front of him.

Christine stood in the doorway, a pistol in her hand. "Frank, we need to go."

Frank shook his head. "No. Christine, he's got it. My lock. The one from my head."

"Frank, you're not making sense."

Zed seemed to have regained some of his composure. "Hello, Dr. Osmond. Would you please remind Frank that he is out of jail temporarily and that waving a knife at a Regulation-abiding citizen will not help his case for permanent release?"

Christine held out her hand to Frank. There was no color in her face. Frank realized she was terrified. "Come on, Frank."

Frank turned back to the desk. He grabbed the box, pulling it out of Zed's hands. He set it on the table. The Cassandra lock looked perfect, the way it always had in his head.

Frank moved the knife toward Zed. "What happens if I open it?"

"What?" Christine asked. "Frank, don't open it. We don't know what will happen."

"Yeah. That's why I'm asking. So how about it, Zed? What happens if I open it?"

It was a long time before Zed answered. "If you open that box, I leave. You are on your own. I'll leave this town to the Unfeathered."

Frank looked at Zed, tried looking into his eyes the way Zed had looked into Frank's, but all he saw was emptiness. Even the fear he had seen before was gone.

"That's all I get?" Frank asked.

"That's all you get."

"How about if I start cutting you?"

Zed shrugged. "I might say a few more things, but would you believe them? You already know the important stuff. That box keeps the Unfeathered away. What else do you need to know?"

Frank didn't believe him, at least not fully. He knew Zed was lying, but he wasn't sure about which part. Frank really wanted to try the Cassandra lock.

He picked up the box and held it to his ear. It made a soft ticking sound.

"Frank, no," Christine said.

Frank reached for the lock and twisted it, squeezing in exactly the right place and pulling at just the right angle. The lock snapped open, and joy sprang up within Frank. The lock worked the way he had always imagined it would.

He removed the lock and opened the latch. He lifted the box's wooden lid.

The four sides of the box collapsed outward onto the desk. The box was empty.

"That will be very difficult to replace," Zed said.

The room was silent for a long moment. Then, in the distance, Frank heard a noise that sounded a bit like singing.

Christine put a hand to her mouth. "Oh, Frank. What have you done?"

"He's killed you all," Zed said.

THE BAD THING THAT HAPPENED

I.

On the night the world changed, Christine was lying awake in bed trying not to look at the clock. She had struggled with insomnia all her life and that night she hadn't slept for a moment. She knew what all the experts said, the strategies to fight it. But the experts weren't there, lying in bed hour after hour with their minds racing, growing more stressed, more worried about how tired they would be the next day. Christine had been, and she was bored and worried and tired of the experts. She picked up her iPad to queue up an old episode of Alias. If she couldn't sleep, at least she could have some vicarious excitement with Sydney Bristow.

Jake was fast asleep and snoring. The man could sleep through anything. When there was a thunderstorm, Christine would toss and turn all night, waking up anew at each thunderclap. In the morning, Jake would look out the window and say, "Oh look, it rained." It hardly seemed fair.

A little circle icon on her iPad spun as it attempted to connect to the Internet. The connection had been down when Christine went to bed four hours ago, but she was hoping it would be working by now. No such luck. It wasn't a surprise, really. Internet outages were all too common there in the mountains. She got up and walked toward the bathroom.

That was when she heard it.

The sound came from outside. It wasn't a human noise or a machine noise. It was an animal noise, but unlike anything Christine had ever heard before. It was like a cross between a bird and a bear. Most disturbing of all, it wasn't a constant tone. The noise fluctuated. It sounded almost like singing.

Christine froze in the middle of the bedroom, halfway between the bed and the bathroom door. Damn, that thing was loud. It had to be right under the window. She rubbed her arms. That noise, it wasn't right. It wasn't natural. She turned back toward the bed and said in a loud whisper, "Jake."

To her surprise, the response came immediately. "I hear it."

In a way, that frightened her more than the noise itself. The noise had woken up Jake, and nothing woke up Jake.

"What is that?" Jake asked.

"I don't know. Some kind of bird or something."

Jake pushed off the covers and stepped out of bed. He was dressed in only his boxers. "Whatever it is, it's right outside the window." He crossed the room to the window and opened the blinds. He craned his neck back and forth. The noise continued. "Well, I don't see anything."

"Do you think it could be in the house?"

"What? No. God, no." But he didn't look completely convinced.

"I'm going to check on Trevor."

Jake nodded. "I'm going to go outside and see if I can see anything."

Christine nodded and left the bedroom. The noise was almost as loud out here. The longer it continued, the more pronounced the melody became. It hurt her head to listen. It was like no song she had ever heard. She couldn't quite tell if it was one creature making that sound or dozens of them.

She opened the door to Trevor's bedroom. The boy was sitting up in his bed.

"Hey," she said. "You okay?"

"Mommy, there's singing."

"I know honey. You want to go back to sleep?"

He shook his head. "No, Mommy. I'm scared. Can I come with you?"

Christine paused. She rarely let him sleep in their bed, but this was different. Christine didn't want Trevor out of her sight.

"Okay," she said. "You can sleep with me. Bring your pillow."

Trevor visibly relaxed at this unexpected boon. He grabbed his pillow, his favorite stuffed animal, Mr. Bear, and climbed out of bed. Christine took him by the hand.

"What's that singing, Mommy?"

"I don't know. Daddy is checking it out."

When they reached the bedroom, Trevor hopped onto the bed. He sat on top of the covers, his legs crossed. The moonlight through the window illuminated the Phineas and Ferb logo on his pajamas.

Christine gave him her best mother glare. "This isn't a party. Climb under the covers and go to sleep."

"But they're still singing. I can't sleep when they're singing."

"Maybe not, but you can try."

Trevor, resigned to his fate, slid under the covers.

Christine moved to the window and looked out. The streetlights gave her a pretty good view of what was happening below. To her surprise, Jake wasn't standing under the window looking up at the house. He was close to the road, looking straight into the sky. And he wasn't alone. The neighbors on both sides were out in their yards too, all of them looking up.

What was going on out there?

Christine looked across the street and saw that neighbor, too, was standing at the end of his driveway. All Christine knew about the man was his name, although they had been neighbors for almost two years. Ed Snell. He was in his late-sixties by Christine's estimation, and he lived alone. The man kept to himself.

How much more scary must it be, she wondered, to wake up to that noise and not have anyone else in the house? Fear was like a weight, Christine thought. When there were multiple people in the house, you could spread the fear, lessening each person's load. But if you lived alone you would have to keep all that fear for yourself.

While Christine was still considering that thought, a white shape fell from the sky onto Ed Snell. No, Christine realized. It wasn't falling. It was flying. The shape swooped down, grabbed Ed, and turned back skyward, taking the man with it.

Christine put her hand to her mouth, stifling a scream.

"What is it, Mommy?" Trevor asked.

Christine didn't answer.

The white shape circled through the air, once, twice, three times, and released Ed. He landed in the Hinkle's front yard, thirty feet from Jake.

Jake ran toward Snell's unmoving form. He was almost to the man when the white shape appeared again, swooping toward the ground. Christine put a hand to the window pane. She wanted to scream to Jake, but he was too far away.

Jake saw the shape too, and he stopped, stumbling backwards.

The white creature landed on top of Snell, its feet on his chest, and it raised its head to the sky and sang. Christine saw the creature clearly for the first time and terror shot through her heart.

It was like a bird, a giant featherless bird. The creature was so white it almost glowed under the streetlights. Its wings were big fleshy things like the wings of a bat. It was unnatural. It was terrifying.

Christine felt a tiny hand slip into her own. She hadn't realized Trevor was standing beside her.

"What is it?" he asked.

Christine tried for a moment to think of something comforting to say, something that would make the boy feel safe, but nothing came to mind. She squeezed his hand, hoping that would help a little. "I don't know," she said.

Another white shape shot down from the sky. It landed next to the first. Then another joined it. And another. Soon there were six of them all gathered around Ed Snell's body. They stood in a circle around him, their beaks open and pointed to the sky in a terrible song.

Then the song stopped, and they struck.

Trevor screamed as the first beak sank into Snell's neck. Christine put her hand over his eyes.

The creatures moved with uncanny speed, stabbing at Snell's body with their long thin beaks and then pulling them back, covered in blood, bits of flesh and intestines.

The creatures feasted for a long time on the man, their mouths hungrily thrusting into him again and again.

"They're eating that man, Mommy. Is Daddy going to save him?"

Christine still had her hand over her son's eyes, but it was too late. He had already seen what he had seen.

"Trev, the man's already dead. They aren't hurting him." She wasn't sure if that would comfort the boy. She had said it partly to convince herself that it was true.

She turned her gaze to Jake. He sat on the ground, unmoving, staring at the bird creatures. Christine wanted to knock on the window, or maybe open it and yell down to him, but she also didn't want to do anything that might call attention to Jake. The bird creatures still might be hungry when they finished with Snell.

There was only one thing to do. She would go downstairs, go outside, and get her man. She'd drag him in if she had to. There was no other option. Trevor would be fine. She'd have to make sure he understood to keep the doors and windows shut and not open them no matter what.

She opened her mouth to speak, but no words came. Jake was moving.

He stood up slowly and took a step forward.

"No," Christine said.

Jake was walking the wrong direction. He was moving toward the creatures.

"No," Christine said again, far too quietly for anyone but Trevor to hear.

Jake moved slowly and deliberately. Christine saw the gun in his arms. Jake stopped fifteen feet from his downed neighbor. He raised his rifle and took careful aim.

"Daddy's going to save that man. I knew it!"

Christine realized she was no longer covering her son's

eyes. She was too afraid to move. Her eyes were glued to her husband.

Jake held his rifle pointed at the creatures for what seemed an eternity. He shifted his feet a little, corrected his aim, and fired.

The shot echoed through the neighborhood. The closest bird creature's head exploded, raining brains and blood on its flock mates behind it as it collapsed.

Jake stood frozen. Christine willed him to move, to run. But he stood firm. The other creatures didn't seem to notice. They continued their feast.

"Get out of there," Christine whispered.

Jake cocked his rifle and fired again, dropping another one of the creatures. Again none of the others seemed to notice.

Jake fired again. And again. Now there were only two left.

The one closest to Jake had its back to him. Jake raised his rifle and took aim. Before he could fire, the creature lifted its head and turned to him.

Christine gasped.

It tilted its head as if trying to interpret what this man and his rifle meant. Then it lifted its bloody beak to the sky and began to sing. The other remaining bird creature stopped feeding and looked at its singing compatriot. Another white shape appeared in the sky, and then another.

Jake fired, silencing the bird creature and its song. Then he turned and bolted for the house.

As Christine watched, the remaining bird creature returned to its meal. It picked apart poor Mr. Ed Snell until there was nothing left but bones.

2.

Four days later the killings had stopped, the Regulations had been put in place, and Rook Mountain had been changed forever.

Christine knocked on the door of a large conference room in City Hall. They were calling the room the Command Center. It was a place for Zed and his inner circle to meet and do whatever it was they were doing since the town had been saved.

A short, thin man Christine didn't recognize opened the door wide enough to stick his head through. He didn't speak —he just waited.

"Hi," Christine said. "I was wondering if I could talk to Zed for a minute. I have some information I think he might like to hear."

The man looked Christine in the eye, and Christine felt a quick jolt, like a bolt of electricity running through her brain.

The man nodded. "Come in." He led her through the large room to a desk in one corner. Zed sat behind the desk, furiously writing on a form of some sort. That seemed odd to Christine. What kind of paperwork could there really be at this point?

The short, thin man cleared his throat and Zed looked up. He saw Christine and smiled.

Christine was a little shocked at the sight of him. She had been at City Hall the day the Regulations were voted into law, but she had been near the back. She hadn't gotten a clear look at Zed. The last time she had seen him up close had been when he was knocking on doors a couple of years ago. Then he had been subservient, odd but polite. Now he looked like a man transformed. He wore a blue turtleneck tight enough to show off his muscular physique. He looked tired, which was understandable, Christine supposed, but he also had a charismatic glow about him. He oozed confidence.

"Hi," Christine said, holding out her hand. "I'm Christine Hinkle."

Zed took her hand, and his smile grew even wider. "Yes. You're a doctor, right?"

Christine nodded.

"We are going to need you, I promise you that. Not many doctors in town." Zed held her hand a moment too long before finally releasing it. "But we can talk about that later. What brings you by today?"

"Well, first of all, thank you for what you did for our town."

Zed waved her thanks away. "My pleasure. It's my town too, you know."

Christine smiled. "Yes, of course. The reason I came down here is that I think I might have something useful."

Zed tilted his head. "Oh? What's that?"

"The first night those creatures attacked, my husband managed to shoot a couple of them. Five, actually."

Zed laughed out loud. "Good Lord! That's incredible. Did you hear that, Jack?"

"I did," the short, thin man said. "That's mighty impressive."

"Absolutely," Zed said. "Tell your husband I said that's some great shooting."

"I will. The thing is we still have the bodies."

The smile fell from Zed's face. "What do you mean?"

"The creatures' bodies. You know Maria's Pizzeria downtown? They recently closed, but their walk-in freezer is still functional. We've been keeping them there."

Zed folded his hands. "Why on earth would you do that?"

Christine paused. This wasn't the reaction she had been expecting. "We were attacked by a species never seen before. We have to study them."

Zed chuckled and leaned back in his chair. "Doctor Hinkle, I understand your impulse, and I think your heart is in the right place. You are a person of science, and thank God for that. We are going to need you. But in this case, your instinct is incorrect."

"We need to learn everything we can about these creatures. Studying their anatomy could be the key to stopping them if they ever get through your barrier."

"Let me explain, doctor," Zed said. "I haven't put up a barrier. I've managed to make us invisible to these creatures, these... let's call them the Unfeathered. There is nothing stopping the Unfeathered from coming into town except that they can't tell it exists. If I've done my job, and I think I have, they will feel a slight discomfort, a natural aversion to this place."

Christine's eyes narrowed. That wasn't quite how he had explained it that day at City Hall. Truth be told, he hadn't explained it much at all. He had just said that he could stop them.

"The only way the Unfeathered will come into the town," Zed continued, "is if they have a reason stronger than the natural aversion I've put in place. The most likely reason would be a person going out of town. Once they have attacked a person, they will keep on attacking and, if the person fled back to town, the Unfeathered would follow. Hence the Regulations. What might be some other reasons? We don't know."

"That's why we need to study them. There is so much we don't know."

"Or maybe having those bodies, the bodies of their fallen brothers, could draw them here."

"That's a big leap," Christine said. "We have no reason to think that."

Zed sighed. "Doctor Hinkle, we've put this town back on track. Keeping those bodies is too big a risk. We have to burn them immediately."

"Maybe we should let the town know we have them. Let the people decide."

Zed pulled out a pocket watch and opened it. Christine saw a symbol on the watch—a broken clock. "That won't be necessary. Jack, can you send someone over to Maria's to pick up the bodies right away?"

Jack nodded. "I'll send Russ over there. He's got that pickup."

"Good," Zed said. He looked up at Christine, that glowing, confident smile back on his face. "Doctor, I appreciate you bringing this to me. I hope you trust that I know what I'm doing. My friends and I have a little saying: trust is a must. It's truer now than ever before."

Christine didn't know what to say, so she nodded.

"Goodbye, doctor. We'll talk soon. I have big plans for you. We need your help to keep this town running."

Christine turned to go. As she left, she heard Zed call after her, "And say hello to your husband for me. I have big plans for him, too."

SEVEN NIGHTS IN ROOK MOUNTAIN

NIGHT ONE

"He's killed you all," Zed said.

Frank looked at the five pieces of wood on the table. The pieces that had been a box until he unlocked it and it fell apart. He turned to Christine.

"No, it's okay," Frank said. "There was nothing in the box. That couldn't be what was keeping the Unfeathered away."

Zed twisted his face into a grimace. "It wasn't what was in the box. It was the box itself."

Christine looked at Zed. The gun hung from her hand. "You can fix it, right? You can fix the box?"

Zed picked up one of the pieces of wood and turned it over in his hand. "No," he said. "I can't. Whatever power it had is gone."

Frank looked at Christine. "Listen, it's all going to be okay."

"No, you listen," Christine said.

Frank listened, and he heard it in the distance. The sound of them coming. The sound of singing.

"The Birdies," Zed said. "Isn't that what you call them, doctor?"

Christine didn't answer.

"First they'll come in the night for people who happen to be outside," Zed said. "But then they will grow bolder. It won't be long before your homes aren't enough to protect you. Then they'll start attacking in the daytime." He turned the piece of wood in his hand over and over.

Frank looked down and saw that his hand was shaking.

Zed set the piece of wood on the desk. "I'm leaving." He held out his hand to Frank. "Give me the knife. I need it where I am going."

Frank hesitated. His instinct was to give the man what he asked for. On the other hand, Frank's instincts had given him nothing but trouble so far. "No way."

Zed stood up. "That's what I figured. I suggest you two stay here for the night. It's going to be ugly out there."

He marched across the room, giving Frank and Christine a final frown as he slipped through the open door. There was a flash of blue light as he shut the door behind him.

Christine put her hands to her head. "Frank, what have you done?"

"I know. I'm sorry. I thought he was lying."

"Everything Will and I have been working for, everything Jake was working for, it's all ruined. We—" She looked up, startled. "We have to go."

"What? No, we have to stay inside."

"It's Trevor. He's at Carl's. They were going to camp out in Carl's backyard."

Frank gave a quick nod. "Let's go."

She ran out the door. He started to follow her, then stopped. He remembered Jake's message to Sally Badwater. "If Frank comes, tell him to bring the Cassandra lock."

Frank swept the Cassandra lock off the table, stuffed it into his pocket, and followed Christine.

"We'll take my car," Christine said. "I'm closer. But I want to have my hands free if any of those bastards come at us. You're driving."

Frank glanced at the gun in her hand. "Maybe I should be the one doing the shooting."

Christine gave him a hard look. "When's the last time you shot a gun? A decade ago? Besides, I've always been a better shot than you or your brother."

Frank didn't say anything. She tossed him the keys. He got into the driver's side.

"Carl lives over on Locust Avenue," Christine said. "You remember where that is?"

"Yeah." Frank gripped the wheel.

"What is it? Time's a bit of a factor here, man."

Frank cleared his throat. He turned toward her. "I'm sorry, Christine. For everything. For killing Brett. For leaving you and Jake to deal with all this bullshit. For opening that box."

Christine's expression didn't change. "You don't have to apologize. You're family. And even though that was a dumbass move in there, it certainly proved you aren't on the side of the Zed Heads."

"Zed Heads?" Frank smiled.

"That's what we call Zed's disciples. Let's get going."

Frank pulled out and hit the gas hard.

Christine said, "We should have told you the score that first night. We've learned to be a little paranoid."

Frank shrugged. "I understand. You do what you have to and it changes you. I know that."

"Anyway, if we get through this night, you're staying with us."

"Good. I get the feeling I'm not exactly welcome at the Hansens'."

Christine grinned. "I got that impression as well when they called me. Turn on State Street. It's faster."

Frank pulled a hard left onto State Street. "What did you mean earlier when you said I'd messed up what you and Will were working for?"

Christine looked up, her eyes scanning the sky. "Did you see how scared Zed was of that knife? We think the things with the broken clock symbol can hurt him."

Frank glanced at Christine. Her eyes were still glued to the sky. "You gonna give me some more details or don't you trust me yet?"

"You help me get my son and I'll give you more details than you ever wanted to know. Locust is the next turn."

The singing was getting louder.

"You see them?" Christine asked. "They're high, but they're there. They leave a little white glow behind them when they fly, freaky little bastards."

"Christine, do you think Jake's still alive?"

Christine finally took her eyes off the sky and looked at him. "I know he is."

Two minutes later, they pulled into Carl's driveway. Christine knocked on the door. When Carl's father answered, she said five words. "Send Trevor out. They're back."

NIGHT TWO

Will handed Frank the shotgun. "You sure about this?"

Frank took the gun. Between that and the pistol stored away in his shoulder holster, he was ready. "I'm sure. It's my fault we're in this damn mess." He glanced at the open gun cabinet. "You were never an NRA type guy in the Before."

Will shoved another box into his backpack, then zipped it shut. "I was a lot of things in the Before. In this town, with those things out there and the Zed Heads in charge, I thought I could use some firearms. There never was a shortage of them here."

"You know, I'm a little surprised. A guy like Zed takes power, I would think the first thing he'd do is round up everybody's weapons."

Will smiled. "Yeah, I thought that too. But having a gun makes people around here feel a little more comfortable, a little more free. The Zed Heads are all about making you feel free even if you aren't." He threw the backpack into his truck. "Besides, if you have a gun and you aren't afraid to wave it around they have a much better excuse to shoot you."

They climbed in Will's truck and rolled out of the garage. The sun was almost down, but the singing hadn't started yet.

"I've been meaning to ask you something," Will said. "When you held the knife with the broken clock, did you feel anything?"

"What do you mean?"

Will shrugged. "When I pick up the objects... it's hard to explain, but my mind sort of goes empty. I lose track of where I am. Sometimes I get little intuitions about what the objects are for, but mostly I just go blank. It doesn't happen to Christine or the others. I was wondering if you might have felt it."

"Drifting," Frank said. "You're talking about drifting. It didn't happen to me when I held the knife, but it does happen to me. I don't know why."

"You ask me, it's creepy. Like I'm losing myself a little."

Frank knew exactly what he meant, but talking about it made him uncomfortable. "You don't have to come with me tonight," Frank said.

"Yeah I do." He grinned at Frank. "I won the coin toss."

Frank chuckled. "I don't think I've ever seen Christine so disappointed."

"She really likes to shoot stuff."

They drove in silence through the neighborhood before turning onto the highway that led to the edge of town.

After they got home on Monday night, Will and Christine had told Frank all about their theories on the items with the broken clock symbol. How Jake had discovered the first one. How they had started finding more of them. Jake had been so sure he could take Zed down if they could find a couple more items.

Will pulled off the road and onto a long driveway. Frank shifted in his seat nervously. "You sure about this? We could probably get along without them."

"Maybe," Will said. "But I'd rather have three more guns by our side. The Unfeathered killed Ty's brother Kurt eight years ago. However mad they are at you, they are madder at the Birdies. Besides… this is going to be hilarious."

The car rolled to a stop in front of Ty Hansen's cabin. Three men, Ty, Gus, and Gus's brother Teddy, were all standing in the driveway. Each was heavily armed.

Will rolled down the window. "You boys ready?"

Gus spit on the ground. "I'm ready." He nodded toward Frank. "I ain't too pleased with this one, but I'm ready."

Ty smiled. His swollen nose gave his face an even more menacing look. His neck was a mess of deep purple bruises from where the chain had dug into his throat. He climbed into the back seat right behind Frank.

Ty reached up and clapped Frank on the shoulder. "You got a nice jab, man. That nut shot was a little cheap, but I'll let it slide."

Frank turned in his seat to look back at the man. "Yeah, look, I'm really sorry about last night. I should have handled things differently."

Ty bobbed his head back and forth for a minute as if weighing what Frank had said. "Well, I guess you could have taken me out faster with a good blow to the head. But don't be too hard on yourself. Breaking my nose was a nice way to go. Messed me up for the rest of the fight. I could hardly see anything."

Will had told Frank that Ty wouldn't be mad at him, that Ty Hansen brawled for fun and would respect Frank for besting him. Frank didn't believe it would be quite so easy.

"You didn't have to take my truck, though. That was low."

"Don't be a sore loser," Will said. "You got the truck back."

Ty nodded. "It was worth it for a good fight. Next time we'll do it at your place. I won't knock, though. I'll come in through the window."

Frank wasn't sure if it was because the broken nose was muddling the inflection, but he had no idea whether or not Ty was joking.

"What's the plan?" Teddy asked. He was a few years younger than Gus and thin as a twig. It was a hard thinness, though; the man was all long limbs and lean muscle.

Will said, "I figured we would start down by Fifth Avenue Baptist. See if we can't draw a few out down there. Then maybe work our way up to State Street."

Frank looked toward the back seat. "You guys all killed these things before?"

"Yep, nearly every weekend," Gus said. "We liked to put a little animal out across the town line and then shoot the bastards for target practice."

"Guess I'm the only virgin then," Frank said. "Any tips?"

Ty smiled. "Aim for the head. As far as I can tell, they don't have nuts so your usual technique probably won't work."

NIGHT THREE

The sun wasn't down yet, but it was getting close. Trevor sat in the living room, staring at the sky through the picture window. How long would it be until they came again? How long until the singing started?

He didn't remember much about the first time the Unfeathered had come, the time before the Regulations. He had only been four years old. What he did remember was images, bits and pieces like snippets from a movie he had fallen asleep while watching.

He remembered lying in bed, listening to the song. He remembered his mother's hand covering his eyes. He remembered that scared look on his parents' faces. He remembered long beaks covered in blood.

Trevor took a deep breath. That was a long time ago. Things were different—he was different. He wasn't a little boy anymore. So why did he still feel so afraid?

There had been a town meeting that afternoon for all the adults. Everyone at school had been talking about it. Afterward, Will said it had been the usual type of meeting - lots of talking and no deciding. Mom hadn't been at the meeting. She had been at the clinic all day with those who'd been injured. The town had been lucky so far. Six injuries and only one death. Folks in Rook Mountain knew enough to get inside and lock the windows when they heard that particular song.

School had been weird. The teachers tried to keep a brave face, and they upped the talk about how the Beyond students were the future of Rook Mountain and all that. But Trevor knew there were only two questions on everyone's minds: How had the birds gotten into town and where was Zed?

Uncle Frank was already gone for the night—he'd left to hunt the Unfeathered with the Hansens again. Trevor had asked if he could go, but both Uncle Frank and Will had given him a look that said he might as well not ask again.

He squinted up into the darkening sky, watching for any streaks of white.

There was a knock at the door. The noise was so loud and unexpected that Trevor almost leapt to his feet. He went to the door and looked out the little window. There were five boys standing out there, all older than Trevor. Trevor knew them, though he wasn't sure of all their names. They were his classmates from the Beyond Academy.

Trevor opened the door wide enough to stick his head out.

The boy in front crossed his arms. His name was Sam something, Trevor knew, and he was one of the popular kids, if there was such a thing among the brainiacs at the Beyond Academy.

"What's up, Hinkle?"

"Hey guys," Trevor said. The words felt awkward leaving his mouth but he couldn't think of anything else to say.

"Listen," Sam said. "We weren't sure whether to invite you given who your dad was. But then we remembered what Zed said. You're a Beyond man. It doesn't matter what your dad did. So you can come."

Trevor stared at them, hoping one of them would elaborate. They didn't. So Trevor asked, "Come where?"

Sam nodded toward the sky. "The Unfeathered are back. We are Beyond Academy. Where do you think?"

Trevor tried not to let his face betray him. They were just kids... whatever the teachers said, they were just kids. Were they really going to fight monsters? At the same time, Trevor couldn't deny the heat of excitement warming his belly. It would feel so good to be out there fighting instead of cowered inside waiting for the adults to do something.

Finally, Trevor nodded. "Okay. Let me ask my step-dad."

A couple of the boys laughed. Sam smiled. "You really think he's gonna say yes to this? You think any of our parents would?"

Trevor knew Sam was right. The only way this was going to happen was if he didn't ask permission. "What do I need to bring?"

Some of the kids laughed again, but it was a joyous laughter this time. A short boy whose name Trevor didn't know said, "That's the best part. They let us into the Beyond Academy's armory. We've got more guns than you've ever seen. All you need is your trigger finger."

Trevor wasn't sure what to ask first. Who had let them into the Armory? Where were the guns? Also, the Beyond Academy has an armory? Instead he said, "One second. I'll be right out."

Trevor ducked back inside without waiting for an answer. He wasn't going to ask permission, but he also didn't want his mom and Will to think he'd been plucked into the sky or something. He grabbed a pad of paper off the counter and jotted a quick note. He tore off the piece of paper and stuck it under a magnet on the fridge.

He grabbed his hooded sweatshirt and walked out the door.

It was almost a half hour later when Will found the note:

Mom/Will,

I'm spending the night with some friends from school. I'll explain in the morning. Please don't worry. I'm safe.

Trev

NIGHT FOUR

They were surrounded.

Frank stood with his back to the Hansen men. The Hansens had their guns trained on the four Birdies gathered around them. Frank's eyes were on the sky, quickly scanning for the tell-tale white shapes. The four on the ground were troubling, but it was the possibility of an unexpected attack from above that really worried Frank.

The Unfeathered didn't move. Neither did the men.

As one, the Unfeathered turned their beaks to the sky and began to sing.

"Shit," Gus said. "They are calling for reinforcements."

"Drop 'em!" shouted Frank. He turned his gun on the Birdie closest to him.

One moment and four ear-splitting gunshots later, three of the creatures fell to the ground. The fourth, the one closest to Ty, thrust its beak forward and snapped at Ty's leg. Another gunshot rang out, and the fourth creature hit the ground, a piece of denim from Ty's jeans hanging from its beak.

The four men turned toward the sound of the final gunshot and saw Sean Lee standing in front of his police car, firearm raised.

"You all right?" Sean asked Ty.

The big man was gripping his leg. Blood oozed between his fingers. "Yeah," he groaned. "I could use a bandage, but I'll live."

"I can't believe you missed, Ty," Teddy said. "That thing was like ten feet away."

Ty gritted his teeth. "It was moving like a snake."

"Thanks for the assist, Officer," Gus said.

As Sean approached, Frank gave him a cold stare, and Sean sent the same right back. The two men hadn't spoke since that night at Sean's house. Frank wasn't avoiding Sean, not exactly anyway. Confronting Sean about turning him in to Zed was definitely on his to-do list. His anger at the police officer was never far from his mind. But things were a little hectic with the monsters attacking town every night. Frank and the Hansen men were piling up Unfeathered bodies all over town while most people huddled inside their homes. The guys purposely attracted the creatures, and when they cornered one, they gave it time to call for help before killing it. Depending who you talked to, Frank and the Hansens were either public annoyances or folk heroes.

Frank glanced down and saw the remains of the thing the Birdies had been feeding on when he and the Hansens had stumbled upon them. He wasn't sure what the poor animal had been until he noticed the collar around its neck. It was a smallish dog. A beagle, maybe. It was hard to tell with so much of the flesh missing. Frank was fairly confident it had been a hound dog of some sort. Frank looked away. He had a soft spot for animals, and it made him sad to see that dog and think about what its last moments must have been like.

"Gentlemen, I think you better head home and do it quick," Sean said.

The men looked at each other. Frank said, "Did we do something wrong, Officer?"

"Maybe we made you boys look bad by killing too many Birdies?" Gus asked.

"Ain't no shortage of the bastards," Teddy said. "Plenty to go around."

"No, nothing like that," Sean said. "It's your families at home I'm worried about."

"Our families are fine," Gus said. "They stay inside after dark. No need to worry."

"We're getting some reports tonight from the outskirts of town. The Unfeathered are getting more aggressive out there. They're attacking windows. I hear they slammed into the front door of one house over and over until the damn thing buckled."

Frank felt the familiar wave of guilt crash over him.

"Nothing against your cabins," Sean said, "but I'm not sure how they'll hold up to giant birds flying into them."

Gus looked at Ty and Teddy. "Let's go."

"I'll follow you there," Frank said.

"I'd suggest you get your family further into town," Sean said. "We have some vacant apartments downtown. You are welcome to use them for a bit until this thing blows over."

Ty gave Sean a hard stare. "You want us to retreat? Leave our homes to these creatures?"

Sean looked him in the eye. "Yes sir, I do."

Gus frowned. "Let's check out the situation before we get crazy."

Gus, Ty, and Teddy walked to the car. Sean tapped Frank on the shoulder. "Hey, you ride with me. We need to talk." Frank only paused for a moment before nodding.

Sean pulled his squad car in front of Gus's beater pickup. All three Hansen men were jammed into the truck's front seat. Sean sped down the road with his sirens blaring and his lights flashing. Even still, Gus kept right on Sean's bumper the whole way.

Sean waited until they were a few blocks away before he spoke. "Frank, what the hell is going on? What happened to Zed?"

Frank glanced at the sky. "After you called him, you mean?"

"Yeah, I called him," Sean said. "I thought if anyone could keep you from doing something stupid, it would be him. Looks like I was wrong."

"You were wrong. Can't nothing keep me from doing something stupid."

"What happened? What did you do?"

Frank shrugged. "I opened Zed's box. Then Zed left."

"Where'd he go?"

"He didn't say. He seemed like the cryptic type." Frank brushed the thick, black blood of the Unfeathered off his jacket sleeve and onto the car's upholstery. "I'm sorry, Sean. This is all my fault. Zed said that I've killed us all, and I think he might have been right."

"We'll find a way," Sean said. "We're going to stop these bastards yet."

Frank stared straight ahead. "There ain't no we. You sold me out. Even if you had good intentions, you still betrayed me."

By the time they made it to the cabins the Unfeathered had already smashed through every door and window. They found Gus's youngest son unharmed, hiding under his bed. Gus's wife wasn't so lucky. All that was left of her was a pile of bones in the kitchen.

NIGHT FIVE

The students were collecting the feet of the Unfeathered. They lined them up along the end of the gymnasium in rows. The collection was now four rows deep.

The feet were interesting in a purely academic way, Wendy had to admit. Each foot had three toes with long claws curving out of the end. The feet were a solid fifteen inches long, and they were pure white, like the rest of the creatures' bodies. The number of joints on each long toe varied, anywhere from three to seven. Pretty fascinating, if you didn't think about the fact that each foot had been chopped off the leg of a monster by one of the Beyond Academy's teenage students.

Wendy surveyed the gym once again, scanning for anyone who might need medical attention, a shoulder to cry on, or even a little pep talk. She was the only female faculty member at the Beyond Academy and she had been left to act as Den Mother to students taking a break from their hunting. She had mixed feelings about it. On the one hand, it was incredibly sexist. On the other hand, if she had been given her choice of assignments, it would have been the one she picked.

It wasn't that she was against fighting the Unfeathered. If it had been just her, she would have been out there kicking ass. She was much more ambivalent about enlisting teenagers to fight the battle. Other faculty members were out there acting as field generals, devising strategies and showing the students where to point their weapons.

They had been lucky so far. No Beyond Academy students had been killed. There were a few injuries, but none too serious. How long that luck would last was anyone's guess.

A group of ten students shuffled into the gym followed by Ned Carlile, the science teacher.

The returning kids looked beyond tired. They were different than they had been a few days ago. They walked past without a word, approached a group of tables set up at the north end of the gym, and began disassembling their rifles to clean them.

Ned Carlile shuffled over to Wendy. "Everybody doing okay here?"

Wendy nodded. "Everybody's okay. Spirits aren't exactly high at the moment, but what can we expect?"

"Supplies holding up okay?"

"Yeah." In addition to the gym, she had also been put in charge of the armory. "Unless we're planning on invading a small country, the ammo will last for the near future. How's it going out there?"

Ned shook his head. "I don't know Wendy. These kids... they're amazing. A real tribute to the Rook Mountain spirit. They are professional and efficient. They listen to orders without question. They protect their brothers and sisters."

"Then what's the problem?"

"It's the creatures. I'm starting to think they're smarter than we thought. They attack people on the streets when they have the chance, but they're focusing most of their efforts on the edges of town. They're destroying house by house and slowly moving inward."

Wendy tried to imagine whether such a thing was possible. "Do you really think they have the intelligence to be that methodical?"

Ned shrugged. "It might be planning, or it might be that there are more of them on the edge of town. Either way, the result is the same."

"What do you think is going to happen?"

Ned glanced around before speaking. "Honestly? If they keep moving inward, the town won't last another week."

Wendy took a deep breath. There were things she could control and things she couldn't. She could make sure everyone who stepped into this gym was safe and comfortable, but she couldn't make sure they would survive long term. All she could do was stay in the moment and do her best.

"Have you seen Trevor Hinkle?" Wendy asked. "I thought he was with you a couple nights back."

Ned nodded. "He was. The kid was good, too. Everything Zed hoped he would be. Fought like the devil himself. I haven't seen him in two nights, though. I suspect his family is keeping him at home."

"Good. I wanted to make sure he was okay."

"Some of the boys wanted to head over there and liberate him. Let his family know he's needed. I talked them out of it. I figured it was best not to go looking for trouble."

"Good call."

Wendy was glad Trevor was home. She wanted the boy to be safe. She knew she couldn't wait much longer. Soon she would have to visit the Osmond house and give Trevor the gift from his father.

NIGHT SIX

It was one of those times when Christine missed cell phones.

Will, Frank, and the Hansens were out in the streets again tonight, fighting their endless and increasingly futile battle against the Unfeathered. Tonight they had taken the fight to Meadow Park, Rook Mountain's largest subdivision. It was a newer section of town featuring street after street of well-kept middle-class homes. The Unfeathered were getting uncomfortably close to the subdivision, and the guys were hoping to push them back a little.

It would have been nice to check in with Will every once in awhile to make sure he wasn't bleeding out in a gutter or something. But, no cell phones. She knew he would call if he had the chance.

Speaking of calling... she glanced at her watch. It was 9:03. She walked across the makeshift hospital, past the quickly filling gurneys, and made her way to the phone mounted on the wall. She picked it up and dialed a quick seven digits.

Trevor answered on the third ring. "Still here, Mom."

"Okay," Christine said. Ever since Trevor had gone out with his school friends a few nights ago, she wasn't taking anything for granted. She called him every hour on the hour to make sure he was home. If there had been any other choice, she would have stayed home with him, but the town needed its doctor. Will had stayed home with him the last two nights, but tonight she hadn't been able to talk him out of going out to fight. Will said he was doing more to protect his family out there than if he stayed home. Christine wasn't so sure. They were killing lots of the Unfeathered, and in the end that could save some lives. On the other hand, those things seemed endless.

Christine asked, "How's it going there? Any singing?"

"A little, but it's far away."

"Good. Got your gun out?"

"Of course, Mom."

"Good. Keep the safety on unless you need to shoot something." Something in life had gone horribly wrong, Christine knew, for her to feel comforted by the thought of her twelve-year-old son with a loaded rifle.

She had considered bringing him with her. At least she would have known he was safe. They were set up in the spacious basement of the Fifth Avenue Baptist Church. Though it had been designed for potluck dinners and Bible studies, the room was working out nicely. There was plenty of space, and it stayed cool even with all the people. The building itself was among the most solidly built in Rook Mountain. Christine hoped it wouldn't come to that, but the Unfeathered would have a hell of a time getting in here if they attacked.

In the end, she had decided against bringing Trevor. She wanted to limit how much death the boy had to see, and here he would see plenty. Most of the people who were brought here were passed the point of saving with her limited triage skills and resources. There had been two deaths already tonight.

The Osmond home was near the center of town, and there hadn't been much Unfeathered activity nearby except for the occasional stray flier. Trevor was armed and he knew how to use the weapon. Leaving him home alone was a risk, a terrible risk, but it was a calculated one. The neighbors on both sides were watching the house and had promised to call her if any Birdies showed up in the neighborhood.

"Doc!" someone yelled from across the room.

Christine sighed. "I gotta go. Be safe. I'll call you at ten."

"You don't have to."

"Yeah, I do. Love you. Bye."

"Bye."

Christine hung up and made her way toward the man who had called out to her. His name was Martin Grady. A bird had crashed through the window of his home on the outskirts of town last night. It had taken a sizable chunk of his right leg before his wife had blown its head off with a shotgun. She sat next to him now. She'd been holding his hand since Christine had arrived three hours ago.

Christine sat in the folding chair on the other side of the cot from Mrs. Grady. "How you doing, Mr. Grady?" Christine didn't like the distant look in the man's eyes.

It was Mrs. Grady who spoke. As she did, she gave Christine a look that couldn't have been far off from the one she had given the bird creature before she shot it dead. "He's in pain, doctor. You need to help him. He's not a complainer and if he says he's in pain then by God he is."

Christine hated this part She reached out and took the woman's hand. "I believe you. But we are low on supplies, and injured people are pouring in here. He's had all the pain medication I can spare at the moment.

Mr. Grady pulled her hand away. "Please."

"I've done all I can for now. It'll be a rough night, but I believe he is going to make it. In the morning, I'll reevaluate our supplies and let you know."

She turned and marched away before Mrs. Grady had a chance to respond.

The door at the top of the stairs opened with a crash and a man stumbled into the basement. It was Henry Strauss. He had a two-inch cut on his right cheek and the blood was dripping down onto his shoulder. Christine hurried over to him. "Henry, let me take a look at that cut. Any other injuries?" She pulled on a pair of latex gloves.

Henry shook his head. "No, that's not why I'm here. Christine, they've taken Meadow Park. The Unfeathered have taken Meadow Park."

Hours later, Will, Frank, and the Hansens staggered into the gymnasium, escorting a dozen wounded men and women. The guys looked like Christine felt – near total exhaustion. They stood by, their eyes distant and hollow, while she tended to the new arrivals. After she had seen to the most pressing of their wounds, Christine pulled Frank and Will away from the others.

"Tell me," she said. "How bad is it out there?"

Will shook his head.

"We're losing," Frank said. "They're gaining ground. A few more days, maybe a week, and it will be over."

Christine didn't respond. She didn't know how.

"I'm sorry." Frank's voice was barely louder than a whisper. "Zed was right. I've killed us. I've killed you. And Jake... I let down Jake. He called to his brother for help, and I failed him."

Will's head snapped around. "Wait. What do you mean he called to his brother?"

"When he talked to Sally Badwater, he asked for my help."

"What exactly did he say?"

Frank swallowed hard before he spoke. "Tell my brother to meet me at the quarry. And if Frank comes, tell him to bring the Cassandra lock."

Will and Christine looked at each other.

"We have to get Sean," Christine said.

"Why?" Frank asked.

Will grimaced. "We know what Jake's message means."

Night Seven

The sun was starting to sink by the time they all gathered at Sean's house. Christine had managed to get a few hours of sleep and Sean had only gotten off his shift fifteen minutes ago. They didn't have much time before the singing would start; they would have to talk fast. Will, Christine, and

Frank met in Sean's living room. Sean's face, as usual, was unreadable.

"A couple of months after Regulation Day, a farmer named Dan Johnson brought me a cane with the broken clock symbol on it," Sean said. "He'd found it half buried in his field. One of the Regulations says any item with that symbol needs to be turned in to the police or selectmen."

"Regulation 2," Frank said. "I remember."

"Yeah. Regulation 2. That cane was the first Reg 2 item anyone had turned in, and I told Dan Johnson to keep quiet about it. I knew even then how badly Zed wanted those objects. He came and spoke to us at the station about them. He called them the Tools. He said to avoid touching them as much as possible. And when he talked about them, his eyes were... greedy. I don't know how else to say it. They were greedy."

Frank nodded. "I saw that look too. When he saw the knife."

Sean continued. "I was supposed to hand it over to the selectmen immediately. Thing is, life in Rook Mountain was already getting pretty weird. People had taken to the Regulations. They were actually excited about enforcing them. I was seeing it more every day. I'd get called to a scene and by the time I got there, the people had already taken matters into their own hands. Something inside me didn't want to give Zed any more power than he already had. So instead of calling the selectmen, I called my friends. And we decided to hang on to the cane."

"We started calling ourselves the Unregulated," Christine said with a smile. "It was Sean, Jake, Will, Wendy, Todd, and me. That was when we realized some people react differently to the Tools. Will picked up the cane and everything changed."

"Remember when I said that I zone out when I touch the Tools?" Will asked. "Drifting, I think you called it? There's a little more to it than that. I see things. The Tools, they show me what they're for."

"What do you mean?" Frank asked.

"They are Tools, right?" Sean asked. "They have to have a purpose. And the purpose of the cane is to find the other Tools."

"The minute I picked up the cane and touched the broken clock symbol, it sort of came to life in my hands," Will said. "It started vibrating. And it was pulling me somewhere. It was like a divining rod. Except it wasn't finding water. It was finding the Tools. We found the first one buried out by the cabins. It was a lighter."

"We were off and running," Sean said. "We started using the cane to look for other Tools. It wasn't long before we found this." He pulled out a small object wrapped in an old t- shirt. He slowly unwrapped it and held it up for the others to see.

Frank gasped.

A wave of déjà vu swept over him. His emotions—guilt, anger, despair, fear—swirled within him at the sight of it. It was a silver coin with the symbol of the broken clock.

"Where did you get that?" Frank asked.

"Brett's ex-wife had it," Christine said. "When the cane led us to her house, she was more than happy to hand it over. She didn't want anything to do with the coin. She told us Brett had it with him the day he died. That was when we started piecing things together."

"What's it do?" asked Frank.

"I don't know," Will said. "Not exactly. But when I held it, I felt death. I know that sounds weird, but I don't know how else to describe it. That coin radiates death. The Tools seem to want things. The cane wants to find its brothers. The mirror wants to pull you in. But this coin? It wants everything to die."

"I felt it," Frank said. "The day I... I killed Brett. That coin touched my foot and I felt so angry."

"The Tools affect people differently," Christine said. "Some people, like me and Sean, they don't seem to affect at all. Others, like Will, are more sensitive to them. We think that you are as sensitive to them as Will is, but maybe in a different way."

Frank felt a flash of anger at that comment. What did she mean? She had no idea what he'd been through or felt the day Brett died. Then he stopped. Were those thoughts and feelings his own? Or was he being affected by the coin?

"I think," Frank said, "that I'm feeling it now."

Will grimaced. "Yeah, me too. I can feel the hate coming off the damn thing. Here's the worst part. You have to touch the broken clock symbol to activate the Tools. That coin is not even turned on. There's no doubt in my mind that the coin is more powerful than the rest of the Tools put together."

Frank squeezed his eyes shut. Was it possible? Had he been under the influence of this thing, this Tool, when he killed Brett? He replayed the scene in his mind. He had punched Brett in the stomach. That move had been all Frank. But then the coin had rolled out of Brett's bag, and Frank had flown into a killing rage.

"This is what we've been protecting," Christine said. "This is the Tool Zed wants above all the others. We think this is why he came here in the first place."

"You think Zed is powerful now?" Will asked. "If he had that coin, it would be game over. He'd have what he wanted and he'd have no use for the town anymore. I don't know for sure, but it's possible that the moment he touched that thing, every living creature in Rook Mountain would die. The coin's that powerful." Will paused and looked at the floor. "We've done things. I've done things. I've killed. What I did was wrong, but it was all to protect this coin. I knew Zed was watching me closely, and I had to be above suspicion. We all did."

"That's why you turned me in to Zed that day?" Frank asked Sean.

Sean nodded. "I'm sorry, Frank. I knew they would find out you'd been here. If it came out that I knew you were breaking into City Hall and I didn't say anything, they would take a really close look at me. And my home. I couldn't risk that."

Frank nodded. He understood. For maybe the first time, he was starting to understand that this was bigger than him.

"When we found the coin, we agreed that we had to keep it separate from the other Tools," Christine said. "Sean was the least likely to fall under suspicion, so we left it with him."

Will sighed. "It was a burden knowing this thing even existed. I can't imagine what it must have been like having it in your home."

Frank thought for a moment. "You said this had something to do with Jake's message to Sally Badwater?"

Christine nodded. "It was our code. In case one of us were caught and needed to get a message to the others. 'Meet me at the quarry' meant the coin might be in danger. It meant that we needed to move the coin."

"How would Jake know the coin was in danger?"

None of them had an answer for that.

"Okay," Frank said. "What about this? Why did he say,

'Tell my brother'? Why would he use your code to give me a message?"

Will and Christine exchanged a glance.

"Things were different after you went to prison," Christine said. "Jake was more upset than he let on. After Regulation Day, when they stopped allowing visitors at the prison, he felt like he had lost a brother."

"He and I were spending a lot more time together," Will said. "He said he considered me a surrogate brother. We even started calling each other brother."

"So when Jake said, 'Tell my brother to meet me at the quarry'..." Frank said.

"That message was for me," Will said. "What I don't understand is why he was so cryptic. Why not say 'Tell Will to meet me at the quarry,' or 'Tell Christine to meet me at the quarry'?"

"I don't know," Frank said. "What about the other part? 'If Frank comes, tell him to bring the Cassandra lock.'"

"Maybe those were two separate thoughts," Christine said. "Maybe what he meant was, 'Tell Will to meet me at the quarry. And if Frank comes, tell him to bring the Cassandra lock.'"

"Guys," Sean said. "I don't mean to break up the speculation session, but the sun is dropping fast. I'll do what Jake said and move the coin. I know somewhere else I can hide it. But we need to get out there."

"You're right. Let's get going." Frank nodded toward the coin that was resting on the coffee table. "And put that thing away. I don't want to see it ever again."

MORNING

The night had been hell, but it was almost sunrise.

They had relocated the surviving residents of Meadow Park into three main locations downtown: The Middle School, the High School, and Anderson Elementary. All three were centrally located and had plenty of rooms. Still, the scene at all three locations was grim—they had long ago run out of cots and movable beds. The residents of Rook Mountain were jammed in like refugees, lying on the floor in sleeping bags or blankets. Whatever artifacts they had been able to salvage from their homes were jammed into garbage bags and paper sacks and stacked next to where they lay.

Frank, Will, the Hansens, the Beyond Academy students, and some other men from town patrolled the downtown area throughout the night, taking out the few Unfeathered that flew into their paths. Will had brought Trevor with him this time; the Unfeathered were getting too close to the Osmond home now, and the boy had proved himself to be both careful and effective in the fight.

Compared to the last few nights, it was quiet. There were attacks, but the creatures came in groups of twos and threes. Not like last night's wave of Unfeathered that descended on Meadow Park as if by some silent command. It was almost as if the creatures were gathering themselves, preparing a final assault to destroy the residents of Rook Mountain once and for all.

In Fifth Avenue Baptist, Christine and her band of helpers dragged themselves from cot to cot, caring for the injured. The death toll was above twenty, and it would likely be twenty-five in the next few hours.

Sean too was having a difficult time remembering when he'd last slept. There were a few smaller neighborhoods the Unfeathered had attacked that had been overshadowed by the battle at Meadow Park. It was in these smaller neighborhoods that Sean and his partner were working tonight. They fought the creatures when they could and convinced residents to leave when the battles were lost.

Wendy remained at the Academy, making sure her student-soldiers had what they needed, from weapons to food to the occasional nap. She hadn't seen most of the faculty members in days, and she had no idea who was alive and who was dead. She concentrated on what she could control, and she kept the terrible machine of the Beyond Academy rolling through the night.

Becky Raymond wandered through Rook Mountain middle school, wondering what the hell she was doing there. The board of selectmen had agreed to spread out, to have a presence at the places throughout town where people would need the most help. The idea was to give people a sense of normalcy and convince them the selectmen still had a handle on things. Mostly she had been walking the halls, smiling and waving at people when she remembered to do so.

If she looked at it objectively, Becky had to admit that the selectmen had handled things pretty well, all things considered. They'd had emergency plans in case the Unfeathered got into town and attacked en masse, but the plans had all seemed theoretical. Why would they ever need to use those plans? They had Zed.

With the plans, some improvisation, and the help of a few great people like Doctor Christine Osmond and Frank Hinkle, they were managing to muddle through. But Becky felt no sense of pride or achievement in what they had done. It was all temporary. Sometime in the next few nights, the Unfeathered would reach downtown, and then it would only be a matter of time before there was no one left in Rook Mountain. The plans wouldn't save them. The Regulations wouldn't save them. And the board of selectmen, as powerful as it had seemed seven days ago, would not be able to save them.

But that was only part of the despair that clung to her like a weight. At the center of the despair was a question—a question which might never be answered.

Where was Zed?

For ten years, Becky had followed Zed, and she truly loved the man. Not in a romantic sense, for she knew he was beyond such things, and she believed that she was as well. She loved him like a soldier loves a trusted general. He had accepted her when she was an attendant at a Road Runner gas station, and he had believed in her even then. He had showed her how to be a better person, how to demand more from herself than she ever had before. And then he had shown her impossible things. He had told her secrets few had ever known and taught her skills few possessed.

The people of Rook Mountain had laughed at him. They had mocked Becky and Zed's other followers. They'd called them the Zed Heads. But still Zed had prepared for the evil he knew was coming, and when it came he had saved the town.

He had placed Becky and his other followers into the seats of power and taken none of the power for himself. He had counseled them and guided them when they needed it and he had asked for nothing in return. He was, without question, the greatest man Becky had ever known.

And then he had disappeared.

At first she thought someone had taken him against his will. That he had been kidnapped or maybe even murdered. Perhaps Jake Hinkle had finally returned to finish the job he had started eight years ago.

But... the more she thought about it, the less likely that seemed.

Zed was a man of great power; he would not be easy to kill. Even if someone had succeeded in killing him, no one —not even the selectmen—had a key to the room that held the box. And even if someone had found the key, the box itself was locked with an unpickable lock of Zed's own design.

She had considered that maybe someone had tortured the information out of him, but Becky had seen Zed in some rough situations. She wasn't sure he could be tortured.

It wasn't until after Becky started losing her Abilities that she accepted that Zed might be dead.

Zed had shared his Abilities with his six closest followers the day before he gave the town the Regulations. He'd given them the Ability to travel anywhere in town by simply thinking of the destination. He'd given them the Ability to read minds and hearts by looking deeply into a person's eyes.

Over the past seven days, Becky's Abilities had faded and then disappeared altogether. Now she was driving from place to place and could only guess what others were think-ing. That could only mean Zed was dead, right?

Becky looked out the window of the school and saw the first hint of sunlight on the eastern horizon. She walked toward the front door. It had become a bit of a ritual over the last seven days in Rook Mountain. At sunrise, people left their homes and went outside, celebrating another day of life.

A voice Becky didn't recognize echoed through the halls. "Sunrise!"

As she walked, the displaced Rook Mountain citizens poured out of the classrooms and joined her. They walked out together, almost defiantly, and they all turned to the east. It wasn't light yet, not quite, but the Unfeathered never attacked this close to dawn.

The refugees at the High School next door were also coming out onto the street. Among the group, Becky saw Frank Hinkle and Will Osmond, their clothes tattered and stained with the blood of the Unfeathered. For such a large group, it was uncanny how quiet they all were. A few people were chatting. Becky saw some police officers talking in hushed tones near the curb, but most of the people were quiet. They all stood facing east, watching the rising sun.

It was a good moment. Not a happy one, but at least a moment filled with relief. They had made it through another night.

Becky felt a sense of peace settle over the crowd but, underneath that, the dread was already creeping in. The beginning of the day meant the countdown to the end of it. Sundown was coming.

Becky watched the sun peek over the mountains to the east. Then a murmur worked its way through the crowd. It started small, like a group of people all whispering at once, and it grew into a wave of chatter.

Becky's eyes went to the skies. She scanned back and forth, looking for any white shapes, but she saw nothing. Then she looked down and saw him.

He was walking down the middle of State Street, coming from the east. He wore a long coat that hid his form, and he was still too far off to see the details of his face, but Becky knew him from the way he walked.

She stepped forward, pushing her way through the crowd, past the terrified and shocked people of Rook Mountain, until she was at the street. A hush fell over the crowd as he drew close enough for the people to realize who it was walking toward them.

Becky's throat clenched as the emotions ran through her, and she fell to her knees.

Zed smiled at her and held out his hand. She took it and rose to her feet.

His eyes were a familiar deep gray and his smile was as warm as ever. He squeezed her hand and then released it.

Then he turned away from her and spoke to the crowd. Though he didn't yell, his voice carried easily and echoed off the buildings.

"My friends," he said, "I am so sorry for what you've been through these last seven days. I'm so sorry that I was not here to protect you."

Becky scanned the crowd. Their eyes looked hungry and pleading. They needed an explanation. They needed to know why their hero failed them.

"You've all lost so much," Zed said, "and you deserve to know why."

A murmur of approval rolled through the crowd.

"Eight years ago I made a box. The box had one purpose —keep the Unfeathered away. The fact that we are all alive today is evidence that it did its job. I locked the box away in a room in City Hall, and I secured it with a lock I designed myself. I was confident that the box was safe. I was wrong. Seven days ago, the box was destroyed."

Zed held up his hands to the crowd as if to calm them. "I take full responsibility for what happened. I was overconfident. I was too trusting. Things had been so good for so long that I forgot there are people who don't share our dedication to the common good. I forgot that some people break things and start fires and hurt people for no good reason. It's always been that way and it always will be. I can't change that. But I should have done a better job protecting you from those people.

"Unfortunately the box I made wasn't easy to replace. The construction materials were, well, let's just say you can't get them around here. I didn't know if I would ever be able to rebuild the box, but I had no choice. I had to try. Time was of the essence. As soon as the box was destroyed, I left without a word to anyone. I went to some places and did some things I hoped I would never have to do again. The cost was high, but in the end I was successful."

Zed reached into his coat. With a flourish, he pulled out a box identical to the one he had presented on Regulation Day eight years ago. The crowd gasped. Then it began to cheer.

The people clapped, stomped their feet and screamed with joy and relief. Becky felt her own eyes fill with tears. It was so beautiful. Zed had done it again. He'd saved the town.

Zed held the box aloft as the people cheered. He smiled and nodded at the crowd, a look of wonder on his face, as if he too couldn't believe this happy occurrence. After a long while, he held up a hand to silence the crowd.

"We are safe," Zed said, "But we have so much work to do. First, we have a lot of homes that need rebuilding. A lot of you lost everything, and I won't rest until you have everything you had before and more. We also need to take time to grieve. That is no less hard and no less important than the rebuilding. After that, the real work begins."

Becky watched the crowd watching Zed. He had them now like he never had before. They would make him king if he asked.

"We have to make sure this never happens again. And that starts today. There's a man here who doesn't have the same values that we hold so dear. He's repaid this town's kindness with betrayal. And for the last seven days he has laughed while the rest of you have suffered."

Zed looked back and forth across the crowd. "Frank Hinkle! Come forward and answer for your crimes!"

Becky gasped, and much of the crowd did with her. There was a disturbance back near the High School. The crowd parted and two men pulled Frank Hinkle forward. Becky recognized one of the men as Henry Strauss.

The two men dragged Frank in front of Zed, one man holding each arm.

"Come back to mess with us some more?" Frank asked. His voice sounded weak and hollow compared to Zed's.

"Frank Hinkle," Zed said, his voice booming through the street. "Seven nights ago, you broke into City Hall and destroyed the box, bringing death and destruction to Rook Mountain. Do you have anything to say for yourself?"

There was something in Frank's eyes that reminded Becky of a wild animal. "I've been fighting those flying bastards every night. I've been trying to protect the town. What have you been doing?"

Zed smiled. "While you have been trying to save the town, I have actually been doing it." He turned toward the crowd. "You see, my friends? You see how our enemies act? They will do anything to deflect responsibility for their actions. Frank Hinkle is no friend of mine, he's no friend of the Regulations, and he is no friend of Rook Mountain. And, sadly, he is not alone. But I have hope.

"That's why on this day I propose a new law—and a new phase for Rook Mountain. If we really want to provide a future for our children, this is the one and only path. My friends, let me tell you about Regulation 19."

THE UNREGULATED (PART 1)

They met in Will's cabin because it was the smallest of their homes. They crowded in a loose circle in the living room. Jake and Christine sat close together on the couch with an uncomfortable Sean wedged in on the far end. Wendy was in the green recliner. Will sat on a dining room chair he had dragged into the living room for this little meeting. Todd was on the floor, his back against the arm of the couch.

Their seating positions might have seemed casual, but all of their lines of sight were carefully planned. The doors to the lone bedroom and bathroom were wide open and mirrors had been strategically placed near them. Every corner of the cabin that could be seen by at least one of the members of the group. Wendy had told them that Zed and his Zed Heads—the leaders of the town now—wouldn't appear in a spot where they could be seen. They always appeared behind a closed door.

Was the information accurate? Like so much else these days, the group had no idea. Better safe than sorry. In this little band of Rook Mountain subversives, trust was definitely not a must.

It had been almost a year since Regulation Day, and the town had fallen into new patterns. There had been a number of incidents. People had broken Regulations, and those people had been punished according to the new laws of Zed. For the most part, people behaved as if their lives had always been this way. They went to their jobs - many of the jobs newly created by the Zed Heads - and they went shopping and they spent time outdoors (but never across the town line). The lack of resistance or even questions was disturbing to those gathered in the room. As far as they knew, no one else was all that bothered by the Regulations.

Over the past nine months, they had acquired the cane, the knife, the coin, and the lighter. Last night, Will and Sean had found another item.

Will glanced at the bathroom to make sure it was still empty, and then he turned his attention back to the object on the table.

"What's the story, Will?" asked Todd. Todd was the most outspoken member of the group. He had been the first to suggest they keep the cane, even before they had discovered its power to find other Tools. He was the most public about his feelings on the Zed Heads. In a way, it was great to have an extroverted natural leader like Todd in the group. On the other hand, it made Will nervous. If anyone was going to accidentally expose their group, it would probably be Todd.

"We found it in a field off Lakeland Drive," Will said. "We were driving around and the cane started going crazy. It led us right to it."

"And you haven't tried it?" Wendy asked.

Will shook his head. "We stuck to the agreement. It's been hard, though. The curiosity's been killing me. So if no one objects..." He leaned forward to pick up the object on the table.

"Wait," Jake said. "We have to do the other thing first."

"Come on," Will said. "We all know the score."

"Jake's right," Todd said. "People are forgetting. They are starting to see all of this as normal. I see it every day at work. Somebody new gets detained, and my co-workers are joking about playing dice for their clothes. We have to keep reminding ourselves."

"Yeah, but we aren't like that," Will said. "We're here, aren't we?"

"They deserve to be remembered," Jake said.

Will looked at Jake for a long moment, and then he gave a little nod.

Christine grabbed a thin three-ring binder off the arm of the couch and opened it to the last page. "We have three new entries this week. On Wednesday, September 25th, Tyra Underwell was caught breaking Regulation 6 outside her home. Her sentence was carried out immediately by three of her neighbors who removed her left hand." Christine looked up from the paper. "And if I may editorialize for a moment, her lovely and talented doctor missed dinner in order to save the rest of her arm. Moving on, on Thursday, September 26th, Fran Cantor was caught breaking Regulation 1 and her sentence was carried out immediately by the Rook Mountain police officer who caught her trying to cross the town line." She glanced at Sean.

"That would have been Eli Jennings," Sean said.

"Okay. On Saturday, September 28th, thirteen-year-old Gracie Holden broke Regulation 16. Her biology teacher carried out her sentence in front of the class, branding her with the number sixteen on her cheek."

"You're kidding," Wendy said. "I didn't know about that one. I taught Gracie last year. How did I not hear about this?"

"That's what I'm saying," Todd said. "It's barely even news anymore."

"With one death this week, that brings the total to seventy-four executions since Regulation Day." Christine closed the book with a sigh.

"That was uplifting," Will said. "Now, if I may?"

Jake nodded.

Will picked up the hand-held mirror and studied it for a moment. He ran his fingers over the broken clock symbol.

It was Wendy who had told the group about Zed's obsession with the Tools. After her breakup with Frank, she had dabbled in becoming a Zed Head. She'd spent enough time with them that Zed had gone beyond the usual peace and wisdom talk he pitched to the dabblers and moved on to some of the real stuff. Wendy had heard him talk about Regulation Day in intricate detail long before it happened. He talked about the powers he would give to his followers. He had also talked to her about the ten Tools. He had the pocket watch already, but he intended to find the other nine.

All the talk of monster birds and magic pocket watches had seemed like nonsense at the time, but it had been enough to frighten her off. She had left the group only a few months before Regulation Day. If she'd only waited a bit longer, she might be sitting on the board of selectmen today.

Will took a deep breath, and then he pushed the broken clock on the mirror.

The group waited. Will was listening, waiting for the mirror to tell him what it wanted. When it did, he stood up, shuffled to the kitchen, and took out a paring knife.

"What are you doing?" Sean asked. He stood up and eased his way toward Will.

Will sliced open the palm of his left hand. He squeezed the hand shut. He saw a drop of blood fall from his fist and land on the face of the mirror. When the blood hit the mirror, it didn't stop. It kept falling into the silvery surface and Will felt himself being pulled along after it. Powerless to stop, Will fell downward, head first.

A shimmering liquid surrounded him, and all sound disappeared. In the distance, he saw something, and he knew it was his destination. He felt something pulling on his legs, and he was back in the kitchen. His friends stood around him, their faces drawn with concern. Will put a shaky hand to his face, expecting to feel the wet residue of the shimmering liquid, but his had came away dry.

"What the hell, man?" Todd asked. "You all right?"

"It..." Will wasn't sure how to describe what had happened. "It wanted to pull me in."

"Yeah, it did a pretty good job, too," Christine said. "Sean grabbed your legs before you disappeared into that thing."

"It was trying to take me somewhere," Will said. "I could see it in the distance. There were trees, but not like we have around here. These were huge. Redwoods maybe."

"Wait," Jake said. "You're saying that mirror is a door to another place?"

The group was quiet for a long moment while everyone digested the news. Then Todd grinned. "Will, you did it. You found our ticket out of Rook Mountain. We can go there and bring back help for the town."

Will shook his head. "I'm not so sure. That place looked... different. We don't even know if you could get back here. Could be a one-way ride."

"One way or not," Todd said, "Five minutes ago we were trapped in this town. You've just found our escape pod."

7

REGULATION 19

I.

Trevor sat in the back of the minivan hoping they couldn't see his hands shaking.

The guys in the front of the van were Ned Elwood and Carlos Serrano. He had never talked to them before this morning, but he had seen them around town and watched them with awe. They were Resource Expansion Specialists. RESpys. Trevor had dreamed of being a RESpy since he was five years old. RESpys were cool. They could leave town, and they did so every day.

And today Trevor was leaving town with them.

It had been four days since Zed returned to town and once again stopped the Unfeathered. Four days since Regulation 19 was passed into law. Four days since Uncle Frank had been the first person found guilty under Regulation 19.

Trevor was still reeling. He couldn't quite get his mind around it. It didn't seem real. He felt angry and sad about what had happened to Uncle Frank. At the same time, he felt angry and ashamed at what Uncle Frank had done. Uncle Frank had seemed like a good guy. He had been a hero during the fighting against the Unfeathered. But in the end he had turned out to be a terrorist, just like Dad.

Trevor had stayed in bed that whole next day wanting nothing more than to curl up and die. Hinkles were terrorists. Hinkles betrayed the town. He had asked Will if it would be all right to change his last name to Osmond. It had been a tough decision for Trevor. He was the last Hinkle, after all. But maybe the Hinkle name didn't deserve to live on. Will was kind of a dick sometimes, but at least he wasn't a traitor. He'd proven that by shooting that Regulation breaker up on Rook Mountain.

When Trevor asked him, he had expected Will to be happy. Instead, it was like a dark cloud had crossed over Will's face. "I'd be proud and honored to have you take my name," Will said. "But I don't think it would be right. Your dad and your uncle left you that name. They left you a lot to live up to."

"Yeah, maybe if I go on a shooting spree I'll live up to their legacy," Trevor said. He couldn't help it; he was hurt by Will's reaction.

Will opened his mouth like he wanted to say something, then closed it again. He went back to the book he had been reading. Trevor had wanted to talk to his mom about it, but she had been gone for almost every waking hour the past few days. She was still taking care of those injured by the Unfeathered.

School started again the following day. There was an assembly in the morning and Ms. Janet, the principal, talked about bravery and heroism and blah, blah, blah. It all washed over Trevor. He had been there for part of it and he had fought against the Unfeathered with all his might, but it seemed like a dream now.

People were looking at him funny. Not only was he the

son of Jake Hinkle, he was also the nephew of Frank Hinkle. No one mentioned it, but he could tell that everyone was thinking it. Trevor did his best to pay attention and concentrate on his lessons. It was difficult, though. It all seemed pointless.

After lunch, an announcement came over the PA calling Trevor Hinkle to the office. The hot ball of worry that had been growing in his stomach for the last two days suddenly erupted into a flame of panic.

At the office, the lady working the desk showed him into a room and told him to wait. After a few minutes, Zed walked in. He smiled at Trevor and shook his hand. Zed looked into Trevor's eyes a little too long, but Trevor looked right back, meeting his gaze. He wouldn't be intimidated, no matter what happened next. Zed was the first to look away.

"Trevor, I wanted to let you know that I'm very impressed with the things I'm hearing about you. You really made a difference last week. You fought the Unfeathered and did a great job of it from what I hear."

Trevor didn't say anything.

"Something on your mind?" Zed asked. "Go ahead and say it."

Trevor hesitated, not sure if he should say what he was thinking. But what did it matter? It was probably going to be his last day at Beyond Academy anyway. He'd be shocked if the meeting didn't end with him getting expelled.

"My uncle Frank fought the Unfeathered too, but no one's thanking him."

Zed waved his hand dismissively. "That's not really the same thing, is it? If a man burns down a house, you don't thank him for pouring a bucket of water on the fire. Anyway, I'm impressed. You've been through a lot, and this week you had to suffer another family member letting you down. But I think you are a special young man, Trevor. I'd like to offer you a unique opportunity."

And now, one day later, Trevor was sitting in a van with two legendary RESpys, driving toward the edge of town with no intention of stopping when they got there.

Ride alongs with RESpys were a Beyond Academy tradition. The teachers and the students all talked about it. But it was usually an honor reserved for upperclassmen, not freshmen a couple of weeks into their first semester.

Trevor wasn't about to complain. True, he didn't understand exactly why he had been selected, but he was living his dream. He was about to see what really lay beyond the city limits of Rook Mountain.

"Half mile out," Ned said from the passenger seat.

Carlos glanced at Trevor in the rear view mirror. "So you ready for us to pull back the curtain and show you how we leave town?"

"Yeah, I'm ready." Trevor hoped his voice sounded more confident to them than it did in his own ears. Trevor, like every other civilian in Rook Mountain, had no idea how the RESpys left town safely. It was a violation of Regulation 9 to even ask.

Carlos pointed toward the dashboard. It took Trevor a moment to figure out what the RESpy wanted him to see. A wooden block was mounted on the dashboard. The block was about an inch tall, and it was painted the same color as the rest of the vehicle's interior.

Ned gave the wooden block a little pat. "As long as we have this thing, it's like we haven't left town."

Trevor licked his lips, trying to find the courage to ask a follow-up question. After a lifetime of being taught not to talk about the strange goings-on in Rook Mountain, this was no easy task. "How does it work?"

"You know that box Zed made? This is like a smaller version. It keeps the Unfeathered away. But it only protects a very small area. Take a few steps away from the car and it'll be lunch time for the Birdies."

A device that kept the Unfeathered away? And it was portable? Unbidden, visions of the open road flashed in Trevor's mind.

As if reading his thoughts, Ned said, "A few years ago, we had a RESPy named Walter Quinn who thought one of these wooden blocks was his permanent ticket out of town. He jumped in a RESPy vehicle and hit the road. Zed waited until Quinn was a good seventy miles out, and then he shut off the wooden block. Quinn's bones are out near Abingdon, Virginia. Still in the driver's seat of his car. The Unfeathered smashed in the windows and ate him where he sat."

"How'd Zed shut it off?"

Ned shrugged. "However Zed does what he does. Anyway, last week when Zed's box was broken these blocks stopped working too. Thank God Zed came back and put things right."

"This is it," Carlos said.

Trevor felt his heart pounding in his chest. He saw the white line on the road getting closer and closer as the car sped forward. Then they were on top of it. Past it.

And suddenly it was dark. The stars sparkled overhead with a brilliant clarity.

Trevor looked out the windows at the landscape around him. He took a deep, slow breath to see how it felt. "Why is it dark?"

He looked up and saw Ned looking back at him in the

rear view mirror, a smirk on his face. "It's always dark out here."

The trees flickered past as the van tore down the empty highway. Trevor had expected to see the Unfeathered everywhere, but he didn't see any of the creatures. Everything looked desolate and empty.

"Where are the Unfeathered?" Trevor asked.

"They're around," Carlos said. "Mostly holed up in the woods. But they'd be here fast enough if we didn't have our device running. They'd catch our scent and be on us right quick."

"Is that how they sense us? They smell us?"

"How the hell should we know? They just do. Close your mouth and open your eyes. You might see a thing or two."

Trevor turned back to the window and watched the trees roll by.

He had his first glimpse of something strange a few minutes later. Near the side of the road, a bird, the normal feathered kind, hung motionless in the air. It was like a snapshot, a picture of a bird in flight. He saw it in the beams of the car's headlights as they approached, and it disappeared from sight as they sped past it.

"Did you see that?" Trevor asked. "That bird was, like, frozen in the air."

Carlos grinned. "Yeah, we've seen that one a time or two."

They drove on, over bridges and past trees. A few times they passed cars abandoned in the middle of the road. Ned seemed to know when these cars were coming up and he easily avoided them. Neither he nor Carlos commented on the vehicles.

Trevor couldn't help himself. He had to ask. "Have these cars been here a long time?"

"Yep," Ned said.

"What happened to the drivers?"

Carlos and Ned exchanged a glance and grinned at each other like kids on the way to a surprise party. "What do you think happened to them?"

Trevor opened his mouth to say he had no idea, but then stopped. There was a pretty good chance that had been a rhetorical question.

They drove in tense silence for a few minutes. When Carlos spoke again, Trevor almost yelped in surprise.

"Usually we would be driving a much larger vehicle. One of the semi trucks. Or a flatbed. We have a tanker truck we use for collecting fuel. It's nonstop. You should know that if you are thinking about becoming a RESPy. It's amazing how much one little town consumes in a week. After a while, it gets so you see every person in Rook Mountain as just another bottomless pit of consumption. We bust our asses hauling everything we can into the town, but it is never enough. It never ends."

Trevor resisted the urge to speak again and waited for Carlos to continue.

"So, like I say, we would usually use something much bigger. We like to use the van for these ride alongs. The whole thing seems a little more real in a van. Our mission today is simple. Halloween is coming and the town needs candy. We're going to pick up a few boxes. Elizabethton still has some we can tap into."

"Really?" Trevor asked. He had expected something grander, more vital than candy.

"Yep. Just a few boxes of candy. Walk before you can run, my man. Plus, can you imagine all the pissed off parents if we ran out of candy rations on Halloween? There would be a riot, an actual riot." Carlos looked back at Trevor and grinned. "So when you look at it that way, we're saving lives here."

The van sped past another car stopped in the road. As they approached, Trevor looked through the window and what he saw almost made him scream.

"Holy shit!" Trevor said. "There's a person in that car!"

"Yep," Ned said.

"We have to help him! The Unfeathered could be here any minute!"

Carlos chuckled. "The Unfeathered only like the living and the breathing, and that guy ain't either. Not exactly, anyway."

Five minutes later, the van pulled into the parking lot of a CVS pharmacy. Ned spun the car around, threw it in reverse, and backed up almost to the door.

There were only five cars in the parking lot, and two of the cars had people inside them. Motionless people. It was like looking at a photograph.

"Okay kid, listen up," Carlos said. "This is where it goes from a sightseeing trip to real dangerous work. We're going in that CVS to round up some candy. The minute we step outside this van, we are fair game for the Unfeathered. We should be okay inside with the doors shut, but we have to bust ass for the few moments we are outside. Got it?"

"What's with the people?" Trevor asked. "The people in the cars."

"We'll show you inside," Ned said. He pulled out a pistol and looked at it. "Get out your weapon and switch off the safety."

They had given Trevor a pistol for the trip. It felt heavy in Trevor's hands. He clicked off the safety.

"Okay, hands on the door handles," Carlos said. "When I count to three, we run like hell for the door. Got it?"

"Yeah," Trevor said.

"Good. One. Two. Three."

The three men threw open their car doors and leapt out of the vehicle. Ned and Carlos left their car doors wide open, so Trevor followed their lead. He had only taken three steps before he heard the sound of the Unfeathered singing in the distance. It was far off, but he heard another, closer voice join in the song.

Trevor pumped his legs and swung his arms, sprinting after the two RESPys. In front of him, Ned reached the door, still sprinting, and slammed into it. The door banged open, and Carlos and Trevor hustled inside before it clapped shut.

Carlos's eyes scanned the parking lot, then the sky.

"We good?" Ned asked.

"Yeah. We're clear." He turned to Trevor. "We should be safe in here. The Birdies don't usually start smashing into buildings for a few hours. We don't want to be in here all day, but we will have long enough to get the job done."

"You mean getting the candy?" Trevor asked.

Ned smiled. "That too. But that's not our main job. The real reason we are here is you. Zed says that it's time for you to know about the outside world, so we're here to show you." Ned nodded his head toward Trevor's left.

Trevor turned, and what he saw made the breath catch in his throat. A woman was standing behind the cash register. A man stood in front of the checkout counter. Neither of them was moving. The checkout lady had a Baby Ruth candy bar in her hand, poised over the scanner. Her mouth was half open as if she was speaking.

Trevor walked slowly toward them. "What's wrong with them?"

"Technically? Nothing's wrong with them. They're just paused." Carlos took a few steps toward the frozen people.

"It's like this everywhere," Ned said. "Johnson City. Bristol. I've been as far as Charlotte fulfilling some special orders, and it's the same thing everywhere. Everywhere but Rook Mountain."

Trevor reached his hand out toward the man in front of the counter. His hand hovered a few inches from the man's face.

"Go ahead," Carlos said. He rapped on the man's cheek with his knuckle, producing a strange thud. "You can't hurt them. I mean, you really can't. You could take a chainsaw to their necks and it wouldn't so much as scratch them."

"Sure can take their stuff, though," Ned said. He reached into the man's back pocket and pulled out a wallet. He let go of the wallet and it snapped back into the man's pocket like it was attached to a bungee cord. "Well, for a second anyway. Stuff doesn't want to move. It goes back to the way we found it the second we let it go. Until we get it in the van."

Trevor put his hand on the man's cheek. It was hard as stone. "But what happened? What did this to them?"

"Well, the way Zed tells it," Carlos said, "nothing happened to them. They are perfectly fine. It's us in Rook Mountain that got screwed up."

"Zed says Rook Mountain got knocked out of time," Ned said. "It's like we are in a hole in time. We are living in between one moment and the next. Technically, it's still 2014. For the rest of the world anyway."

Trevor turned a slow circle, scanning the paused world around him. He'd been living in the same moment for the last eight years?

"When we put stuff from out here into the van, it gets unpaused," Carlos said. "It joins Rook Mountain time. It's like we are pulling the stuff into the hole with us."

"What about people?" Trevor asked. "What happens if you put a person in the van?"

Carlos shook his head. "Doesn't work like that. People can't be moved. They are too strongly tethered to their time-line. It only works for inanimate objects."

"And liquids are even easier, for some reason," added Ned. "They become unpaused as soon as they get within a few feet of the van."

Trevor looked up sharply as something occurred to him. "If we get too far away from the van, do we get paused?"

"No," Carlos said. "Whatever happened to lock us out of time seems to be permanent."

Trevor blinked hard. His head was spinning. "What about the Unfeathered? How do they fit in?"

Carlos sighed. "We really aren't sure. But our best guess is that this 'time between times' is their territory. Normally they're the only ones who live here. That's why they're so hostile to us. They see us as invaders."

"Listen, Trevor," Ned said. "We know this is a lot to take in. Zed will sit down with you when we get back and answer all of your questions. Take a minute to look around and let it sink in. We'll handle the candy."

Trevor nodded absently. While Carlos and Ned carried armloads of boxes of candy from the store to the car, Trevor wandered. He found a few other customers and workers, all frozen in the moment. There was a little girl in aisle eight who couldn't have been more than four years old. She was dressed in pajamas, and she gripped her mother's hand. The other hand was by her face, the index finger buried in her nose. It was so bizarre and unreal that Trevor wanted to cry. Imagine being frozen for all time with your finger up your nose.

But from her perspective, she wasn't frozen, was she? For

her, this one second would click to the next without any pause. Trevor, his family, maybe even his future kids, would all live and die while that little girl picked her nose.

"Yo, Trevor, you ready?"

Trevor headed to the front of the store.

Carlos put his hand on Trevor's shoulder. "Listen kid, you're in the club now. The people of Rook Mountain don't know this and they can't know it."

"Why not?" Trevor asked.

Carlos frowned. "Sometimes it's easier to think that something is wrong with the rest of the world rather than thinking something is wrong with you."

Ned peeked out through the glass door. "I count six Unfeathered circling. Pretty high up, but they'll dive quickly enough when we head out."

"Okay," Carlos said. He looked at Trevor. "You ready?"

"Yes," Trevor said.

2.

Frank sat on a metal folding chair in a hot little room that smelled of Lysol. His sweaty hands were chained to the table. Even with the nice carpet and colorful paint job, the room reminded him of the office where Becky Raymond had offered to release him from jail. It had seemed like a sweet deal at the time, but in retrospect he should have told her to go to hell.

The last three days had been dark times for Frank, and things didn't look to be lightening up anytime soon. He'd been hauled up in front of the whole town and called a trai-tor. It wasn't the first time he had faced public wrath. After he killed Brett there had been a lot of outrage. Unemployed redneck kills upstanding working man with two daughters.

That was the way the media spun it. There had been a lot of calling for the death penalty. People longing aloud for the days of swift public hangings.

But the thing three days ago had been different. Frank wasn't a scapegoat people could get angry with to forget their own problems; instead, Frank was being called out as the source of their problems. The death toll was still uncertain, but it was twenty-five at a minimum. Not to mention all the people whose homes had been destroyed. The town had been like a seething pack of animals. They wanted his blood. Zed could have come up with anything and the town would have agreed as long as it involved Frank's death. Crucifixion or flaying or beheading, none of it seemed off the table.

But Zed had been thinking long term, and for once Frank was grateful for that fact. It might have satisfied the town to give Frank a flashy death, but Regulation 19 would take care of the Frank problem. Regulation 19 said that Zed or the selectmen could, at their discretion, enact a special punishment for any regulation breaker. A punishment Zed called 'The Away'.

Zed and his Board of Zed Heads had just been given nearly limitless power, though no one realized it quite yet.

Maybe Frank should have tried harder. Maybe he should have denied everything. Not that it would have helped. The people were eating out of Zed's hand. But Frank could have tried. The one thing that kept his mouth shut during his public non-trial was that, on some level, he agreed with Zed. The whole thing was his fault.

The door opened and Zed walked in, an easy smile on his face. He was dressed in khakis and a brightly colored t-shirt. He slid into the chair across from Frank.

"Morning! They treating you okay?"

Frank nodded slowly. "Yeah, I guess. All things considered."

Zed's smile widened a little. "That'll change. It may seem hard to believe, but these are the good times compared to what's coming. I'm almost done building the device. Tomorrow's the big day."

Frank tried to ignore the man's comments. "So how does this work? This erasing me from existence thing."

"Ah!" Zed held up a single finger, "I'm glad you asked. It's kind of beautiful in its own way." He reached into his pocket and pulled out a small object. Frank recognized it immediately. It was another Cassandra lock. How many of them did the guy have? "Time is like a lock with a bolt none of us can move. It seems unbreakable. Try to fight it and it doesn't matter. It carries us along and there's nothing we can do about it."

He tugged on the Cassandra lock to demonstrate the futility of opening it.

"It won't open. We don't have the key."

"You're saying it's a deadlock," Frank said. "That's the term for a bolted lock that can only be opened with a key. Like the kind of lock they use on prison doors."

"A deadlock. I like that." Zed looked pleased. "It's impossible to open this giant lock we call time. Unless you know exactly where to apply pressure." Zed twisted the Cassandra lock and it opened with a snap.

Frank raised his eyebrow. "You're telling me you unlocked time?"

Zed laughed a surprisingly high-pitched laugh. "No, not at all! I'm not as sophisticated as all that. I'm much more childish. I like to poke holes in things. I poke little holes in space so that my friends and I can transport ourselves around town. I poke holes in people's minds so I can see what's inside. And, in a very limited way, I poke holes in time."

"What does that mean?"

The smile never seemed to leave Zed's face. "Frank, you're not a stupid man, so don't ask stupid questions. The town of Rook Mountain is in one of these holes in time. I made a nice little hole for us to live in. Tomorrow I'm going to poke another hole, a hole within a hole, one might say, and I'm going to drop you into it. You won't die, not right away. But you will live out the rest of your abbreviated life alone and frightened in a place you can't hope to understand. It's not a nice place you are going, Frank. Trust me, I've dipped my toe in those waters and I don't plan to return."

Frank felt a chill pass through him. It was as if he were seeing Zed for the first time. Zed wasn't merely a creepy, opportunistic man with some impressive parlor tricks; Zed was something truly evil.

Zed leaned forward and put his hands over Frank's. They were ice cold.

"Frank, this isn't the end for you. There is still a chance. Regulation 19 or not, I can still save you. And I want to."

Frank waited. He took long slow breaths. Whatever Zed said, he wasn't going to get his hopes up. He wasn't going to take the bait.

Zed said, "The knife with the broken clock. Where did you get it?"

Frank stared at the table. He didn't want to meet Zed's eyes; he was afraid what the man might see.

"It's as simple as that. Tell me about the knife, and you can go back to prison. You'll be wearing an orange jumper and playing cards for Twinkies in two hours. All you have to do is tell me what I want to know."

Frank waited, but this time Zed didn't break the silence. He sat there with that creepy smile on his face. Eventually Frank said, "Sorry, Zed. Can't help you."

Zed sighed and nodded. "Okay. That is understandable. You are protecting someone. Maybe it's the good Doctor Christine. Maybe it's Will. Maybe it's those Hansen boys you were running with all week. Honestly? I don't care. I respect your loyalty. I won't make you betray that. So let me change my offer. I don't care where you got the knife. I only care where it is now. Tell me where I can find it and you can go back to prison. The moment it's in my hand, you get on a van back to NTCC."

Frank concentrated on his handcuffs.

"Last chance, my friend. We've looked at Christine's house. We've searched those cabins where the Hansens live and everything on that property inside and out. I will find it eventually. Help us both out. I'll save some time and you'll save yourself a horrific death."

Frank kept his eyes on this handcuffs. If Zed had searched the cabins, why hadn't he searched the shed? Why hadn't he found the freezer?

Zed sighed. "I wish I had the device ready. I'd send you into the hole for a few minutes. I'll bet your lips would be a bit looser after that. If you think the Unfeathered sing, just you wait!"

Frank kept his eyes on the table. "Anything else?"

Zed reached into his pocket and pulled out the pocket watch. "You see this? You know what I've been able to do with this thing? I've stopped myself from aging. I've built devices that can stop the Unfeathered. I've poked holes in time itself, holes that every person in this town will carry around with them wherever they go for as long as they live.

You get the knife and what do you do with it? You wave it in my face like it's a prison shiv."

Frank said nothing.

Zed chuckled. "In a way, I'm glad you didn't tell me. That would be almost like cheating. It'd be like...like looking at the answers to a crossword puzzle before you're finished with it. You don't get it. Your brother didn't either. I've got all the time in the world to find the knife and the other Tools. They attract one another, and they are gathering in this town. More slowly than I would like, but they are gathering. Sometime in the next few hundred years this town is going to burn out, mark my words. And when every last person in Rook Mountain is dead, I will crawl out of this little hole in time. I'll have what I came here for and I'll be infinitely stronger than when I went in. And to the rest of the world no time will have passed at all. So tell me or don't tell me. I'm having fun either way."

Frank looked up, not into Zed's eyes, but at his mouth. "Why don't you poke a hole in my mind and see what I know?"

Zed's smile wavered for a moment. "When I looked into your brother's head, it was murky. There were things there, lots of things, but it was difficult to make them out. It's the same with your nephew. But you are different. You know what I see when I look in your head? I see locks and nothing else. How do you do that?"

"Anything else?" Frank asked again.

Zed stood up. "You're a cold one." He turned to go, and then turned back. "Let me tell you something. When I first came to Rook Mountain and knocked on all those doors, I looked into every eye in town. There was only one person who frightened me. You. You were the only one who even gave me pause. I knew that if you put your mind to it, you had a chance to stop me. You and your locks. Your locks were interesting, so I paid that neighbor of yours to steal them. And then you went ahead and took care of my problem for me. Got yourself locked up."

Zed leaned close to Frank. "You have great weakness in you, my friend. Trust doesn't come easy to you. Maybe you could have been the hero once, but that time has long past. The best you can hope for now is to save yourself. I'll give you one more chance. Tell me about the knife."

Frank said nothing.

Zed sighed. "You know, you should really take the long view every once in a while. Reality gets weaker the deeper you go, and the hole I'm going to throw you in is mighty deep. When the Ones Who Sing come after you, you'll wish you had swallowed your pride. Enjoy your evening."

3.

Will opened the door leading to the attached garage and he saw Christine sitting on the ground with the knife, the lighter, the key, the cane, the mirror, and the frozen head of an Unfeathered spread out in front of her.

"Honey, what are you doing?" he asked.

She didn't look up. She set the key on top of the knife. "We don't have much time. They are sending Frank away in the morning. Whatever the hell that means."

Will stepped down into the garage and pulled the door shut behind him. "Yes, but what are you doing? What are these things doing here?"

"You know what Jake always said. What we all said. These objects work together somehow. We need to find the right combination."

"Christine, these should be locked up. What if Becky Raymond stopped by? Or Zed himself?"

Christine slapped her palm against the concrete floor. "What are we doing here, Will? What have we been doing all these years? He kills our people, he keeps us under his thumb, and we just drive around town at night with this damn cane hoping to find something useful."

"You know what we're doing. We're protecting the coin. We've been smart about it. That's why we're not dead. We've been beyond reproach. That day on Rook Mountain, I didn't hesitate. I killed Jessie Cooper even though every part of me wanted to run out of town alongside her. Because that's what I had to do. What's one life compared to the lives of everyone in this town? Everyone in this world? We've built such solid reputations that no one even looked at us twice when your brother-in-law turned out to be a traitor. We are protecting the things we have to protect. Trevor is safe. And so is the coin."

Christine looked up at Will. Her eyes were filled with tears. "Everything we've ever tried has been a failure. Todd is dead. Jake is gone, probably forever. And now Frank. When is it enough? When do we finally stand up to him?"

"Jake wanted to fight. Look how far it got him. We have to be strong even if it means losing Frank."

"They are brainwashing my son in that school. How much longer before we lose him too? Look around us, we have weapons. We have the knife. We have the head and the lighter."

"Honey, I don't think—"

"Shut up!" she yelled. "Shut up and come here."

He knelt down next to her and held her in his arms. They cried together.

4.

Frank lay on the cot in his jail cell, missing the good old days of prison. If he had to spend his last night in a cell, he wished it could have been his cell at NTCC.

The heavy metal door swung open, and Frank resisted the urge to leap to his feet. Guards didn't like jumpy prisoners. It wasn't a guard who stepped into the cell—it was Wendy.

Frank looked at her for a long moment, not sure how to react. It had been almost ten years since he had last seen her. She hadn't come to the trial. But here she was now, in his jail cell.

He stood up and stepped toward her. "How did you get in here?"

Wendy shrugged. "I'm an instructor at the Beyond Academy. People kind of let us do what we want. I told the guard I was here on Academy business and he stepped out of my way."

Frank nodded absently. He didn't know much about the Academy but he wasn't about to start asking Wendy questions about her job. Not now.

"How you been?" he asked. He didn't realize how stupid the question sounded until it was out of his mouth.

There were tears in Wendy's eyes. "I'm so sorry this all happened."

Frank smiled and shrugged. "I am too."

She looked great standing there, as good as she had ten years ago. She glanced back at the door.

"Did Christine and Will tell you what happened to Jake? How he went away?"

Frank nodded. They had told him the story the day after Frank broke Zed's box. "I'm not sure I fully understand it all, but they told me."

"Did they tell you where it happened?"

Frank shook his head.

"It was at my house. I was the last one to see him before he disappeared."

Frank didn't know what to say. He didn't know why Wendy had felt the need to come here, to tell him this.

"Frank, I believe that you're special. If anyone can survive what Zed's got planned for tomorrow, it's you. I've been trying to think of some way to help you. All I came up with was this." She handed him an envelope. The name Trevor was written on the envelope in Jake's distinctive handwriting.

"Jake gave me that letter before he disappeared. He asked me to give it to Trevor when he was old enough to understand what's happened to Rook Mountain."

Frank looked up at her. "The kid's smart, Wendy. I'm sure he'd love a letter from his father. What are you waiting for?"

"I agree. It's time. I'm going to give it to him soon. I haven't opened it. I don't know what it says. But I thought maybe there was a chance it might be able to help you somehow."

"You want me to open my brother's letter to his son?" Frank asked.

"No," Wendy said. "I want you to decide for yourself. What if there's something in the letter that can help you survive?"

"What if there isn't?"

Frank looked at the envelope for a long moment and then tore it open. He read it silently, and then folded it and slid it back into the envelope. "There's nothing in there that can help me. Give it to Trevor." He looked up at Wendy. "Thank you, though. Thank you for trying."

Wendy took the envelope. "I won't be coming tomorrow. I can't watch them do that to you."

Frank nodded. He understood. "Can I ask you something?"

"Of course."

"You used to run around with Will and Christine and Jake, right? Looking for the Tools?"

"I did."

"Then I guess you know Will and Christine have some of them."

Wendy glanced back at the door and then nodded. "We believed that the Tools were stronger together than apart. If we could find enough of them, we thought maybe we could take down Zed."

"Zed said they've searched the cabins and that whole property," Frank said. "Why didn't they find the Tools?"

A slow smile appeared on Wendy's face. "You don't know? I thought Will and Christine would have told you."

"It's been a little hectic."

"They put everything in that freezer in the shed and locked it with one of your locks. Becky Raymond came out and personally oversaw the search of the place. When she went into the shed, she didn't even try to open the freezer. It was like she didn't even know it was there."

"How could that be?" Frank asked.

Wendy's smile widened. "It was because of your lock." She tilted her head. "Wait. I have something else for you." She reached into her pocket and pulled out a small lock. It was a Fox, the first original model Frank had designed. It opened without a key if you knew the right place to twist it.

Now it was Frank's turn to smile. "You kept it?"

"It was always my lucky charm, remember?" She put it into his hand.

"Wendy, no. They are going to take it away from me. I'd rather you keep it."

Wendy shook her head. "Keep it locked and they won't find it. Not if you don't want them to. It'll be like the lock on the freezer out at the cabins. They won't even see it."

"You can't know that."

"Yes, I can. Hold on to the lock, and remember that no matter what they do to you, they can't take away who you are. Like I said, Frank, you're special."

5.

Frank waited on a raised platform in front of City Hall. Two people stood next to him. He recognized one as Anita Lawrence. The other was a man he had never seen before. He had no idea what either of them had done or why they were standing there. The crowd was rolling in at a steady pace. There were eight police officers around Frank and his fellow convicts, presumably in case the prisoners started making trouble. He spotted Christine standing near the edge of the stage, her roller bag of medical gear by her side.

One of the police officers stepped forward and held up a gold necklace. A golden loop roughly the size of a peach pit hung from the chain. He addressed the prisoners.

He said, "At the time your sentence is carried out, this marker will be placed around your neck. Do not remove it at any time. This marker will protect you from the Unfeathered. It will also let you know when your sentence is over. When it begins to flash red, that means you have one hour remaining in your sentence. Return to this exact spot immediately. Failure to return to the same spot you left will result in further discipline." He glanced at Frank. "Except you of course. You ain't coming back. Any questions?"

It seemed impossible to Frank but the two people to his left didn't have any questions. Frank had about a million, but he didn't think the officer would have the answers, so he too kept quiet.

Frank looked into the crowd and saw Will, his arm around Trevor. Will gave him a little smile. Trevor looked sad, terrified, and much younger than twelve. Frank decided not to look at the kid anymore. Frank was afraid he might start crying. It wasn't that he was too manly to shed a couple tears; he just didn't want to give Zed and the Zed Heads the satisfaction. So Frank turned his attention to the people filling the street in front of the platform.

It was amazing to see how many people had turned out to see him punished. Way more than had come to Jake's wedding. At least Frank had that to comfort him.

He took a deep breath and tried to take stock of his feelings. All morning he had been waiting for the terror to hit him. There was fear, but it wasn't the crippling kind he had expected. He only felt the emotion that had been his constant companion for as long as he could remember: anger. The way this was playing out wasn't fair. Zed and his cult of freaks were going to win.

Frank heard the roar of the crowd before he saw Zed. The tall man stepped onto the stage and waved to his adoring public. There was nothing somber about his demeanor—he wore the broad easy smile that was as much a part of his uniform as the khakis and solid colored t-shirts.

Zed walked to Frank and put a hand on his shoulder. "Nice turnout. It's a shame you won't be around to see how this ends." Zed gave him a wink and turned to the crowd.

When he spoke again, his voice carried as if projected over a PA. "Good morning, Rook Mountain." The people answered with a roar, like it was a Strange Brood concert or something.

Zed waited for them to quiet, then said, "I'm so glad you are all here to bear witness today. This is a historic occasion for our great town. Regulation 19 goes into law today and with it comes the first three punishments. 'Any person found guilty of an act against the people of Rook Mountain will serve an immediate sentence, the length of which will be determined by the board of selectmen.' Simple enough in theory, but I think you will find its impact will be incredible. Crime will drop. Civic pride will rise. Rook Mountain will grow even stronger in our unity and our goal of building a better future for our children. And that all begins today."

The crowd cheered again. Frank was finding it hard to concentrate on Zed's words. That little pit of fear inside of him was growing.

"Let's begin," Zed said. He turned to face Anita. He spoke again in his unnaturally amplified voice. "Anita Lawrence, you have been found guilty of Breaking and Entering and Theft. While your neighbor fought for her life against the Unfeathered, you stole her jewelry. You have been sentenced to three hours Away. Do you have anything to say before your sentence is carried out?"

Anita's mouth was a thin white line. "This is ridiculous. I don't understand what is happening."

Zed put a hand on her shoulder. "You will, sister."

He held out his hand, and the police officer handed him the gold necklace with the little gold loop hanging from it. Zed leaned forward and put the necklace around Anita's neck. Frank's mind flashed to the end scene in Star Wars when Princess Leia put medals on the heroes. Everyone but poor Chewie.

Zed said, "Under Regulation 19, your sentence begins

now." He poked the little gold loop with his finger. And suddenly Anita changed.

The crowd gasped.

A moment ago, Anita had been clean and tidy, her hair neatly pulled back into a ponytail. Now she looked like a woman who had been chased through a field of thorn bushes. Her clothes were torn, and small cuts crisscrossed her face. Her hair was down and chunks of it were missing, leaving gaps large enough to show her bloody scalp. Her face was dirty. Her cheeks were gray with little streaks where her tears had run down.

She spoke in a hoarse, scratchy yell. "My God, the people there. They ain't real. They hurt me. They hurt me bad, and they ain't even real. They..." Her words trailed off as she began to cry.

Zed removed the necklace and then put his arm around her. "Shhh. You're safe, sister. Your debt is paid."

The man next to Frank took a step back. "What the hell just happened? You ain't doing anything like that to me."

Zed turned to face the man, and his face grew cold. "Earl Garrison. You have been found guilty of stealing your mother-in-laws' rations and neglecting her in the face of danger from the Unfeathered. She died because you didn't care enough to take her somewhere safe after her neighborhood was lost. You have been sentenced to two months Away. Do you have anything to say before your sentence is carried out?"

Earl pointed to Anita. "Yo man, I don't know what happened to her, but I don't want none of that. Send me up to NTCC. I don't want no part of that other thing."

Zed nodded to the police officers standing on the side of the stage. Two of them came forward and held Earl's arms down by his side. Zed slipped the necklace over his head.

"Under Regulation 19, your sentence begins now."

"Yo, this ain't right! I should be allowed to know what's going on here. I—" Zed pressed the gold loop with his finger, and Earl changed.

The man looked years older. He was naked except for the necklace, and his chest and legs were covered with half-healed cuts. His head was a mess of dried blood and stubble as if his hair had been shaved with a dull knife.

Earl didn't speak. He squinted out at the crowd as if the sun was too much for him. He lifted his right hand to shield his eyes. The hand ended in five jagged nubs where his fingers had been only moments before.

Earl tried to take a step forward, and he collapsed into Zed. His breath came in ragged gasps.

"Your debt is paid, brother," Zed said. He nodded to the police officers. Someone stepped up and wrapped a blanket around Earl.

The pit of fear in Frank's stomach exploded into a cold chasm. There it was. The terror he had been waiting for all morning.

Zed turned to him. "Your turn." He felt the two police officers behind him grab his arms. Zed slipped the necklace over Frank's head. The gold loop was heavy against his chest. Frank had expected the crowd to cheer when his time came, but they gave him only silence.

Christine moved so fast that Frank barely had time to register what she was doing. One moment she was standing on the side of the stage, the next moment she stood behind Zed. She had the knife, the one with the symbol of the broken clock. She snapped the knife open and held it to Zed's neck.

"No," she said. Her voice was quiet, almost a whisper. "No. You let him go."

"Doctor," Zed said, "What are you doing?" He still smiled his broad smile, but there was a quiver in his voice.

The eight police officers drew their weapons and pointed them at Christine. Zed waved them away.

Frank glanced to his right and saw Will crouching near the front of the stage, unzipping a backpack. Zed and the police officers hadn't noticed him yet. All of their attention was on Christine. Will reached into the backpack and pulled out a roundish white object. It took Frank a moment to recognize it: the Birdie head from the freezer at the Hansens'. Will set the head on the stage and pulled something out of his pocket. The lighter with the broken clock symbol. He flipped the lid open and held it near the head.

Frank's eyes scanned the crowd for Trevor, but he didn't see the boy.

Christine grabbed Zed's shoulder and swung him around a quarter turn, the knife still pressed to his neck. Will was ten feet directly in front of them.

Zed's eyes widened when he saw Will. "Take it easy. Let's talk this through."

Christine nodded to Will.

Will flicked the lighter and it burst to life. "How do you like my book learning now, Zed?" He moved the flame to the beak. As soon as the fire touched the head, it burst into flames as if it were made of old newspaper. The decapitated head's eyes shot open and it opened its beak and let out its familiar song.

Christine yelled to the crowd, "Go home! They're coming. The Unfeathered are coming! Go home before it's too late."

One, then two, then three white specks appeared in the sky overhead. They were high up, but they were slowly circling. Their distant voices joined the song of their brother on the stage.

The crowd moved like a living thing, wriggling and squirming away from the stage. A few people screamed in terror as they noticed the Birdies circling above, lazily looping lower toward the ground.

Frank felt the hands on his arms fall away. He wanted to run, to help Christine and Will, but he had no idea how. He stood and waited.

Zed's smile was gone now, replaced with a snarl. He turned and spoke to the crowd, and his voice echoed off the surrounding buildings. "Wait. Stop."

To Frank's surprise, they did. They froze, almost all of them, and turned to look at the stage.

Zed turned his head and looked back over his shoulder at Christine. "Here. Let me help you." He grabbed the hand holding the knife and pulled it hard across his own neck. . Christine stepped back, her mouth hanging open.

Blood poured from Zed's neck, darkening his purple t-shirt. He turned and took a step toward Christine. "Is that what you wanted? Did you want to cut my throat? Watch me bleed out like an animal in front of my town?"

He grabbed the knife from Christine's hand and tossed it down onto the stage. He walked over, pulled the blanket from the crouching and shivering Earl Garrison, and wiped the blood off his neck.

Frank felt the breath catch in his throat. Zed's throat was whole and uninjured under the blood. It was as if the cut had healed in only a moment.

Zed took three quick steps toward Will and tossed the blanket over the blazing head, smothering the flames. The song stopped. The three Birdies in the sky circled one more time as if listening for the song, then shot into the clouds above.

The police officers leapt forward, one tackling Christine to the ground and another grabbing Will.

"They never learn, do they?" Zed said. He was pacing across the front of the stage now, addressing the crowd. "The enemies of justice are everywhere. They are hiding among us."

He turned toward Christine, pinned to the stage by the officer who had tackled her. "Among our most trusted citizens. But understand this, my friends. They cannot hide, not for long. Because they despise justice so much that they can't help but reveal themselves in the face of it, as we have seen here today.

"These two people we considered friends—" He spat out the word like a curse. "—have shown themselves to be enemies of Rook Mountain. So they, like all enemies of Rook Mountain, will be judged under Regulation 19. In our town, justice cannot, will not, be stopped."

"Uncle Frank." The voice came from behind him.

"But let's finish what we started," Zed said. "Frank Hinkle, for acts of terrorism against the city of Rook Mountain, you have been sentenced to spend the rest of your natural life Away. You will not be given the chance to speak. Your actions have spoken louder than your words ever could."

Frank turned and saw Trevor crouched down near him. He held out his hand, palm up, to Frank. The open knife was resting in it.

Quick as he could, Frank reached for the knife. Even as he was reaching for it, he thought he saw a hint of a smile returning to Zed's face.

Frank's hand was almost there, almost touching the

knife, but Zed was faster. His finger shot toward the gold loop resting on Frank's chest.

Frank kept reaching. His hand was almost to the weapon. Another inch and he'd have it.

Then the world blinked out of existence.

THE UNREGULATED (PART 2)

Jake and Todd were at the river. In spite of spending most evenings driving around town with the cane, waiting for it to detect something, the group was in the middle of a long dry spell. Since the mirror, they hadn't found anything.

Todd and Jake had spent the last few nights out at the Gray River. The cane hummed like crazy out there, drawing itself toward a spot in the water. Digging in the river bed was messy, dangerous work, and they had yet to turn up anything. Tonight the group had decided that Jake and Todd would dig out there again while Wendy and Will used the cane to search another part of town.

Jake and Todd approached the river. Todd was a few yards ahead of Jake. Jake almost crashed into him when Todd stopped at the top of the embankment. Then he saw what had caused his friend to freeze.

Zed stood near the edge of the water, arms crossed and that ever-present smile on his face. "Evening, gentlemen."

"Hello, Zed," Todd said. Jake stepped forward alongside his friend, but he didn't say anything.

"The police are on their way," Zed said.

"We haven't done anything wrong," Todd said.

Zed shrugged. "We'll think of something. I've been watching you two since last night. I appreciate your independent spirit. Still, I don't see the need for all the clandestine stuff."

"Really?" Todd asked. "People are being killed. Branded. You've trapped us all in this town and told us to like our prison. You don't understand why we might not be super public with our objections?"

Zed chuckled. "No, you misunderstood. I don't know why you are still objecting at all. I won. This town is mine. There's nothing to fight."

"We disagree," Jake said, finding his voice. It sounded weak.

Zed swiveled his head toward Jake. "Okay. That's your prerogative, as the song says. You keep on disagreeing." He pulled out a pocket watch and looked at it. "Do you have any idea how closely the Tools are tied together? I knew a Tool was being used in town. My watch knew. At first I thought maybe it was the mirror, but then I realized it was the cane. After that, it was pretty easy to fool the thing, to lead whoever was using it out here. And then last night you two showed up. So, tell me, where is it? Where's the cane?"

"We're done talking," Todd said.

"Maybe it's time for us to go," Jake said.

Zed turned toward Jake. "Maybe I'll feed that little boy of yours to the Unfeathered. Maybe I'll take your wife home with me some night. I could do either of those things and no one would stop me. I might do it just for laughs."

Jake didn't think, he acted. He reached into his coat and pulled out his pistol. He pointed it at Zed and took three steps forward.

"No one else dies," Jake said. Then he fired.

It was a clean shot. It hit exactly where Jake had meant it to: Zed's forehead. A dark hole appeared above Zed's left eye. Zed fell backward onto the ground and put a hand to his forehead. Slowly, he got up and took a step forward, staggering like a drunk. He rubbed at the spot on his forehead vigorously with the palm of his hand. He took the hand away and the bullet hole was gone.

The smile never left his face.

"Whoa," Zed said. "I was not expecting that. Maybe I underestimated you. Maybe we got the wrong Hinkle locked up over at NTCC."

Jake raised his pistol again, careful to not let the barrel shake.

Zed shook his head. "Come on, really?" His hand snaked out quicker than Jake would have thought possible, and he grabbed the pistol, ripping it from Jake's hand.

Todd's hand went into his jacket. Zed pointed the weapon at him. "Empty hands, friend. Hold them up so I can see them."

Todd raised his hands. It looked ridiculous to Jake, like a movie. He had never seen anyone put their hands up in real life.

"I'll be honest," Zed said. "I don't like either of you. You are dangerous. Let me show you what I mean."

Zed fired. Todd was dead before he hit the ground. Jake screamed, ran to his friend and fell to his knees next to the body. He turned back to Zed, but before he could speak a squad car pulled off the side of the road.

Jake didn't know if these officers would be his saviors or his executioners. The way Sean talked about the police force, it could go either way.

Zed was waving his arms, signaling for the officers to hurry over. They stepped out of their squad car.

"Guys!" yelled Zed. "We need your help! We've got a man hurt over here!"

The police officers hustled forward. Jake recognized Gary Stampard. Gary had been a jock back in high school, but his point guard days were about seventy pounds behind him. His stomach strained the limits of his uniform. His partner was an older guy with a stereotypical cop mustache. Don Franklin. Don had busted Jake a few times back in Jake's hell-raising days. The fact that he knew both of them was both a comfort and a concern. Would they be more or less likely to help him?

"Zed. Jake. What's going on out here?" Officer Franklin asked.

Zed fired two shots into Franklin's face, and then turned and shot Stampard. Zed's accuracy was lethal. Both men fell down dead.

Zed swung the gun around and pointed it at Jake.

Jake froze in his crouched position next to Todd's body. He didn't think he could have moved if he'd wanted to. His legs were shaking and his breath felt strange. The world looked a little fuzzy around the edges.

Jake thought, This is what it feels like to know you are about to die.

"Don't make me shoot you," Zed said.

"Todd didn't make you shoot him. Neither did Gary and Don."

"That's true. You made me shoot them. You pulled your gun and fired it. Without your predilection for violence, this whole thing would have been a lot less bloody."

Zed licked his lips. From Jake's vantage point near the ground, Zed looked impossibly tall.

"Why'd you come here tonight?" Jake asked. "What do you want?"

"The way I see it, I came out here to think, as I often do, and I stumbled upon you and Todd breaking some Regulations. I haven't decided which ones yet, but it hardly matters, does it?"

Jake said nothing, so Zed continued.

"I ran to the nearest house and called the police, reporting some suspicious activity at the river, but I knew the police might be too late. I had to investigate. So I came back out here and hid in the bushes, watching you and Todd. Imagine my surprise when you two started arguing. It sounded like Todd was trying to talk you out of leaving town, and you were saying it was the only way, that you didn't care who got hurt as a result of your actions. One thing led to another, and you pulled out a weapon and ended the argument. I was shocked and too afraid to come out of my hiding spot. I didn't even come out when Officers Stampard and Franklin showed up and you ambushed them. Then I found my courage, came out, and wrestled the weapon away from you. It was terrifying. A real nightmare." Zed shook his head sadly.

"You're crazy if you think anyone's going to believe that."

"Maybe," Zed said. "Still, I like my odds. I'm the hero of Rook Mountain. You're a redneck who tried to jump his station by marrying a pretty doctor. People around here know what you really are. How many times were you arrested as a teenager? Plus, the murder weapon is a pistol registered to you."

Jake eased his hand under his dead friend's jacket.

Zed crouched down next to Jake. "Is Dr. Christine involved in your little conspiracy? If she is, I'll find out. How about your friend the teacher? I'll be watching him, too. They take one step outside the Regulations, and they are mine. I know you have the cane. Where is it? "

Zed raised the gun and placed the barrel against Jake's forehead. The metal was hot on Jake's skin.

Jake thought of Trevor and wondered what kind of man the boy would turn out to be. He mouthed a silent prayer. His hand tightened around the gun in Todd's shoulder holster.

"Look at me Jake."

Jake did. The creepiest thing about Zed was his genuine smile. He always seemed delighted.

"Hmm, your mind is cloudy. I can't make out much of what I need in there. Too bad. I do see some cabins that seem important. I'll have to check those out." Zed sighed. "Be smart here. You are going to die either way—"

Jake ripped the gun out of Todd's holster and shoved it into Zed's mouth before the man finished his sentence. Jake pulled the trigger, and chunks of skull and brain matter exploded from the back of Zed's head. Jake fired again. And again. He kept firing until the gun was empty. Then he put his foot against Zed's chest and pushed him off the gun.

Zed fell backwards with a moan. He lay on the ground twitching.

Jake had no illusions that Zed was dead. But the man hadn't gotten up yet, either. Jake might still have time to do one last thing for Rook Mountain. He jumped into his car and drove toward the center of town.

8

AWAY

I.

The world flickered, and then everything was different.

The first and most visceral difference was the temperature. It was as if the heat had been sucked off Frank's skin and a cold emptiness was left in its place. It was maybe not cold, but it was crisp, the type of weather where one would have liked to wear a sweater.

The light was different too. The world was illuminated by an ultra-diffused, grayish light. Frank looked up and, while there didn't seem to be any clouds above, he couldn't see the sun. It was as if the entire sky was glowing—there was no visible light source.

Frank's eyes darted around him, trying to take in everything at once. It was sensory overload, and he felt his breath coming faster as he tried to understand what was happening to him.

The people of Rook Mountain were frozen where they had been moments ago. There was Trevor, with his hand stretched out. There was Will, an angry snarl on his face as a police officer pinned him to the stage. Zed stood directly in front of him, that creepy smile taking up most of the real estate on his face, his finger poised millimeters from Frank's chest. The police officer to Zed's left had his mouth open in a shout, and speckles of saliva were frozen in the air in front of him.

It was as if the world had been paused. All of it except Frank. He suddenly understood how the other prisoners had served their sentences in only moments.

But the frozen people weren't the only change.

Dozens of the Unfeathered covered the area, and they were definitely not frozen. There were three of them on stage and many more scattered throughout the crowd. They strutted casually, occasionally pecking at one of the frozen people as if eating invisible bugs off their skin. These Unfeathered looked different than the ones Frank fought last week. The shorter beaks and more defined facial features gave these Unfeathered a look that was part bat and part emu. There seemed to be more variety among them, too. The one closest to Frank had long, finger-like protrusions at the end of its wings.

Frank stumbled backwards as the Unfeathered came near, and he crashed into what felt like a stone wall. He looked back and saw it was the police officer who had been standing behind him. The Unfeathered passed by Frank like he wasn't there.

Frank glanced down at the necklace around his neck. Zed had said it would protect him from the Unfeathered. Looked like he hadn't been lying. About that part, at least.

That was no reason to go unprotected, though. Frank reached for the gun holstered on the police officer's side. He pulled on the holster's strap and unbuckled it. As soon as he released it, it snapped back shut. He touched the officer's face. It was hard as rock. His face, his hair, his hands, they were all part of the unmovable statue that was this man.

Frank eased himself out from between Zed's outstretched finger and the officer behind him. He walked around the stage, touching things, trying to understand his new world. He found that he could pick up objects off the ground, like the microphone lying unused near the front of the stage, but as soon as he let them go, they snapped back to their original locations as if pulled by a strong magnet.

More than once he crossed paths with one of the wandering Unfeathered. They took no notice of him. Gaining a little more confidence, Frank inched close to one of them, stretched out his hand, and brushed his fingers against the creature's wing. The Birdie shook itself as if a fly had landed on it, but it didn't turn toward Frank.

A thick swarm of Unfeathered passing overhead. It was then he noticed something else: the creatures weren't singing. Frank had rarely seen an Unfeathered that wasn't singing its terrible song or feeding. But these creatures, even the countless cloud of them in the sky, were absolutely silent but for the flapping of their wings.

Frank walked up to Zed and spat in his face. It was less satisfying than he thought it would be; the moment the spit hit Zed, it disappeared. It seemed not even his saliva could affect the rest of the world here.

He slid off the stage and walked through the crowd. He held out his hands as he walked, letting the cold hard skin of the people brush against his palms. It was strange looking into their frozen faces. Some were somber. Some expressionless. But a disturbing amount of them looked gleeful, their faces frozen masks of delight as they watched the punishment being doled out up on the stage. Frank had known many of these people his whole life, but that didn't stop them from getting their sadistic jollies watching him get the punishment they felt he had coming to him.

Suddenly the Unfeathered all froze as if listening. Then, as one, they took off into the air and flew away. Frank had a sudden sinking feeling in the pit of his stomach. The creatures had looked frightened. Whatever frightened the Unfeathered would probably not mean good news for Frank.

A low humming began. Then a higher note joined it. Then another.

It was a song, but not a song of the Unfeathered. This was something else. Frank remembered what Zed had told him. "When the Ones Who Sing come after you, you might wish you had swallowed your pride."

Frank backed up until he was against the stage. He looked out into the crowd, waiting.

He saw a shadow moving through the crowd. Then another.

No, they weren't shadows. They were dark shapes, vaguely like that of a man, though their edges seemed to shift and blur. They moved quickly, twisting their way through the crowd. Where moments ago there had been three of them there were now dozens. The shapes divided and merged, as if they were all part of some single, ever-changing mass.

The singing grew louder, so loud that Frank felt the urge to put his hands over his ears. He resisted it, afraid that any movement might draw their attention. He concentrated on staying perfectly still, his back pressed against the stage.

More voices joined the deafening chorus, and somehow the cacophony of notes began to form words. It was like no language Frank had ever heard, but it was also perfectly understandable, like a language he had always known somewhere deep inside. They were singing a single word.

"Frankkk."

Frank's breath caught in his throat. How did they know him? What did they want?

"Frankkk."

Frank tried to pick one of the shapes out in the crowd and follow it with his eyes, but he found he couldn't see the shape when he looked at it directly. It disappeared. It was only when he didn't focus, when he took in the scene as a whole, that he could see them.

That poor woman on the stage had been right. They weren't real. But they were.

"Frankkk. You are almost free."

The shapes moved closer to him. He pressed himself harder against the stage. He wanted to run, but where? The shapes were all around him. The Ones Who Sing circled closer, their ever-changing song growing even louder.

One of the shapes brushed up against his leg and he heard a ripping sound. He looked down. His jeans were ripped and there was a long cut on his thigh.

"Frankk," the song continued. "Come to us as a dog to its master, and we will feed you."

One brushed past his head, and he felt a clump of his hair being ripped out.

"Get away!" he yelled.

"Come to us as a master to his dog, and we will give you three truths."

Another brushed past his arm, and a new gash appeared in his skin.

"Come to us as a friend, and we will take your flesh."

They were brushing against him two at a time, so quickly he lost track of his wounds.

"Come to us as an enemy, and we will take your life."

Frank put his arms up to cover his face. He fell to his knees to cover as much of himself as he could.

"Come to us, Frankk. Come to us."

The song stopped, and they were gone.

2.

Bad as the Ones Who Sing were, it didn't take Frank long to realize that they might not be his biggest problem.

He stood in the produce section of Food City in front of a beautiful stack of Honey Crisp apples. Honey Crisps were his favorite. Will always said they were so good because they came from the North, but Will was an idiot.

Frank decided to try again.

He reached out and picked up the apple on the top of the stack. It was shiny and red, like an apple you'd see in a commercial. It looked delicious. Frank licked his lips and slowly brought the apple to his mouth, imagining how it would taste if only—if only!—he could eat it. He brought his teeth down gently this time. His mouth still hurt from the last attempt. But the result was the same. It was like trying to bite into stone.

He glanced down at his hand and saw he was dripping blood onto the apple. He hadn't taken the time to count his cuts, but there had to be a dozen. Thankfully, none of them seemed too deep. Still, between the cuts and the blood smeared all over him, he probably looked like something from a Tarantino movie.

He had been up and down the aisles, and it was all the same. At first he had hoped it was only produce, so he had tried the meat. When that hadn't worked, he had moved on to the more processed foods. But everything from the peanut butter to the Twinkies was inedible.

Frank dropped the apple, but it didn't even have the decency to fall down. It snapped back to its rightful place on the top of the stack.

The food situation was worrisome, but he could go for a few weeks without food if he had to. Much more troubling was the lack of water. He could turn on a faucet, but no water came out. He had tried the fountain near City Hall downtown, but the water in the fountain was rock solid. The bottled water at the store was the same. He needed water if he was going to make it more than a couple of days, but he was out of ideas. Poor Earl Garrison had survived here for two months. How had he done it?

The words of The Ones Who Sing came back to Frank: *"Come to us as a dog comes to its master, and we will feed you."*

As a dog comes to its master. Begging, thought Frank. They wanted him to beg. He wasn't quite that desperate, not yet anyway. Then Frank thought of another part of the song: *"Come to us as a friend and we will take your flesh."* He thought of Earl's hand with its missing fingers.

Frank sighed. He had only been there a couple of hours, by his estimation. The situation wasn't dire yet, but he had to think ahead, to figure it out, if he wanted to survive. He made his way to the front of the store and looked out the glass door. He was relieved to see three Unfeathered standing in the parking lot. One stood near Sally Badwater of all people, idly pecking at her face. It was as if they ate something off the frozen people. If they survived off that, was it something that could also sustain Frank?

He sighed and opened the door. He wasn't ready to start licking Sally Badwater yet, but give it a few hours.

Frank stopped a few feet in front of one of the Unfeathered. After spending the whole of last week fighting these creatures, it was odd to stand so close to one without either of them trying to kill each other.

Frank glanced down at the gold loop resting on his chest. Zed had told him this would protect him from the Unfeathered, but Zed said a lot of things. Maybe the necklace was what was keeping him trapped here in this place where time didn't move.

Slowly, Frank lifted the necklace over his head and set it on the ground. He took a deep breath and let go of the chain.

No sooner had his fingers lost contact with the metal than the creature fifteen feet in front of him snapped his head toward Frank and looked right at him. It opened its stunted beak and let out a weak cry. It was a pathetic version of the song the Unfeathered usually sang, but it was recognizable nonetheless. The other Unfeathered scattered throughout the parking lot all turned toward Frank.

Frank glanced at Sally Badwater. Damn it. She remained frozen.

Frank grabbed the necklace off the pavement and put it over his head. The Unfeathered closed their beaks and went back to their lackadaisical business.

Frank made his way through town. He had no clear destination. He needed to think, and he knew that the best solutions often presented themselves when he let both his mind and body wander.

After a while, he found himself back at City Hall. He looked out over the makeshift stage. He didn't much care to see that again, so he turned the other way and opened the door to City Hall.

He meandered through the hallways. He stopped in front of the sixth door on the left, the door that had held

Zed's box. He let the scenarios play in his mind for a moment. If only he hadn't opened the box. If only Sean hadn't ratted him out to Zed. If only Zed hadn't returned. If only the people of his hometown had stood up for him. In the end, though, there were only two people he could blame for his current situation: himself and Zed.

One of those two people was already paying for his sins. If Frank survived this place, he vowed that Zed would pay, too.

As Frank stared at the door, he heard a low familiar hum, and his heart jumped with terror. Other voices joined the first more quickly this time as the song grew.

"Come to us. We will sustain you."

Frank silently cursed himself for going into City Hall. If he had been outside, he would have seen the Unfeathered scatter. Inside, he had been caught unaware.

Though the voices were many, Frank saw a single dark shape at the end of the hallway. It flickered as it approached him, hovering motionless for a moment, and then traveling ten feet in less than a second.

"Come eat from our hand. Our price is small."

"I've seen your damn price," Frank muttered. "I'd like to keep all my fingers, thanks."

He wasn't going to wait this time while they/it carved him up like a Christmas ham. He turned and ran toward the exit. He rounded a corner, and there was the dark shape. Frank didn't hesitate. He ducked around it and kept running. He felt his hand slice open as it brushed against the shape. He didn't stop.

He crashed into the door and threw it open. As he ran outside, he risked a glance over his shoulder. The dark shape was following close behind him. But now that he was in open space, he sprinted. The stage was directly in front of him.

The shape glided past him, cutting his shoulder. It split in front of him, forming a dozen dark shapes.

"Come to us as a friend. We will take your flesh."

They formed a semicircle around Frank, pinning him against the stage once again. Frank saw Zed up there, his face frozen in a grin. He would have done anything wipe that smile off Zed's face. Then Frank saw something else on the stage.

He pulled himself up onto the waist-high structure. He struggled to his feet and ran to Trevor.

Trevor's hand was still outstretched, and the knife was still resting in his hand. Trevor had wanted Frank to have the knife, but Frank had been a fraction of a second too slow. Or maybe not.

Frank grabbed the knife. He said a silent prayer and opened it, knowing it would snap shut as soon as he let go of the blade. But it didn't. And it didn't feel like everything else here did. It felt like metal, not stone.

A dark shape drifted toward him, and Frank swiped at it with the blade. He hit the thing in what he guessed was its shoulder. To Frank's surprise, the blade sliced through the shape and a piece of it fell to the ground. As the blade struck, there was a momentary pause in the creature's song like a record skipping.

Frank lunged at the shape's head, but the shape was already retreating. The song faded, and the Ones Who Sing were gone.

3.

The next thing Frank did was try to stab Zed in the eye.

He was disappointed but not surprised when the blade made no mark on the stone skin.

Next Frank set the knife on the stage and let go. It didn't snap back to Trevor's hand. The Tools didn't seem to follow the same rules as the rest of the things in this place. Frank walked over to where Will lay on the stage. The lighter with the broken clock symbol lay on the ground next to him.

Frank picked up the lighter, opened it, and flicked the thumb wheel. It lit on the first try. Good. He had fire and a weapon. He was becoming pretty advanced by caveman standards. What else?

He suddenly thought of Zed's pocket watch. Was there a chance Zed had it on him? Frank walked to Zed and immediately saw the pocket watch. Zed held it clutched in his left hand.

No matter how Frank tried, he couldn't get the watch out of Zed's stone-like hand. He tried cutting and prying with the knife blade, and he tried burning Zed's hand with the lighter. Neither worked. He couldn't get the watch away from Zed.

Well, at least he had fire. Now if only he had something to cook. His eyes drifted to the Unfeathered. No. Not yet. He wouldn't eat that abomination unless he had no other choice.

Frank wandered over to the fountain with its motionless streams of water hanging in the air. He knew he couldn't drink them, but they sure looked wet. His thirst was beginning to get the better of him. He stabbed the water with the knife. The blade bounced off. He lit the lighter and dropped it onto the water. It hit water's solid surface with a thud.

He had to move on. This fountain was only making him thirstier.

Just as he was about to pick up the lighter, something

occurred to him. He pressed the broken clock symbol on the lighter. For a moment, nothing happened. Then the water began to change. Moisture pooled up around the lighter and it slowly began to sink. The water was melting. Like ice.

The lighter had brought the dead Birdie back to life. It was doing the same for the water.

Frank forced himself to wait until there was a good size puddle around the lighter. It was submerged, but the flame didn't go out. Frank reached into the water and grabbed the lighter. Then he sank his face into the pool and drank with long thirsty gulps. He couldn't help but laugh as he felt the wetness dripping down his face. He had water. He had a weapon. He had fire.

He might be able to survive in this place.

4.

Frank took another bite of the meat and wiped his greasy fingers on the tattered remains of his pants. It wasn't exactly delicious, but he wasn't eating for pleasure. He had to keep his strength up.

By his estimation, he had been there for a little more than two weeks. It was difficult to tell because there was no night. There was always the same amount of hazy light coming from the sky. He tried to use his body to judge the passing time. He slept until his bladder woke him up, and then he stayed awake until his body had told him to eat three times, and then he slept again. It wasn't an exact science but it was all he had. He was starting to wonder how much sleep he was really getting, though. The last few days he had felt dead tired.

He had gotten over his squeamishness at eating the Unfeathered. Killing them was easy; they didn't notice him until the moment he cut their throats. The real trick turned out to be cooking them. While he did have fire, he didn't have anything that would burn. Wood, paper, fabric; they were all inflammable here. Luckily he remembered Will's little on-stage demonstration with the head. The Unfeathered themselves were pretty flammable. So he lit the meat, waited until it was nicely charred, and put it out. It wasn't tasty, but it worked.

He had learned to cook only small pieces of the meat at a time. As Will had demonstrated, the lighter seemed to temporarily bring things back to life. Frank had discovered with small enough pieces of meat it was difficult to tell whether it was alive.

He'd spent much of his time looking for the other Tools. He had the knife and the lighter, but the cane, the mirror, and the key were all still missing. He'd searched the shed at the cabin. He'd searched Will and Christine's house. No luck. Will and Christine had hidden the other Tools somewhere new. He found the coin at Sean's house, but he decided to leave that one where it lay.

He'd also spent time discovering the limitations of the Tools. The lighter unpaused liquids, but it didn't seem to have any effect on solids. He could drink water, juice, and sodas as long as he could remove the lid long enough to apply a flame directly to paused liquid. Applying the flame to food items with high water content like applesauce produced a mixed result—the water eventually drained out, but the solid portion remained paused. The lighter had no effect on the humans or solid foods.

Frank had become skilled at avoiding the Ones Who Sing. It was all about watching the Unfeathered and clearing out when they did. The few times he had gotten caught, Frank fought off the Ones Who Sing with minimal damage. The real trouble was any time he went to sleep. By the time their song was loud enough to wake him, it was too late.

It had only happened once so far, but he had been lucky to escape. Even still, they had taken a small piece of his ear before he managed to fight them off.

He couldn't live like that forever, he knew. Some night he would wake to find them too thick to escape. They considered him an enemy now, and the song said, *"Come to us as an enemy and we will take your life."*

He had to figure something out.

He'd been thinking a lot about the song they sang to him on his first day. *"Come to us as a dog to its master and we will give you food. Come to us as a friend and we will take your flesh. Come to us as an enemy and we will take your life."* He understood all of that. But there had been another part.

"Come to us as a master to his dog and we will give you three truths."

That was the part he kept thinking about. What were the three truths? Would they tell him how to get out of there? And how exactly did a master come to his dog? With confidence? With love? He didn't know.

Three days later, he was sleeping near the fountain when they came. That was the moment, half asleep, that he figured it out.

As they swarmed around him, he began to whistle.

5.

At first, the whistling didn't seem to do anything. The shapes sped around him, brushing past him, cutting him, singing their haunting song. Then Frank listened for a moment and adjusted his whistle. He matched the pitch to the song.

Suddenly, for the first time, he could hear them as individuals instead of as part of the whole.

"He joins!"

"A new voice in the song! A little voice!"

"The Little One has joined the song."

Frank kept whistling.

Then, as one, the shapes sang, *"Three truths are yours to know. What three truths would you ask, Little One?"*

Frank wasn't sure how he felt about being called Little One, but at least they weren't cutting pieces off of him. He said, "How do I return home?"

The voices separated and babbled too quickly to follow, as if they were conferring among themselves. Then they said, *"You are home, Little One. Are you not of Rook Mountain?"*

"Yes, but how do I get back into time?"

"Ah, there's a wiser question, Little One. Time is a prison for your kind. It's a river that carries you so fast that you cannot experience the sights on the passing banks. Why do you wish to return to your prison?"

"I—I need to help my friends who are there."

"You are locked outside of time, Little One. You wear the lock around your neck. You must unlock it with the key."

"The key?" Frank asked. "What if I don't have a key?"

"Then find it. Or make it. Or pick the lock. Are you not the people who build powerful machines to cough smoke into the air and who traveled to the moon itself? Can you truly not open a lock? You try our patience, Little One. Ask your second question."

Frank thought hard before speaking. He had heard too many stories of genies and wishes to screw it up. They didn't seem to be counting follow up questions, so that was something.

"There is a man named Zed. How do I kill him?"

The voices rumbled in something like anger. *"We know of this man. The boy who found the watch. Or was it the watch who found the boy?"*

The throng seemed to be at odds on this matter, but the voices soon reunified and continued. *"He has taken the Town of Rook Mountain and moved it out of the river of time. He has put it into a stagnant pool where time cannot flow and the town will grow putrid. He sent you and the other two as peace offerings, but we are not at peace. He cannot be killed by any means we know, Little One, or he would be dead."*

"Then how can I put Rook Mountain back in the… river of time?"

"That is the same thing you asked before. Your kind will always be in the river unless they are locked out of it. For Rook Mountain, there is another lock and another key. You risk our anger by repeating your questions, Little One. Ask your last question, and we will give your last truth."

Frank's mind was racing. One last question. Before he could even think, he blurted it out. "Where's my brother? Where is Jake Hinkle?"

"Ah, we know this name, too. We know it well. He is our—" Here the voices split once again and Frank heard multiple words at once.

"Friend."

"Enemy."

"Rival."

"Champion."

"Oppressor."

"Brother."

The voices joined back together. *"The one you speak of stands outside the river of time. He stands on its edge like a fisherman, pulling out those who swim by as it suits him."*

"Is he locked out, too?"

Another babbling laugh. *"No, Little One. He chose to step out. We do not know all, but we do know this: you will never see Jake Hinkle again."*

Frank started to speak, but the voices cut him off.

"Little One, will you join us? Will you join our throng?"

Frank looked out at the shapes around him. They almost appeared to be dancing.

"Join us. Your kind flows in the river of time, but the river of time flows in us. Join us and time will be your plaything."

Frank thought of Trevor, still standing on the stage holding out his hand. "Would I be able to help my friends?"

The babbling laugh came again. *"No, those Little Ones will be of no consequence to you once you are in our throng. They matter no more than a flash of light at the edge of the universe."*

"Then no," Frank said. "I won't join you."

"Very well, Little One. We will not answer your call again. Next time we see you, we will take your flesh."

Frank held up the knife. "And I will take yours." But they were already gone.

Frank held the gold loop dangling from his necklace up to his face. He tried to see it as a lock. If he were designing a lock like this, how would he do it? How would it open? The Ones Who Sing had told him to find a key. There was only one key in this town that might work to unlock the necklace. He just had to find it.

It took a very long time, but he did.

THE UNREGULATED (PART 3)

Jake Hinkle sped through town, frantically looking in his mirrors and expecting to see the flashing lights of a squad car closing in on him. So far there didn't seem to be anybody following him. That was a good thing, because once they arrested him, he would have missed his opportunity. He would either join Frank in prison or—more likely—he would join Todd in the morgue. Those things couldn't happen. Not yet. There was more left to do.

He wondered where they would look for him first. There were a couple of possibilities. The most obvious was home. He'd give anything to kiss Christine and hold Trevor one more time. But he couldn't do either of those things, and probably would never do either of those things again, because home would be the first place they would look for him. If he went there, he would be captured. He wouldn't get to do the other thing, the thing he needed to do for his family.

Another possibility was the cabins. Two of them were empty with Frank and Brett gone. He could probably go there and hide out for a while. He knew those woods like no one else, save maybe Christine. He could evade them for a good long time if he didn't mind living wild. But all that would do was delay the inevitable. It wouldn't help his friends or family. Eventually, he would slip up or they would get lucky.

There was only one destination. He had to go there, even though going there would mean the end of him.

He reached the house at a little after two in the morning. She should be home by now, and, if he knew the owner of this house, she would be awake, maybe winding down with a glass of wine while watching old episodes of The Twilight Zone on Blu-ray.

He took a deep breath and knocked, rapping on the door frame three times with his knuckles. Twenty seconds later the porch light came on and the curtains rustled as she peeked out. Then the door opened a crack.

"Jake, what are you doing here?" Wendy asked. "You scared the hell out of me."

"Sorry. Let me in. We need to talk."

"Is everything okay?"

He shook his head. "It's bad. I need your help."

She opened the door and shooed him in. Jake saw a half empty glass of red wine on the end table. The TV was on.

"No!" a voice said from the TV. "No, it's nothing of the sort! I didn't blow the lights out. I swear I didn't! Someone's pulling a gag or something!"

The Twilight Zone.

Another voice from the TV said, "A gag? A gag? Charlie, there's a man lying dead in the street, and you killed him. Does that look like a gag to you?"

Wendy turned off the TV and sat down on the couch. Her face was drawn with concern. "Tell me."

He told her, starting with Zed showing up. He told her

about shooting Zed and about Zed shooting Todd and the cops.

"So he knows?" Wendy asked. "He knows about us?"

Jake shook his head. "I don't think so. He only knows that Todd and I are involved."

Wendy stood up and started pacing. "We have to call the others. We have to meet right away. Talk this through."

"No. Wendy, listen. We only have one chance. The mirror."

Wendy shook her head. "That's a long shot at best. And even if it does work, we have no idea how long it will take to bring back help. It could be years. Decades. And what are the rest of us supposed to do during that time?"

"You'll wait. You'll be model citizens. You won't meet with each other again and you'll follow every Regulation to the letter. You'll publicly and vocally support Zed and his cronies. You'll give them no reason to suspect you of anything."

"Jake, that's crazy. If we don't stand up to them what's been the point of any of this? They win."

"What's the alternative? This is our shot."

Wendy's face was pale. Jake saw it from her point of view. She had been relaxing in front of the TV in her t-shirt and yoga pants, and in came Jake to tell her that her friend was dead and that the secret war they had been waging for the last six months was over. When he looked at it that way, she was actually taking it pretty well. She sat down on the couch next to him.

"Look, it's not an ideal solution," Jake said, "but I don't know what else to do. This thing... we've been doing our best for a while now, but it isn't working. We aren't going to beat him head-on the way we wanted to. The mirror is our only chance. It's ugly, but it's the only way Trevor and the rest of the kids in this town have a chance at growing up as anything but slaves."

Wendy sighed. "Fine."

"Fine? Like, you agree?"

"Fine like I agree. I only have one favor to ask. Let me be the one to do it."

Jake gritted his teeth. They were wasting time. "That won't work."

"Of course it will," she said. "You have a family. I disappear, who cares? Your son needs you. Don't make him grow up without you."

"Wendy, that doesn't make sense. I'm the one they're after. It has to be me. I don't go and I'm under arrest or dead in the next eight hours."

"Maybe we could frame it so I did the crimes. I could leave a note—"

"Wendy!" he said, a little louder than he had intended. "You know it has to be me. I appreciate the offer. Your heart is in the right place and I'll never forget it. But you know I'm right."

Finally Wendy said, "I'll get the mirror."

She walked out of the living room and left Jake sitting on the couch. He saw the glass of wine and wondered if she had anything stronger. He sure could use a shot of Tennessee whiskey. He couldn't do that, though. He needed his wits for what was about to happen.

Wendy returned and gave him the hand-held mirror. The broken clock symbol was intricately carved on the handle.

"Do you have a..." He mimed cutting his finger.

"Oh. Yeah, let me get something." She returned a moment later with a large serrated kitchen knife.

"Thanks," he said. He set the mirror on his lap and held

his index finger over it. Then he stopped, remembering something. "Do you have some paper? And an envelope?"

"Of course."

Writing it took a while. Words didn't come easy to him in the best of times, and now was not the best of times. Wendy waited quietly, not rushing him. He finished his message, folded up the paper, and stuck it in the envelope.

"When Trevor gets older, old enough to understand, will you give this to him?"

Wendy nodded.

"I'm coming back. I am. But... just in case. There's some things I want to tell him."

"I'll give it to him."

He sighed and picked up the knife. "And ask Will to... to take care of my family."

Wendy nodded again. "Any message for Christine?"

Jake shook his head. "She knows. She knows anything I could want to tell her. She knows what I'm gonna say before I say it. She always has." Jake smiled. "She is going to be pissed, though. I promised her we'd play darts to see who got to use this thing."

Tears leapt into Jake's eyes as he brought the knife toward his skin. Would he ever see his family again? "Wendy," he said, "I'm scared."

Wendy said nothing, but she put an arm around his shoulder.

Jake took a deep breath and nodded to her. She stepped back. He slid the blade hard across the meat of his index finger. Blood pooled around the cut. Jake turned his finger over and let the blood drip onto the mirror. The surface of the mirror shimmered when the blood hit it.

"See ya, Wendy," Jake said. He fell into the mirror.

9

THE BROKEN CLOCK

I.

The moment Zed cut his own throat Christine knew she was in trouble.

She and Will had talked late into the night trying to decide what to do. They had at times argued and at times agreed. They had changed each others' minds and then changed them back. The central point of discussion was that they had been waiting for eight years to make their move, so why exactly were they still waiting?

At first they had been waiting for Jake to return. They had followed his instructions. They stopped meeting and even socializing with Wendy and Sean, the other two remaining members of the Unregulated. But Christine and Will hadn't stopped seeing each other. As they kept more secrets from everyone else in Rook Mountain, their bond grew stronger. Part of it was the honesty they shared only with each other, but the other part of the bond was how deeply and profoundly they both missed Jake.

It was Christine who first brought up that perhaps they should start dating and eventually marry. It made sense from a logistical perspective. They spent so much time together already. And getting remarried would prove to the town that she had moved on. It would help people to stop seeing her killer husband every time they saw her face. So they had dated and gotten married as quickly as seemed appropriate. They had discussed the idea calmly and rationally, but it quickly became clear that it was much more than a marriage of convenience. As they spent more time together, their feelings for each other grew. They were two people living in a desperate situation, and soon they were desperately in love.

So they had remained undercover, living their new lives with Christine as the town doctor and Will teaching high school and eventually taking over the delivery of the certification program. They were polite, community-minded citizens. They told themselves they were doing it all for Trevor and to protect the coin, and that they were only waiting for the right opportunity to take Zed down.

But last night, talking in the garage until the wee hours of the morning, they had realized they might be using carefulness as an excuse to maintain their comfort. What exactly were they waiting for? They had the best chance of anyone in town of taking out Zed. They had five Tools. That was more than Zed himself. And they had reason to believe that they might be able to hurt him with the knife. Christine had seen Zed's face when Frank pulled it out at City Hall. The knife, she was convinced, was the one thing in town that might be able to hurt him.

Acting now was dangerous. They discussed all the usual reasons for inaction: protecting Trevor, giving Jake a chance to do what he needed to do, not wanting the Tools to fall into Zed's hands if they failed. But all the usual reasons seemed hollow. Frank's life was on the line. If they didn't act now, when would they? Sure, it might be putting Trevor at risk, but maybe safety wasn't worth selling your soul.

So they had devised a plan. The knife for Zed and the lighter and the resurrected head to keep the townsfolk at bay. Christine had fully intended to slash Zed's throat whether he let Frank go or not, so she was more than a little surprised when Zed did it for her.

Zed cut his throat, took the knife, and threw it on the ground. He put out the fire, and then Christine felt a police officer tackling her, pinning her to the ground. His knee pushed into the small of her back with painful force, but she was beyond such things. She noticed the pain only as a distant annoyance. Everything took on an air of unreality for her. Her only clear thought played on a loop in her brain: we failed. After waiting eight years, they had taken their shot and failed.

She turned her head as much as she could with her face pressed into the ground, and she saw Will in a similar position. His eyes met hers and she saw the same look of despair on his face that she felt on her own.

Zed was talking, speaking to the crowd as he so loved to do, but Christine wasn't listening. She kept her eyes on her husband. There was no one coming to save them. Jake's mission to bring back reinforcements from Wendy's mirror had failed. All the years of trying to protect Trevor were for naught—even worse, he was in Zed's pocket at that terrible school. Would he be an outcast after this, or would Zed draw him in even deeper?

Christine stared into her husband's eyes and tried to convey what she felt, the one message she desperately wanted to give him. We tried. No regrets.

If she understood Regulation 19 correctly—and she was sure she didn't; no one did at this point—the only possible sentence for her and Will was to be sent 'Away.' The only question was for how long. It was a fairly genius plan really, Christine had to admit. There was something terrifying about serving a ten-year sentence right now in some unknown land, serving the whole sentence in what seemed like the blink of an eye to any onlookers. That was much more terrifying than the prospect of twenty years in NTCC. And now, with Earl's suddenly missing fingers, it would be even more frightening.

Christine squeezed her eyes shut. Whatever 'Away' meant, she and Will would have a firsthand look soon. Regulation 19 didn't seem to leave a lot of room for appeal. The only reason it had taken Frank so long to be sentenced was that Zed had to build that necklace with the gold loop. Now that it was complete, assuming Zed had made more than one of them, it was entirely possible Christine and Will would be convicted and sentenced right on the stage in mere moments. She only hoped that wherever they ended up, they would be together.

Christine twisted her head to see Frank. Two police officers held his arms. Zed approached him, saying things that were meant to sound formal and official, but were really another way of saying, "You're screwed." Zed reached out, touched the gold loop on Frank's necklace, and Frank was gone.

Christine felt herself gasp. It came out much louder than she would have expected considering she was being crushed by a two-hundred-pound cop. Then she realized it wasn't only her own voice she was hearing, but it was the sound of the crowd who had gasped along with her.

This wasn't like the last two times. Those had been shocking enough with the convicted suddenly changing right in front of the crowd, their outward appearance evidence of the time they had spent in the Away. This was different, and, as bad as those first two were, this was worse.

Frank wasn't changed; he was gone. He hadn't been killed; he simply no longer existed. He was gone and he would never return. A wave of nausea washed over Christine. A life had been taken out of the world in a wholly unnatural way. The laws of the universe, both the laws of nature and the laws of morality, had been broken. Christine looked into the crowd and from the disturbed looks on some of their faces, she knew she wasn't the only one feeling it.

Christine turned and noticed Trevor for the first time. When had he stepped onto the stage? He was squatting near where Frank had been a moment ago. He was staring at his outstretched empty hand.

Zed turned and opened his mouth to speak, then stopped. He looked at the crowd for a long moment, and Christine realized he was gauging them, checking their temperature. He had been about to make a triumphant speech, but the bastard was so in tune with his audience that he caught himself. He course corrected even before speaking.

"My friends," he said. "Our path is not easy, and our burden is not light. We do what we do for our children and for the future of this great town. Believe me, I take no joy in what we've had to do. No joy at all. And sadly our work today is not yet done." Zed looked at Will, then at Christine.

Christine's heart sank. She had hoped she would have a little time, maybe to explain things to Trevor, but clearly that was not to be the case. Zed stared at her, his lips pressed together. The effect made his wide smile even more eerie than usual.

A high, long note suddenly filled the air and Christine

instinctively put her hands over her ears. For a moment she thought it was the song of the Unfeathered—it had the same otherworldly feel to it, but it didn't quite sound like them. It sounded like someone whistling.

Christine turned to the crowd and her eyes searched for the source of the sound. She noticed that everyone was looking upward. The sound was coming from above. Her eyes moved up, and she scanned the sky, looking for the Unfeathered. Then she saw him.

Christine gasped. His hair hung past his shoulders and it was more gray than black. He was dressed in strategically tied rags of denim and what looked like an old t-shirt. His face was a crisscross of scars. But there was no mistaking him.

Frank Hinkle stood on the edge of the roof of City Hall, and he was whistling.

2.

The first thing that hit Frank was the light. After living in the cold, diffused glow of the Away for so long, he had forgotten how hot sunlight felt. It hit him like a physical blow. He had trouble gaining his balance and almost tumbled off the roof. What an ending to the grand plan that would have been. He had intended to start whistling the moment he arrived, but that damn light.

He had spent a long time—days? weeks? so hard to tell—trying to find the exact right place to reappear. He had squeezed himself in between stone-statue bodies in the crowd, checked out nearly every possible line of sight in the crowd itself, and even thought about appearing right behind Zed so he could give him a nice sucker punch right in the kidney.

But in the end he had decided that what he was after was shock and awe. The rooftop gave him that and more. From up here it all seemed so manageable and small. It looked like a problem to be solved rather than a city to be saved. He might not be a hero but he had always been a problem solver. He'd gotten back, hadn't he?

He guessed that it had taken him about two years to find the key. That might have been wildly inaccurate. One of the worst parts of the Away had been the absence of the passage of time. His body felt it—oh, how it felt it—but the rest of the world was at a standstill. He aged without knowing how much.

He had started whistling at the Unfeathered one day out of boredom. It had been a day when his belly was full and he couldn't stand to look for the key anymore. The idea occurred to him that if he could imitate the song of the Ones Who Sing, maybe he could learn to imitate the Unfeathered, too.

It hadn't been easy. It had taken a long time, but he had managed to blend in with their song. Even though they couldn't seem to see him, they were able to hear him. Or at least hear his whistle. The Unfeathered in the Away didn't sing often, so that made it more difficult. Over time, he had begun to notice the subtleties in their song. The long, slow call of the 'I've found a safe place' song. The sharp piercing notes of the 'Danger! Flee!' song. The rapid trill of the 'Help!' song.

It had been a fun distraction at first, and then he began using it as a tool. He called the Unfeathered to him as he worked and used them as an early detection system for the Ones Who Sing. He called them when he needed to kill one for food. He sent them away when their smell began to bother him. A few times he had even caused them to attack the Ones Who Sing just to see if he could do it. But they never attacked him. When he whistled, they saw him as one of their own.

After a long while, he had thought of how they might fit into his plan for Rook Mountain.

He'd search the town street by street, house by house. He'd started with any place that had a connection to Will, Christine, Sean, or Wendy. When that hadn't turned up anything, he'd started a more systematic search of the town. Finally, in an office building on the south side of town, he'd discovered an office with Will's name on the door. There was a closet in the office with one of Frank's locks on it. Inside he had found the cane, the mirror, and the key.

Now he stood on the roof of City Hall and whistled a sharp series of notes. The song was high and loud. It was the 'Help!' song. The song that would bring them most quickly. The song that would ensure they attacked everything in sight. The song that would override the effects of the daylight and of Zed's mysterious empty box.

They came even more quickly than he had anticipated. They filled the sky, little moving clusters of white coming from all directions of the compass. Frank kept whistling as he watched their aerial dance. These Unfeathered were quicker than the ones he had grown familiar with in the Away. He had forgotten how deadly the Birdies here could be. He had a moment's doubt—had he doomed the people of Rook Mountain by calling the Unfeathered down?—but he didn't stop whistling.

They came from all directions, but they gathered around him. They swarmed above him like a cloud, a deadly mass of wings, beaks, and claws. He changed the timbre of his whistle, trying to calm them, keep them from attacking as long as he could. He needed them right where they were—above City Hall.

The people in the crowd fled. They ran to their vehicles, into nearby stores, the high school and middle school buildings. But most importantly to Frank, they ran away.

Only a few ran into City Hall. Police officers and the members of Zed's inner circle. Frank knew that only the most dedicated Zed Heads would be thinking of capturing little Frank Hinkle while the sky was filled with monsters.

He only had a few moments. It wouldn't be long before police officers burst through the trapdoor that led to the roof and took Frank down. He couldn't afford to wait much longer. He looked down toward the ground and saw—thank God—that Christine, Will, and Trevor were all out of sight. He only hoped they would know what to do with what he had left them. A lone figure stood on the stage looking up at him. It was hard to tell from this distance, but Frank was almost certain Zed wasn't smiling.

Frank let out a long high note—the call to attack—and the cloud of Unfeathered dove toward the ground.

There was no controlling them now. He had released the feral creatures on the people of Rook Mountain and there would be no take backs.

The flock spread out as they neared the ground. Many pursued the poor members of the crowd who were still searching for cover, but a good-sized group of the creatures headed for the stage—for Zed. A swarm of at least ten Unfeathered fell on him, and he disappeared from sight as they attacked, their beaks raining down with relentless speed. Frank was certain it wouldn't kill Zed, but it would keep him busy for a few minutes.

Frank's need for the Unfeathered was over. He stopped whistling and turned away from the carnage on the ground.

Frank had thought long and hard about what would happen next. He had played out the possible outcomes in his mind hundreds of times and only about half of them ended with him doing any lasting good for the people of Rook Mountain. Even less of the outcomes ended with him surviving the next thirty minutes.

He had planned things out as well as he could, as well as he knew how to in the Away, but a lot had to fall into place for them to have any chance. So much depended on Will, Christine, and Trevor. So much depended on the board of selectmen. So much depended on Zed. Trust was most definitely a must.

Frank stood on the roof and waited for them to arrive.

3.

"Will! Will!"

Will heard his name being called as if from a distance. His eyes were glued to his old friend standing on the roof of City Hall, his suddenly gray hair blowing in the wind. The man up there barely looked human, and he certainly didn't sound it. A mass of white creatures circled above his head. The people around Will were screaming and running away, but he still laid on the stage, transfixed by his friend's dramatic reappearance.

"Will!" the voice said again. Will looked in front of him and saw a pair of sneakered feet. He also saw the open knife on the ground next to his hand. Somehow it must have gotten lost in the skirmish between Zed and Christine. Will reached forward and picked it up. He felt the familiar jolt he always experienced when he touched one of the Tools, and he felt himself beginning to drift.

"Will!" The voice was sharp this time, its patience gone.

Will looked up and saw Trevor staring down at him. Maybe it was the angle, but Trevor looked more grown up than he ever had before.

"Will, we gotta go."

Will nodded absently. He wasn't sure if it was the way he had been knocked to the ground or the events unfolding around him, but everything seemed unreal. It all seemed distant. He shook his head to clear it. Trevor needed him. Christine needed him.

Will said, "Let's get to the car, fast. Where's your mother?"

"No," Trevor said. It wasn't a defiant no, the one Will was so used to hearing lately; it was a 'you don't understand' no. "The police officers. Zed. The selectmen. They all ran into City Hall. They're going after Uncle Frank. We have to help him."

He almost started to say something like, "How are we supposed to help him?" or "We already tried," but he saw the determined, man-with-a-job-to-do look on Trevor's face. It was a look Will had seen on Jake's face many times over the years. A looked of righteous resolve. There would be no talking the kid out of this. And, Will had to admit, Trevor was right. If ever Frank needed their help, it was now. Even if Will had no earthly idea how they could help him.

Will looked down at the knife in his hand and sighed. It was something. It might not be able to cut Zed's throat, but it was something.

Will nodded to Trevor. "Let's go." They stepped off the stage and turned toward City Hall. Then Will stopped. "Wait. Where's your mom?"

At that moment, Frank's whistle from above changed into a high pitched single note, and, like a rain, the Unfeathered descended on them.

They were only fifteen feet from the doors of City Hall. Will threw his arm around Trevor's shoulders and pulled him toward the door. He glanced back at the stage and saw a pile of white wings where Zed had been a moment before. The man would have his work cut out for him getting out of there.

Will grabbed the door to City Hall and pulled it open. He shoved Trevor inside and then followed him, pulling the door shut behind him.

"Your mom," Will said. "Did you see where she went?"

Trevor shook his head. His eyes were still on the attacking Unfeathered outside. "I saw her running. I think she was heading this direction, but I'm not sure." The look of confidence melted from his face. He looked like a scared little boy again, the same way he had looked when Jake had disappeared years ago.

Will put a hand on his shoulder. "I'm sure she made it. She's probably ten steps ahead of us as usual."

Trevor nodded. He turned and glanced down the hallway. "Do you know how to get to the roof?"

Before Will could answer, the door burst open behind them. Greg Darrow stumbled in, his suit rumpled and his hair uncharacteristically messy. He was carrying a baseball bat. Greg was on the board of selectmen. In the days before becoming a Zed Head, he had been a burnout stoner who delivered pizzas, but he had taken to the bureaucratic life-style quickly, traded weed for whiskey, and gained thirty pounds to fill out his cheap suits.

The walkie-talkie clipped to Greg's belt chirped to life. "Darrow! Get your ass up there! Meet on the roof."

Greg Darrow glanced down the hallway, his eyes finding the doorways, scanning them as if looking for the most welcoming candidate.

"Now!" yelled the voice coming from the walkie-talkie. Darrow licked his lips and glanced at Will and Trevor. Then he nodded, as if to himself.

Will had been in the presence of selectmen many times. As the head of the Certification program, he could hardly avoid it. They always prided themselves on their signature entrances and exits. They stepped into a closet or an empty room and shut the door. There was a flash of blue light and they were gone. Will had often wondered what it would be like to be behind that closed door and watch as they disappeared. Would they blink out of existence and reappear elsewhere at the same moment? Would it be like Star Trek, with their bodies slowly dissolving?

As he watched Greg Darrow, Will got his answer.

Greg closed his eyes and pushed his fingers into his temples. His head began to vibrate. Then Greg Darrow melted.

It started with his feet. His shoes seemed to liquefy and drip onto the floor. Then his socks and the lower part of his pants oozed away. Then the skin of his feet melted, joining the liquefied goo puddling under him. Blood first seeped and then poured from his exposed muscles and blood vessels until they too melted. The baseball bat in his hand melted and joined the puddle on the floor. The process worked its way upward and inward, his pants, underwear and shirt dissolving so that his torso was left naked for only a moment until the skin melted and his inner layers were exposed.

Will heard Trevor gasp as Greg's stomach muscles disappeared and his intestines spilled out of their cavity, flopping onto the floor with a splash of blood before they too melted away. Their last glimpse of Darrow was his skinless face floating atop his liquefied body, his mouth open in a silent scream and his brain beginning to show through his melting skull. Then there was a flash of blue light and the whole mess of him disappeared.

Will looked at the clean spot where the liquefied remains of a human being had been only moments before. "Damn. Guess that's why they close the door."

"Will, look," Trevor said. He was pointing toward a door marked STAIRS.

"Let's go," Will said.

Trevor went through the door first and dashed up the stairs. Will followed, pushing himself to keep up. Whatever was at the top of those stairs, Will didn't want Trevor facing it alone.

As they ran, Will thought back to that day on Rook Mountain. The day he killed Jessie Cooper. Maybe if he had been brave enough to break his precious cover things would be different today. He had held onto to his cover for far too long. What he had rationalized as caution was really cowardice. The time spent living with his family, even under the oppression of Zed and the Regulations, had been a precious time. But this—standing up to Zed with his family by his side—was even better.

Trevor reached the top of the steps and started up the ladder to the roof. Will stayed right behind him. Trevor stepped out onto the roof and froze. Will followed, grabbed his stepson and stepped in front of him. He didn't know what Trevor had seen, but he wanted to protect Trevor from whatever it was. Then Will saw it too.

Christine stood near the corner of the roof, a gun in her hand. Three selectmen and the city manager stood in a semi-circle around her. Christine waved the gun back and forth, trying to cover all of them at the same time.

A man lay on the floor between them, a thin stream of blood running from his right ear. It was Frank.

Something hit Will in the back like a sledgehammer. He fell forward, hitting the floor face first. He felt Trevor land on his back a split second later. Then he heard the voice behind him, and the blood seemed to freeze in his veins.

"Excuse me, gentlemen," Zed said.

4.

A moment after Christine noticed Frank standing on the roof of City Hall, she felt the police officer who had been pinning her to the ground roll off. She turned and saw Sean. He had his gun held to the head of the other officer.

"Go," Sean said to Christine. "Help him if you can."

Christine nodded. She reached down, unbuckled the other police officer's holster, and pulled out the man's gun. He grunted his protest, but Christine was already on her feet.

"Let her take it," Sean said to the other officer.

"Thanks," Christine said. Sean nodded.

She looked around the stage and saw that most eyes were still on Frank and the Unfeathered swirling above him. She had to get to Frank before they did. She didn't know what would come next, but she didn't want Frank to face it alone. She turned and ran for City Hall. Christine was inside before the Unfeathered attacked. She paused and looked back, but it was too late. Tears filled her eyes. She knew there was nothing she could do to help Will and Trevor. She had to trust that they would take care of each other. She sprinted to the top of the stairs, hoping she could reach the roof hatch before the Zed Heads did.

At the top, she saw a ladder leading up to an open hatch.

She climbed and stuck her head through. Frank was only a few feet in front of her.

"Hurry! We have to get out of here!"

Frank dropped to his knees. He blinked hard and looked her up and down. It was as if he hadn't seen her in a long time. Christine realized he probably hadn't. There was no denying that Frank looked older even aside from his harshly graying hair. The scars crisscrossing his face probably did little to help, but there were also deep wrinkles on his face, a face so pale it looked like it hadn't been touched by sunlight in years.

She stepped out onto the roof and gave him a hug. He flinched at her touch and didn't hug her back.

"Come on," she said.

Frank shook his head. "No. They're almost here. Listen. The Tools are behind the..." His voice trailed off as he pointed toward the air conditioning unit mounted on the roof next to him. Frank sounded hoarse, and he spoke hesitantly as if unsure of his words.

She looked behind the air conditioner. There they were on the floor. The mirror. The key. The cane. "Where did you get these?" Christine asked.

"Will's office."

She reached down to grab the mirror. A flash of blue light and a pool of thick liquid appeared on the floor next to her. She instinctively took a step back. The smell of the stuff hit her—a rotten, tangy smell—and her stomach turned. The middle of the liquid swirled, revealing a human face. A head formed around the face, and then a neck and a torso. The liquid swirled across the forming body adding muscle to bone, skin to muscle, and finally clothes. The whole process couldn't have taken more than five seconds, and now Selectman Nate Grayson stood before them. A final bit of liquid bridged the gap between Grayson's right hand and the floor, and suddenly he was holding a baseball bat.

Grayson moved before Christine had a chance to react. He took a step toward Frank and swung the bat like a slugger aiming for the stands. He connected, and Frank went down with a groan.

Christine brought the gun up and pointed it at Nate. "Drop the bat, Nate! I will shoot you dead if you so much as raise it again."

Nate glared at her and a guttural growl escaped his throat. His face was pure hatred. He dropped the bat. "There are Regulations for people like you," he said slowly. "You will pay very soon."

Another puddle materialized across the roof, and two other puddles appears a split second later. The first puddle solidified, and Becky Raymond stood facing them. Another Selectman joined her a moment later. Then another. Then there were four of them. It was four against two.

Christine moved behind Frank, trying her best to protect him, moving the barrel of her gun between Becky Raymond and the selectmen, trying her best to cover all of them at once. They weren't attacking, but they weren't backing off, either.

Frank raised himself to his hands and knees and groaned.

The four people looking at Christine reminded her more of rabid animals than government officials. This was a standoff she was destined to lose. If she thought she could shoot them all, she would have done it, but she sensed the other three would charge the instant she fired.

The trapdoor burst open and Christine's heart simultaneously leapt and plummeted as first Trevor and then Will stepped through. Her family was alive, but they probably wouldn't be alive for long.

Then Zed arrived.

5.

Frank heard the voice before he saw Zed. He was still looking at the ground, trying to get his head straight. Even getting to his knees had felt like crawling out of a spinning washing machine. There was no way he was standing up anytime soon. Even through his daze and his ringing ears, he recognized that voice, the last voice he had heard before going Away. The voice of the man he had come here to stop.

He raised his head and looked at Zed. As he did, he saw some blood on the ground and wondered where it was leaking out of him.

Zed stepped forward. His clothes were torn in dozens of places, but he seemed uninjured. Not bad for a man who had just been attacked by a flock of giant bird monsters.

Frank noticed Will and Trevor sprawled on the ground near him. Bad guys up, good guys down. Things weren't going as well as he had hoped. Except for Christine of course. She was still standing, pointing that gun at anyone and everyone.

That damn smile was back on Zed's face. "Are you going to shoot me, doctor? Your first husband tried that. If I remember correctly, he was never seen again."

"It might not kill you, but it would be cathartic," Christine said.

Zed bent down next to Frank. "Now what are we going to do with you?"

Frank tried to answer and instantly wished he hadn't. All that came out was a pathetic grunt. He took a slow breath, and then reached into his pocket and took out the Fox, the lock Wendy gave him the day before he was sent away. He slid it across the ground to Will.

"Lock it," Frank said. He was grateful that words came out at all, and that Will understood. Will closed the lock through the latch on the trapdoor.

"What did you do?" Becky Raymond asked. "The trapdoor looks all... fuzzy. Like it's not there."

Nate Grayson looked up at Zed, panic in his eyes. "They did something. I can't melt off this roof. I know I can't."

"Nobody leaves," Frank said. His voice was little more than a groan. "We finish this here."

Zed sighed, but he was still smiling. "I've tried really hard not to kill you. You have a mind that... well, it's remarkable. Somehow you've closed it up tight. And the locks! They are marvelous. For example, that necklace lock came from your subconscious. Guess I shouldn't be surprised you eventually managed to unlock it. In another time and another place, you could have been great. But you never get out of your own way. You have all these ideas brewing in there and no clue what to do with them. You lack the resolve, the confidence to do something special. You have original ideas, but you lack originality. You are completely predictable."

Frank saw Will helping Trevor to his feet.

Zed stood up and stretched. He had an oddly distant look in his eyes. "There are Tools here. I can feel it... I've never felt so many of them in the same place."

"It enhances your powers, doesn't it?" Frank asked. "Having all these Tools together makes you stronger."

Frank was looking at Zed, but he was really talking to Will. Frank knew that he had to get the knife into Will's hands. Will and his gift at figuring out the purpose of each

Tool. Wendy had told Frank the Tools were meant to be used together. Frank knew that his only chance was to get all the Tools in one place and hope Will's powers of perception came through.

It was risky and it left everything in Will's hands. In some ways, Will was the one Frank trusted least out of all his friends. Zed was wrong about a lot of things, but he was right about one of them: trust was a must. Frank had to trust that Will would find a way.

"I must say," Zed said, "This feels very good." He sounded distracted. Almost not there. "For someone like myself, tuned into the Tools... it's hard to explain. Thank you for bringing them to me, Frank. I will grant you a quick death for that."

Frank saw that Will had the knife in his hand. Will was staring at it with a distant look in his eyes.

Zed's voice was distant as he spoke. "Something is blocking the door out of this place. But with all this power, I think I may be able to send you people... you dangerous people... somewhere far away. Somewhere you will die quickly." He looked down at Frank. "Starting with you."

Frank felt wetness in his shoes. He glanced back and he had to stifle a scream at what he saw. His shoes—and his feet along with them—were melting.

Zed said, "And you, doctor." He turned toward Trevor and Will. "And the boy. And Mr. Book Learning."

Puddles were growing around Will, Trevor, and Christine's feet, puddles of shoes and blood and melting flesh.

"Mom, what's he doing to us?" bellowed Trevor.

Christine's voice sounded shaky. "It's okay, Trev. I love you. We're going to be okay."

The wetness was nearing Frank's knees now. He felt

himself fading. It was so hard to concentrate. Will was still staring at the knife in his hand.

"This isn't working," Zed said. Beads of sweat dotted his forehead. "I don't know what you did to this place, but it's locked tight. I'm going to have to push. I must warn you— this will hurt." Zed squeezed his eyes shut and grunted with effort.

Frank screamed in pain and he heard Christine, Will, and Trevor join him. It felt like his feet were being squeezed in a vice. The agonizing pain was slowly creeping upward.

"Frank!" yelled Will, "Is the cane up here with us? If it is, I need you to push the broken clock symbol on it."

Zed clenched his fists. "Almost through the barrier."

Frank took a deep breath. The pain was like a fire inside of him, but it had also cleared his mind. He pushed the agony aside and slid his hand behind the air conditioner. He pulled out the cane, gripped it with both hands, and pressed the broken clock symbol. The cane shot upward. It was all Frank could do to hold on. The end of the cane smacked against the side of Zed's right pant leg as if drawn there by a strong magnet.

Then everything happened at once.

Will flipped the knife open and stepped toward Zed. He wobbled on his stump of a leg and took another step forward.

Becky Raymond leapt at Will, her fingers extended like claws. She hissed as she dove through the air. She landed on Will, and he fell forward onto his face. The city manager wrapped her legs around him and slashed his cheek with her fingernails. Christine fired, and Becky Raymond's brains hit the floor behind her with a splat.

The three selectmen sprang into motion, two headed for Christine and one headed for Will.

Will raised himself up on one arm. He drew back the knife and then drove it forward, slamming it into Zed's pocket and into the pocket watch.

Zed screamed. There was a cracking sound as loud as a gunshot. The scream and the crack blended together into an ear-piercing combination of agony and white noise.

The sound drifted away and time started again.

6.

The air still tasted the same as it had a moment ago. The wind still whipped around them. But they all knew. They all felt it. Things were different. Things were back. Zed's clock was broken, and the real clock was running again.

They stood in silence on the suddenly dark roof of Rook Mountain City Hall. Zed, the knife still sticking out of his leg, had his head bowed and his fists clenched by his sides.

Christine, Trevor, Will, and Frank's bodies were whole again. Only the echoing memory of pain remained.

Moments ago it had been morning. Now the sky was dark and the stars shone over their heads.

"This all began in the middle of the night," Christine said. "We're back where we started."

Zed raised his head. He was scowling. His face looked different, hardly recognizable without his signature smile. "Yes. We are back where we started. March 27th, 2014. After the lengths I went to in order to quarantine us, to keep what I had to do contained in this one little town, you have brought the world into it again."

"2014?" Will asked. "What does he mean?"

"He means time started again," Frank said. He struggled to get to his feet as he spoke. "For the rest of the world no time has passed. For us, it's been nine years."

"He means we're home," Christine said.

"Yes," Zed said. "Home. But at what cost?" He nodded toward the cane in Frank's hand. "You think you understand the Tools? You think that cane is only useful for finding other Tools? You think the lighter just brings back the dead? You have no idea. You've only scratched the surface of what these things can do."

"I understand that your watch ain't doing shit with that knife through it," Frank said.

"I didn't want to be a mass murderer," Zed said. "I wanted to keep the damage as small as I could. That's why I took Rook Mountain out of time. I figured if I let this one town live out its natural course and die out, I could take what I needed and return not even a moment after I left. There were the Unfeathered to deal with, but I figured that out too, didn't I? But you've ruined it. Now lots more people will have to die."

"You're talking crazy, Zed," Frank said. "You lost."

"Not even close. It's you who's lost. Humanity. I will get the Tools no matter what it takes, and I will use them here instead of outside of time. I'll find the coin and I'll use it. Millions will die. Time itself will pay."

"Time seems to be doing okay." Out of the corner of his eye, Frank saw Christine bending down, picking something up.

"Not for long," Zed said. "You met them. The Ones Who Sing. They can't be allowed to survive. They will devour all, and their prison is weakening. If I have to kill a billion people to stop them, I will do it."

Like a blur, Christine leapt forward. She grabbed the handle of the knife and pulled it out of Zed's leg. In one swift motion, she swung the knife forward, slashing at Zed's throat.

Frank's first thought was, Didn't we already try that?

Then he saw the blood shooting out of Zed's neck and he understood. Christine had cut an artery. The blood sprang out in an arching stream with each beat of Zed's heart.

Christine raised her other hand, the one holding the mirror. Zed's blood hit the mirror and Zed screamed. It took only a moment for the mirror to pull him into its liquid surface. Zed's cry echoed through the night as he disappeared into the mirror.

The broken pocket watch hit the ground with a clang.

Zed was gone.

THE UNREGULATED (PART 4)

Falling into the mirror was like diving into a pool of cold water. Jake felt like he was being pulled down toward something. The liquid—if that's really what it was—was so cold it hurt, sapping the energy from his muscles.

He tried to fight panic as the circular view into Wendy's living room grew smaller and smaller, shrinking until it was the size of a basketball, then a baseball, and finally a pinprick of light.

His lungs were burning now. He tried to relax, to let himself be pulled down toward whatever world waited below.

The group had argued about whether or not to use the mirror. All they knew was that it took you somewhere else. Will said he had seen something far away in the mirror. It was a forest, but the trees looked different than any in Eastern Tennessee. Will was convinced that the mirror was a portal to another place. Possibly another time.

The group had been evenly split on what to do about the new-found information. Christine, Jake, and Todd had been in favor of sending someone into the mirror in the hopes they would find a way to bring help back to Rook Mountain. The mirror, they argued, was their only way out of town and their only chance at outside help. Sean, Will, and Wendy had argued for caution. Leaping blindly into the mirror was potential suicide, they said. They had no idea what was in there and no reason to believe someone who went in would be able to return at all, let alone bring help.

Finally, the group had agreed that the mirror would be used as a last resort. Only if their other plans had failed. Jake just happened to be the first of them to find himself in a situation dire enough to use it.

So there he was, trying not to drown, sinking toward God only knew where.

As he sank, the light dimmed and Jake's clarity of mind seemed to dim with it. A thousand thoughts raced through his head, but they were all blending together, merging into a confusing soup of facts and images. And then, suddenly, one thought hit him with the force of a punch. One thing he had forgotten to do. One thing he needed to do.

He needed to go back. But which way was back?

He took his best guess on what direction was up and swam hard, fighting against the downward pull with all of his strength.

Just when he thought his lungs would explode, when he almost couldn't stand it, he burst through the surface. Gasping for air, he reached up to wipe the liquid out of his eyes, but he found himself completely dry. He blinked, adjusting to the sudden bright sun.

It was daytime. He was outside. Where was he? Where was Wendy's living room with the wine glass and the Twilight Zone? It was hard to think, hard to keep any one thought in his head. It was as if his thoughts had become slippery. Holding on to each one was nearly impossible.

He looked around, trying to orient himself. He was in a parking lot. It looked familiar... yes, this was the Food City parking lot. He felt a pull. The same pull he had felt when he was in the mirror. It was trying to pull him back, to take him downward.

He looked around, panicked. He had come here to tell someone something. Who was it? What had he wanted to say?

The pull was growing stronger. He knew he couldn't fight it for long. He needed to get the job done quickly. Then he saw her, only ten feet away. Sally Badwater. Not the person he had been looking for but she would have to do.

He ran to her, fighting the backwards pull with all the strength in his legs. He reached out and grabbed her shoulder.

She turned around and gasped when she saw him. Why was she so surprised?

He opened his mouth and tried to remember what he had to say, tried to find the words he needed to speak. Zed had said he would be investigating Jake's friends. The coin was in danger. He needed to tell someone. Maybe his friend. His brother. Will. Wait, was that his name? Everything was so confused in his mind. "Tell my brother. Tell my brother to meet me at the quarry."

The words were all jumbled in his head, but he had gotten them out. They would understand. He prayed they would.

The pull on him was stronger now and he almost stopped fighting. Then he remembered one more thing. Zed had a Tool too. Jake needed protection from Zed. He needed time to find help for Rook Mountain. There was only one thing he knew of that could protect him. And only one person who had it. A person who wouldn't hesitate to help Jake if he could.

"And if Frank comes, tell him to bring the Cassandra lock."

Then he stopped fighting.

He crashed back into the liquid almost immediately, almost before he had the chance to take a last deep breath. When he hit the liquid, he went limp, not fighting this time, and his mental clarity returned. He let himself be pulled down toward whatever salvation or damnation lay below. He hoped it would be a place where he could find help for his family. He had failed all of them—Trevor, Christine, Frank, and Will—for far too long. He hoped it would be a place of second chances.

As he rushed through the liquid he saw the figure of another man join him. It was dark and he couldn't make out the details. He could only see a vague shape. Then a third shape appeared. Jake barely had time to register that one at all before the liquid spit him out.

He stood in a forest of towering trees. Will had been right—they weren't the trees of Eastern Tennessee. Jake took a long deep breath of sweet forest air. The woods were alive with sound, the birds singing, the wind in the trees, the buzz of the insects. It felt like a place of peace.

He stood there for a long while enjoying the forest before he saw the object on the ground in front of him. It was a book. Jake picked it up.

The book was bound with rich brown leather. The only marking on the cover was a symbol. For a terrible moment, Jake thought it was the broken clock symbol. But it wasn't. It was similar; it too had a crack running down the length of the image. It was a globe. A broadly drawn representation of the Earth.

Jake tucked the book with the symbol of the broken Earth under his arm and started walking. He had come to find help, and he intended to do so.

IN THE AFTER

1.

One morning, in the middle of May 2014, Wendy Caulfield and Sean Lee knocked on the Osmonds' door. Will looked through the peephole. Between the media, the government, and the scientists investigating the events in Rook Mountain, the Osmonds barely had a moment to themselves. Knocks at the door were far too common these days, and Will, Christine, and Trevor had quickly adjusted to ignoring them when they came unexpectedly.

Frank was still living in their spare bedroom. With the town so overrun with outsiders, it wasn't the best time to look for an apartment. He was keeping busy, distracting himself from the media circus by learning about programming. In prison, he'd had some ideas about locks that could be opened by completing a puzzle on a smart phone. Now that the Internet was back, it seemed like a good time to look into it.

Those were the reasons Frank and the Osmonds told themselves that Frank hadn't moved out. The real reason was that it felt better to be together, to be with the only people who truly understood what it had been like, what had happened on the roof of City Hall that day.

Will opened the door when he saw Wendy and Sean. He invited them in, scanning the street for strange vans or news cameras before shutting the door behind her.

"You doing okay?" Wendy asked.

Will thought about how thoroughly to answer that question and then nodded. "Yeah. We're okay. How about you?"

Wendy did a half-shrug half-nod. "As well as anyone I guess."

Overall, the people of Rook Mountain were handling the situation very well. Sure, there were a few media whores who appeared on every news and talk show that would have them. There were a few who had signed book deals and sold their movie rights. Some good Samaritans had volunteered to spend time with the scientists trying to figure out what had really happened in Rook Mountain and how the population of the town had aged nine years in one night. The former selectmen seemed to be adapting to life without teleportation and mind reading.

Frank kept waiting for someone to show up and tell him it was time to go back to prison, but it hadn't happened yet. He had cut his hair to a more manageable length, but he had left it gray. He kind of liked it that way.

Will looked at Sean. "You brought it?"

Sean nodded. "I'll be glad to get rid of the thing. We should have done this two months ago. Things have been a little..."

"Yeah," Will said. "I know."

"Before we do that, can I talk to Trevor?" Wendy asked. "I have something for him. From Jake."

A few minutes later the group was gathered in the living room. Will had a duffel bag as his feet.

Wendy handed Trevor the envelope.

"Your father wanted me to me to give this to you when you grew up. After everything that's happened, I guess now's the time. I never read it. But I did let Frank read it the night before he was sent Away. I thought... I hoped maybe there would be something in there that would help him. I hope that's okay."

Trevor nodded slowly. "Yeah. Of course."

Trevor took out the single piece of paper and read carefully. When he was finished he didn't say anything, but he passed Christine the note.

"You sure you want me to read this?" she asked.

Trevor said, "You both should."

Christine read it with tears in her eyes, then she passed it to Will. He held it on his lap and read.

Dear Trev,

I am so sorry I have to leave you. I don't know how much you know about what's happened, so I wanted to explain.

One night when you were little, a bad man named Zed somehow managed to cut off Rook Mountain from the rest of the world. This place he put us in was filled with these creatures he called the Unfeathered. He protected us from the Unfeathered as long as we didn't leave town, so people were grateful and they gave him and his friends a lot of power. But the real reason he took us here was so that he would have time to find these objects he calls the Tools. There's a key, a cane, a knife, and a bunch of others. These things have special powers. If he gets them, he will have all the power he wants, and that would be a very bad thing. So me and your mom and some of our friends decided to fight him. I found a way to maybe get us some help, and that's why I am not there with you today.

You may already know some of this. Maybe you know all of

it. But I wanted to tell you in case no one else has told you straight out.

Three other things I need to make sure you know:

1) Your mother is the toughest person I've ever met. She will fight all the monsters in the world to protect you. Trust her and do what she says.

2) Will is a good man. I'm not sure what your relationship with him is like, but you need to trust him too. He loves you like a father. Will and your mother will do anything to protect you. Will has a way of figuring out what the Tools are for. He is sort of in tune with them in a strange way. He hasn't figured out the knife yet, but tell him to keep trying. I know the answer will come to him when he needs it.

3) I will never stop trying to get back to you. I wouldn't have left unless I thought it was the best way to help you. I'll see you again someday. Believe that with all your heart. I know I do.

Love,

Dad

Will set the letter down, walked to the couch, and hugged Christine and Trevor with all his strength.

Frank said, "I'm sorry I never mentioned the letter. I forgot about it after everything that happened."

"Is that why you left me the knife?" Will asked. "On the stage that day?"

Frank nodded. "Jake said the answer would come to you when you needed it. He was right."

"It was a little scary the way the knife spoke to me. It told me exactly what to do."

"Maybe the Tools changed the two of you," Sean said.

"What do you mean?" Frank asked.

"The lighter was buried out there by your cabins. Who knows how long it was there. Maybe it amplified your natural talents. It made your locks stronger, so that people who weren't meant to open them didn't even see they existed. And maybe it upped Will's powers of perception."

Frank couldn't argue. Becky Raymond had searched that shed, and she hadn't even noticed the freezer with his lock on it. It was Frank's lock that had trapped Zed and the selectmen on the roof of City Hall.

After a long moment, Frank turned to Will and said, "Speaking of powers of perception, let me ask you something. In that letter, it seemed like Jake knew you and Christine would get together. How'd he know that?"

Will looked out the window a long time before answering. "After you went to prison, things changed between the three of us. We grew closer. We spent a lot of time together. It's hard to explain the relationship the three of us had. I don't want you to get the wrong idea. Christine and I never did anything behind Jake's back or anything like that... but we were all close. You're right. He knew Christine and I would get together if he were gone. And we knew we would have his blessing."

Trevor cleared his throat. "Can we get to what we came here to do?"

Christine laughed. "You're right. Enough of this touchy-feely stuff. Lay it on the table, Sean."

Sean reached into his coat and set the coin on the coffee table.

Frank looked away. The sight of the thing still made him shiver.

Will unzipped the duffel bag and took out the cane, the key, the mirror, and the lighter. Finally, he brought out the knife.

"If Zed ever makes it back here, he won't find these Tools waiting for him," Will said.

Frank held up his hand. "Zed said that we need to

protect ourselves. That the Ones Who Sing were coming. Do you think maybe we should hold on to them? Just in case?"

"No," Christine said. "I'm done waiting and I'm done being cautious. Zed said, 'death of millions.' We are not letting that thing survive. Do it, Will."

Will brought the knife down on the coin, and it shattered. Then he set the cane on the table and did the same. Then the key. Then the lighter. When he raised the knife over the mirror, Frank held up a hand.

"Wait," he said.

"I thought we agreed these things have to be destroyed," Will said.

"Yeah, I agree. But I have to go into the mirror first."

He continued before any of them could speak. "Jake went through there and we don't know where he ended up. Then we sent Zed through the same way. What if Jake needs help? What if Zed is coming for him and Jake doesn't know it?"

"Frank," Sean said, "I hate to say it, but they might be dead."

"And they might be alive. I have to try. When I was Away, the Ones Who Sing told me that I will never see Jake again, but I have to try. I'm going in. After I'm through, destroy the mirror."

"What if the mirror is the only way back?" Will asked.

"All the more reason to destroy it. We can't leave Zed a way back. But I won't leave Jake there alone."

Christine said, "I think I finally understand the other part of Jake's message to Sally Badwater."

"If Frank comes, tell him to bring the Cassandra lock," Will said.

"He knew you'd come after him." Christine couldn't help but smile.

Frank reached into his pocket and pulled out the Cassandra lock. "I'm way ahead of you."

"Is that the one Zed made?" Christine asked.

"That cheap imitation? No, this is the real deal. I finished it last week." He turned to Sean. "You got a knife? I need to cut myself and I'm not using that thing with the broken clock on it."

"Let me come with you," Trevor said.

Frank shook his head. "I'm sorry, Trevor. The best way to honor your dad is to live your life. Remember his letter. He promised to come back to you, and I'm going to do everything I can to help him keep that promise."

"Before I go, I need to tell you all something," Frank said to the group. "I want to apologize."

"For what?" Christine asked.

"I'm sorry that I wasn't here for you. Zed told me that I was the one person who could have stopped him. He said I could have been the hero. If I hadn't murdered Brett, I would have been here. Maybe things would have gone differently."

"That wasn't you," Sean said. "That was the coin."

"Maybe," Frank said. "But the coin used me. It amplified the anger that was already inside me. I think I could have stopped it."

"But you did save us," Christine said. "It was your locks that let us hide the Tools from Zed. It was your locks that bought us time, time we used to raise Trevor. It was your lock that kept the coin out of Zed's hands. Frank, you were the hero."

Frank smiled at Christine. He didn't know what to say, and he was afraid if he waited much longer he would lose his nerve. He cut his hand, watched the blood fall onto the mirror, and fell in after it.

He didn't fight the downward pull. It was a feeling he knew only too well. He was drifting. And in a few moments he was standing in a forest of tall, strange trees.

2.

The Osmonds lived in Rook Mountain for five more years. The media frenzy eventually died down, but the government and scientific interest never did. Will and Christine kept the knife hidden in their home, the last of the discovered Tools. They told the government about everything that had happened except for the knife. There were three more Tools out there waiting to be discovered, and they wanted to be ready.

When Trevor was seventeen, he told Will and Christine he wanted to go to college out west. He had his eye on a couple of good premed programs, but Christine suspected that 'out west' was the most important part of that equation.

After some discussion, Will and Christine decided that they too would take the opportunity to head west. They loved the rolling mountains and forests of Appalachia, but as Brett Miller had once noted, the dense foliage could be stifling. This place had too many memories and everywhere they looked held reminders of the horror they had lived in for nine years.

Leaving would be hard, especially with Jake and Frank gone and this town the last connection to them. But the Osmonds knew that if Jake and Frank found a way back, they too would be glad to put Rook Mountain in the rear view.

Christine gave the Hansens the cabins and surrounding property. Christine and Will put their house on the market and it sold for a surprisingly large amount. Rook Mountain property values had risen dramatically in recent years. The researchers studying the town had to live somewhere.

At the end of the summer the Osmonds loaded up a U-Haul truck, left Rook Mountain, and never looked back.

In the years that followed, Christine would occasionally see an old object at a garage sale or in an antique store and pick it up, sure she would see the broken clock symbol. But she never did. She would sometimes stare into mirrors, trying to see the face of her first husband or his convict brother or even the wide smile of a man she hoped was dead. But all she ever saw was her own aging reflection.

After a while, these things stopped bothering her. She had her family. She had hope. And she had her knife. Whatever happened next, she was ready.

WHAT'S NEXT?

Dear readers,

Looks like things are back to normal in Rook Mountain. But as you may have figured out already, life will never be normal for Frank and his friends.

Things are about to get even more strange as he uncovers a whole new mystery, encounters an expected family member, and battles a terrifying new foe. All of it is going to lead him to a much deeper understanding of Rook Mountain and Zed's true intentions. But first, he'll need to survive the daylight.

The sequel to Regulation 19 is available now. It's called A Place Without Shadows. Get it at:

http://mybook.to/PlaceWithoutShadows

Thank you for your support, and happy reading!

P.T. Hylton

Printed in Great Britain
by Amazon

32775131R00192